promises,

promises

# Promises, Promises

### A Romp with Plenty of Dykes, a Unicorn, an Ogre, an Oracle, a Quest, a Princess, and True Love with a Happily Ever After

## L-J Baker

Maple Shade, New Jersey

# Promises, Promises

Published in 2011 by Lethe Press, Inc.
118 Heritage Avenue ✦ Maple Shade, NJ 08052-3018
www.lethepressbooks.com ✦ lethepress@aol.com
ISBN: 1-59021-337-8
ISBN-13: 978-1-59021-337-7

This is a work of fiction. Names, characters, places, and incidents are products of the author's imagination or are used fictitiously.

Set in Jenson and LD Honeydukes.
Cover and interior design: Alex Jeffers.
Cover art: Kimball Davis.

LIBRARY OF CONGRESS CATALOGING-IN-PUBLICATION DATA
Baker, L-J.
  Promises, promises : a romp with plenty of dykes, a unicorn, an ogre, an oracle, a quest, a princess, and true love with a happily ever after / L-J Baker.
    p. cm.
  ISBN-13: 978-1-59021-337-7 (pbk. : alk. paper)
  ISBN-10: 1-59021-337-8 (pbk. : alk. paper)
  1. Lesbians--Fiction. 2. Quests (Expeditions)--Fiction. 3. Fantasy fiction. gsafd 4. Humorous fiction. gsafd I. Title.
  PR9639.4.B37P76 2011
  823'.92--dc22
                                    2011006959

I'd like to dedicate this book to my friends on the Lesbian Fiction Forum.

# Acknowledgments

As with all of my books, this one would not have seen print had it not been for the tenacity, persistence, and unflagging faith of Fran. I'd also like to thank the support and encouragement of readers and friends, especially Dejay and Deb. I'm deeply grateful to Steve for taking a chance on a story from a niche within a niche—lesbians, fantasy, and no sex—and turning it into a nifty wee package of a book. Kimball Davis's cover art is simply wicked.

# Chapter One

Sandy Blunt straightened the bottles of the Amazingly Miraculous Manticore's Youthifying Tonic on the shelf, but her thoughts were of creamy skin, large blue eyes, and moist red lips. Ah, the fair Julie....

The doorbell's tinny tinkle cut through Sandy's sighs. A customer. Sandy straightened her tunic as she hurried behind the counter. A dark-haired young woman in a plain brown dress entered the shop. Sandy sagged. Ruth, the girl who lived next door, smiled at Sandy.

"I've brought lunch for you." Ruth set a basket on the counter. "Your mother said to tell you not to eat the apples until you'd finished your sandwiches. And I mended your breeches for you. Your mother won't know they were ever torn."

"Oh," Sandy said. "Thanks."

Ruth bustled behind the counter to fetch a broom. Sandy peeled one of the sandwiches apart to discover cheese and onion filling. It was her favourite, but hardly the sort of lunch you'd find someone rich and successful eating. The onions were a dead giveaway that she didn't have a hot date tonight.

"So, how did you tear your breeches?" Ruth asked.

Sandy frowned. "Life is never as you expect, is it? Take wooing a beautiful girl. I declare her skin is whiter than the purest snow, and she

1

complains that snow means cold. I tell her that her smile would warm me on the bitterest winter night, and she says the blacksmith's daughter warmed her heart by giving her a gold necklace. I tell her that her beauty outshines the perfection of the rose I've brought her, and she complains the rose got squashed when I climbed up to her balcony. I offer her my heart, and she wants wizardly magic—I should change a pumpkin into a convertible coach, or whisk myself up amongst the stars and have a sword fight with some asthmatic cyborg in a black cloak to prove myself worthy of her. I try to serenade her instead, but do I get a kiss? No. I fall off the vine under her balcony, break my lute, and get my breeches ripped by her father's dogs."

"Oh, dear," Ruth said.

"Look at me," Sandy said. "I have my own shop. I don't pick my nose in public. But no girlfriend. My mother sends me lunch every day and still darns my socks for me."

"You could darn them yourself if it bothers you that much."

Sandy stared at her. Ruth looked up from watching where her broom swished across the wooden floor and smiled. Her dimples showed.

"Hey!" Sandy belatedly grabbed the broom handle. "What do you think you're doing?"

"Sweeping. There's a lot of dust in here. It can't be good for—"

Sandy tugged the broom from Ruth's fingers. "Do you know how hard I've had to work to collect this dust? If you go and sweep it away, I'll never sell these." Sandy pointed to the bucket of Mysterious Sneeze Stones, two groats each or three for seven groats.

Ruth peered at one of the shiny pebbles. "It looks like an ordinary stone from the riverbank. What do they do?"

"Do you feel a tingle in your nose? A tickle in the back of your throat? Eyes a bit scratchy and watery? Well, when you walk out of here with a Mysterious Sneeze Stone in your pocket, your symptoms will disappear."

"That's not magic. It's dishonest."

"It's business." Sandy took the pebble from Ruth's hand and dropped it back into the bucket. "Not much of a business, I know. But I will succeed. He doesn't think I can. But I'll show him."

"Him?" Ruth said. "Who?"

"Her father. I told him I'm going to be the richest person in the kingdom. Apart from the king, of course. And I'll do it before my twenty-fifth birthday."

"You have a busy fifteen months ahead of you."

"Then Burgermeister Smelt will rue—" Sandy stopped as Ruth's mild comment sank in. "Are you mocking me?"

"Of course not. I have every faith in you. Oh, dear. So it was Miss Julie Smelt whose balcony you fell off? She is very beautiful. That fair hair. Blue eyes. Perfect skin. Oh, poor Sandy."

Sandy slumped on the stool behind the counter. "What am I going to do? The world is full of gorgeous women. But none for me. Do you know how long it's been since I had a kiss?"

"Perhaps you'd be better picking a woman whose father doesn't own such large dogs."

"And I paid half a silver crown for that bloody lute! If only—"

The doorbell tinkled. A thin woman in a rumpled dark tunic and patched britches sidled in. She shut the door and flattened herself against the wall.

"Hello, Drusilla," Ruth said. "What—"

"Ssh!" Drusilla put a finger to her mouth and cracked the door open to peer outside.

"Who is trying to kill you this time?" Sandy said. "Trolls? Ogres? Dragons? No, it was dragons yesterday. A giant killer hedgehog with a sword in each paw?"

"Assassins," Drusilla whispered. "Eight of them. No, ten."

"And yet you miraculously escaped to bring me the string I sent you to fetch," Sandy said.

"It's safe now." Drusilla left the door and dug a ball of twine from a pocket. "It was a close-run thing. Brotherhood of the Stabbing Blade.

Hello, Ruth. You need not fear for me, dear girl. I am bred from a long line of princely warriors."

Ruth smiled. "Of course you are."

"Don't encourage her," Sandy said.

"I am accustomed to doubt," Drusilla said. "The long years of my exile have taught me patience. I, Drusilla, dispossessed princess of an oppressed people, am ever vigilant for the wiles of evil. That is why I always keep my paring knife sharp. Look. Don't worry, I wiped the blood off it. The first assassin went to a slash. Like this. A disembowelling stroke, thus! A kick to the groin. Stab in the heart. The fifth one I shoved off the bridge. *Splash!* The weight of all those knives concealed under his clothes sank him like a stone. His face screwed up like this. He couldn't breathe. *Blurble. Blurble. Aaarrgh.*"

"Goodness," Ruth said. "How upsetting for you."

Drusilla leaned against the counter and scratched a pimple on her neck. "Daily brushes with death are an occupational hazard for us princesses. I'll have to live with them until a passing band of ill-assorted heroes recognises my royalty beneath my cunning disguise as a shop-assistant and wants to start an uprising to restore me to my father's stolen throne."

Sandy rolled her eyes. "Don't forget the oracle."

"Of course!" Drusilla struck a queenly pose. "I am to remain here, in this humble establishment, because the infallible Oracle of Ring has foretold that the days of exile will end when the noblest scion of my royal house shall travel the known world with the Great Obtuse Mage and perform many valorous deeds."

Ruth's lips quivered as if she struggled to suppress a giggle. "I take it that Sandy Blunt is the Great Obtuse Mage?"

"Don't you two have errands to run for my mother?" Sandy said.

Ruth retrieved her basket from the counter. "Perhaps we'd better leave Sandy to plan how she's going to get rich. Will you escort me to Mrs Blunt's house? To make sure I arrive safely."

Sandy shot Ruth a "don't encourage her" look.

Drusilla offered Ruth a stiff bow. "I and my lethally sharp paring knife are always at your service, dear girl. I, Drusilla, am prepared to spill my secret royal blood for the sake of your safety."

Sandy shook her head and cast a glance up at the ceiling. Ruth smiled, showing her dimples again, and left with Drusilla.

Sandy listlessly toyed with a Mysterious Sneeze Stone on the counter and conceded the appeal of living in a world where you could make things up to suit yourself. Although Drusilla's inhabiting her own warped fairy-tale reality hadn't given her noticeably more luck with women than Sandy had. Wouldn't it be hard to convince yourself that you were kissing an imaginary woman?

Sandy scowled at the door and tried to picture the most beautiful woman in the world walking into her shop. Creamy breasts, rounded hips, smooth hands, neatly trimmed fingernails, cascades of soft, shiny hair.

Sandy sighed. No. It was never going to happen. Perhaps women might find her more attractive when she was rich. After all, it worked a treat for old men. Which only left her with the problem of how to earn a lot of money.

Sandy dropped the Mysterious Sneeze Stone back in the bucket. She needed to think big. Very big. But big what? Surely she had one skill that she was good at.

Sandy glanced around the empty shop and grabbed another two bottles of the Prodigiously Incredible Empericus's Cough Balm. She carried them to the tiny table at the back of the shop and passed one to Drusilla. Drusilla shuffled the tarot cards. Sandy took a long drink. The cough balm burned its way down her insides.

"This is the sort of thing I need to do," Sandy said. "It's pure genius to make cough balm out of brandy. The medicine that everyone wants to take. And it puts your sick kids to sleep."

Drusilla dealt them five cards each. "Haven't you drunk enough of that already?"

Sandy didn't bother pointing out that it was nearly closing time on another slow, dispiriting day that had not earned her fortune. She took another quick swig and picked up her last card. The nine of pentacles. She had a full house in the minor arcana. Sandy smiled. She added two copper groats to the kitty.

"With these cards, I can read your future," Sandy said. "You're going to lose all—"

"No!" Drusilla lunged across the table to clamp a hand on Sandy's mouth. "Ssh! Prophesying the future for one of royal blood is punishable by death!"

Sandy pulled Drusilla's hand from her face. "Uh-huh. It has nothing to do with the fact that you're lousy at poker and I'm going to win every last groat you have. Are you in or—"

The doorbell tinkled.

Sandy jerked her head around. A tall woman in a hooded cloak pushed the door open and surveyed the interior of the shop. The warmth of the spring afternoon made the choice of a cloak unusual, but a customer was a customer. Sandy scrambled to her feet.

"Welcome to Blunt's Spell Emporium," Sandy said. "How may I help you today, madam?"

Enough of the woman's face showed to reveal doubt and distaste on her finely chiselled features. She looked about forty. Gold rings on her pale hands. Long, manicured fingernails. She was straight, then.

"Do these, ah, premises," the woman said, "belong to a fully accredited member of the Most Ancient and Venerable Guild of Magicians, Sorcerers, Witches, and Enchanters, But Not Theatrical Conjurers or Elderly Midwives?"

Sandy bowed unsteadily and regretted those last two bottles of cough balm. "I am the owner of this emporium, ma'am. Sandra Blunt. Witch. I would be honoured to be of service. Perhaps you seek a tonic? A cure? I offer the most discreet—"

A second cloaked woman pushed the first aside and strode into the shop. "You're a witch? But you're so young. Where are your hairy warts?"

Before Sandy's alcohol-soggy brain could think of a flippant reply, the newcomer shoved back her hood. Sandy's breath lodged in her throat. She stared at a tumble of shiny blonde hair, flawless creamy complexion, large hazel eyes, and the most kissable of lips.

"This is a funny place." The beauty wrinkled her adorable little nose. "It's disgustingly dusty. And it smells. You ought to get your servants to clean it better. I want my fortune told. I want to know how long my horrid father is going to keep me rotting away as a spinster in that draughty old pal— Ow!" She glared at her companion. "You pinched me! I've had Daddy flog servants for— Ow!"

"*Lady Beryl*, is your medicine wearing off?" The older woman looked meaningfully and menacingly at the beauty.

Sandy's attention dropped to be enveloped in a perfect, curvaceous bosom swelling with indignation. Beryl. Not the prettiest of names, but any woman who looked like that could get away with worse. What rhymed with Beryl? Smeryl? Teryl? Peril. Hmm. Not exactly romantic.

Drusilla touched Sandy's elbow and whispered in her ear. "I think you ought to be very careful. I suspect—"

"Of course!" Beryl's pout vanished to be replaced by a dazzling smile. "My daddy isn't the king. He's just some common sort of lord."

"Perhaps," the older woman said, "the witch will be able to tell you what lies in your future."

"Oh, yes, you must!" Beryl smiled at Sandy.

Sandy smiled back. Beryl filled her whole world. Beautiful, perfect, loveable Beryl. The room spun. The older woman had to shake her chinking purse in Sandy's face to get her attention.

"Or are you the witch?" Beryl eyed Drusilla. "You have an elusive air of mystery. Shame about the pimples."

Sandy elbowed Drusilla aside. "Lady Beryl, I am the witch. If you will take this seat, I shall work my magic for you."

Sandy hurriedly shoved the cards and copper coins into a pile, thrust the empty bottles of cough balm at Drusilla, and drew a chair out for Beryl. The beauty did not sit until the older woman had wiped the seat with her cloak.

Sandy smiled across the small table. Her knees gently touched Beryl's knees. Beryl did not shift away. She stared at the tarot cards as Sandy gathered them and shuffled. Sandy threw in a showy riffle that owed more to tavern gambling tables than magic school. Beryl's eyes widened. She was impressed. Sandy's insides warmed to more than the brandy swilling around her stomach.

"Now, clear your thoughts," Sandy said, "and concentrate on the questions that you wish answered."

Beryl squeezed her eyes shut and looked so adorable that Sandy went weak with wanting to kiss her.

Drusilla gripped Sandy's shoulder. "I think you should be careful. She—"

Sandy brushed her off.

Beryl even looked pretty when she cut the tarot deck. Sandy received a whiff of a delicate floral perfume. Sandy's imagination drifted off to a grassy bank covered with wildflowers. She and Beryl ran across it, hand in hand. They tumbled onto the springy grass. Together. Pressing against each other. Warm, soft flesh. Kissing.

"Am I going to get married soon?" Beryl said.

"Oh, yes." Sandy imagined herself and Beryl being pronounced wife and wife. *You may now kiss the bride.*

"Whoopee!" Beryl clapped her hands and beamed up at her companion. "This was a good idea of yours, Rochelle! She's not wrinkled and warty like those crones who come to the palace, but she does smell of brandy just like a real witch. And she can tell my future without even looking at the cards! Oh! I'm getting married soon. To be free of my disagreeable old father!"

Drusilla dug a finger into Sandy's back. Sandy shifted out of reach. The older woman fixed a hard, suspicious stare down on Sandy. Sandy remembered what she was supposed to be doing, shook her head to try to jolt her thoughts free of the alcoholic fog, and picked the first three cards off the deck. Beryl stared greedily at them.

"What do they mean?" Beryl pointed to King of Cups. "Is that my prince?"

"Erm. Prince?" Sandy frowned. "You want to marry a prince?"

"Or is that card the princess who will come for me?" Beryl tapped The Empress. "When will she come? When? I must know."

Sandy grinned. "You have already met your True Love."

Beryl's gaze snapped up. "Really? Who— Oh! You don't mean that ugly Prince Ribbit from that stupid kingdom no one has ever heard of? He smells of ponds and eats flies when he thinks no one is watching."

"Not him," Sandy said. "The one who loves you is female."

Beryl's mouth tightened as she considered this. "There was that rather handsome princess who kissed me in the counting house. But I heard she pricked herself, fell asleep, and isn't due to be woken for ninety-five more years. Just goes to show that you can't be too careful around sharp metaphors and phallic symbols."

"Your True Love is unmarried and willing to lay everything she owns—her whole kingdom at your feet," Sandy said.

"I should jolly well hope so," Beryl said. "But how can I ask her if I don't know who she is?"

Sandy reached across to gently clasp a soft warm hand. Beryl jerked free.

"What do you think you're doing, you working-class person?" Beryl said. "You can't touch me!"

"Oh," Sandy said. "I— The cards are confused. I need to examine your palm."

"That's all right, then." Beryl thrust her hand across the table. "You have my permission to touch me. Now, about this princess."

Drusilla tugged Sandy's hair. "I really need to speak with you. There's something you should know about—"

Sandy twisted around to whisper vehemently: "Go away!"

Sandy captured Beryl's hand. A tingling warmth raced under Sandy's skin and went straight to her drunken head.

"In a year and a day," Sandy said, "you and I will be happily married, most beautiful lady."

Beryl frowned. "A year and a day? That's longer than I'd like, but I suppose I can live with it. But I wish you'd concentrate. This is about me. Not you. What do I care if you're getting married? Tell me more about me. What else do you see? I want lots of good things to happen to me to help while away this year until my princess comes. And some presents would be good."

Sandy turned Beryl's hand palm up. She gently stroked it with a finger. Her blood felt as though it were full of tingly bubbles. Love. It must be. She had fallen in love at first sight.

"Well?" Beryl said. "Tell me something nice."

"Your skin... Your skin is so soft and perfect," Sandy said. "It is paler and purer than the mane of the unicorn that roams free in the lands of the frost giants."

"Oh," Beryl said. "A unicorn? I've not seen a unicorn before. So, someone is going to bring this unicorn to me so that I can make the comparison? For everyone to see and marvel at. Yes, I like that a lot. What else are people going to give me?"

Sandy gazed adoringly at Beryl. "Suitors without number could lay gems and trinkets at your feet, but the only jewel worthy of your beauty is the legendary talking pearl earring of the Queen Under the Waves. It would tell you that you are fairer than its previous owner."

Beryl's eyes widened. "Ooh! I like the sound of that. Tell me more, witch."

Drusilla bent, grabbed Sandy's earlobe, and whispered: "You're in grave danger. She's Princess Maybelle! Don't say another—"

"Shut up!" Sandy shoved Drusilla aside. "Go and count the bottles of—of hair tonic we have in the storeroom."

Drusilla chewed her lip and frowned between Sandy and Beryl.

Sandy turned back to Beryl and resumed softly stroking her palm. "My apologies, glorious lady. My assistant has only been in the job a few weeks. Now..."

"You were telling me about all these fabulous things that people are going to bring to me," Beryl said. "I've always rather liked the idea of a magical mirror. Without the wicked stepmother, of course. I don't suppose I'm going to get one?"

"A mirror?" Sandy said. "There is no mirror crafted by man or magic that could accurately reflect such perfection as your beauty. Only the polished scale from the neck of a mature dragon would be clear enough to hold the image of your dazzling self."

Beryl frowned. Sandy had seen no woman frown more beautifully. Oh, yes, this was love. Sandy wanted to dance and recite poetry, but a speck of her brain was just sober enough to realise that she risked falling flat on her face if she tried that. She settled for a longing sigh and a loving smile.

"A dragon scale?" Beryl said. "I'm not sure about that. Still, it would be very valuable, wouldn't it? All right. What else? I was thinking about getting my hair cut and restyled. What do the cards say about that?"

"Your hair..." Sandy stared at the flaxen waves. She would like to stroke them and press them to her face. "Your hair is more golden and lovely than the locks of an elven princess, as everyone would acclaim were you to stand side by side."

Beryl twisted a lock of her hair around a finger. "Elves wear their hair long, don't they? I suppose, then, that means I shouldn't get it cut. Fine. I wasn't that set on the idea. What else? Daddy wants me to continue singing lessons with that slimy creep of a bard. I was hoping he'd drop dead over his lute. Will he?"

"Your voice is so sweet and harmonious, lady," Sandy said, "that an ogre from the Wildlands would lay a flower at your feet when he heard you speak."

"An ogre?" Beryl's nose wrinkled. "Aren't they hairy and horrible? And have bad breath? Couldn't he just send the flower?"

"Even the Green Hermit himself would emerge from his remote hiding place to lie prostrate at the feet of the most gorgeous woman created," Sandy said.

"Oh," the older woman said.

"Green Hermit?" Beryl screwed her beauty into a scowl. "That doesn't sound very complimentary."

"Highness," the older woman said, "the Green Hermit is a notorious misogynist."

"A what?" Beryl asked.

"A man riddled with psychological insecurities about sex and who is afraid of women and blames them for his own failings," the older woman said. "The Green Hermit refused to leave his cave to obey the summons of the High King himself. Because the king was married and the Hermit might come into contact with the queen. Quite what he thought her Majesty would do to him, I'm not sure. He's a bent, nasty, unwashed old man who lives in a cave and has earned himself a reputation for deep thinking by spending the last fifty years meditating on grass. But if he would leave his cave for you, and lie at your feet, that is something special indeed."

"But he doesn't sound like the sort of man I would like lying at my feet," Beryl said.

"You could have a point," the older woman said.

"You would not need to concern yourself with him, most beautiful lady," Sandy said. "He would be but one of the adoring legions."

Beryl smiled. "Adoring legions! Yes. Of course. If this hermit person was too unpleasant lying on the floor, the adoring legions could use him as a door mat. You know, I had no idea that getting my future read could tell me such wonderful things. You've quite put my mind at rest about my hair. Now, what else nice is going to happen to me? What sort of wedding dress is Daddy going to buy me?"

"Your wedding veil will be finer than the finest lace," Sandy said. "It will be a gossamer cobweb spun by the giant spider of—"

"Aaarrgh!" Drusilla staggered out of the storeroom door. She clutched her throat. "Danger! Assassins! Flee for your lives!"

Drusilla whipped out her paring knife and flashed it threateningly into the storeroom. Beryl shot to her feet. The older woman protectively tugged Beryl behind her.

"There's nothing to be alarmed about," Sandy said. "Drusilla—"

"Back, fiend!" Drusilla shouted. "You shall not pass me! You shall harm no one while there is breath in Drusilla's body!"

The older woman dropped her purse on the table and turned to bustle Beryl to the door.

"No!" Sandy shot to her feet. "Wait! There's not really anyone there! She makes all this stuff up."

The women hurried out. Sandy darted around the table. A body slammed into her and knocked her sprawling on the floor. Drusilla sat on her back.

"Get off me!" Sandy flailed at Drusilla. "They're getting away. I have to follow her. Find out where she lives. Let me go!"

"This is for your own good," Drusilla said. "Though I fear I acted too late. I am not as drunk as you, but that cough balm did slow my royal wits."

"Get off!"

"I should have stopped you saying anything. Still, it's not as though you really read her fortune. That might be what saves you from the horrible tortures and gruesome death that await you in the king's dungeon."

"Will you stop that nonsense?" Sandy writhed in vain to dislodge Drusilla. "The woman I love is getting away. I might never find her again."

"I, too, have fallen in love at first sight with her. And, though it pains me to disappoint you, I might have to marry her."

"You?" Sandy tried wrenching Drusilla's leg. "You're madder than I thought."

"I'll invite you to the wedding, of course. If you've not been executed for prophesying for one of royal blood. I did warn you about that."

"Get off me! She's getting away. I'll kill you myself for this!"

The doorbell tinkled. Ruth entered. Her dark eyebrows lifted.

"I'm terribly sorry," Ruth said, "am I interrupting?"

"Can you get her off me?" Sandy said.

"It was for her own good." Drusilla stood and nodded at Ruth. "Good afternoon, dear girl."

Sandy scrambled to her feet and darted to the door. She ran out into the street and frantically looked up and down. She saw no sign of the two cloaked women, but ran down the street anyway.

When Sandy staggered back to the shop, sweating and unhappy, she found the CLOSED sign on the door and Ruth and Drusilla chatting cosily over a cup of tea.

"If you've been drinking, you'd better take some tea before you go home to your mother." Ruth poured Sandy a cup of tea. "Did you run all the way to the palace?"

"Palace?" Sandy clenched a fist and shook it at Drusilla. "I'll never forgive you for this."

"Isn't the palace where Princess Maybelle lives?" Ruth said.

"Yes, dear girl," Drusilla said. "I hope the princess and her companion in disguise did not get waylaid by any of those assassins who lurk in wait for my royal self. I ought to have escorted them back to the palace, with my paring knife at the ready. But my loyalties were torn. Did I do wrong to protect Sandy instead?"

"Sandy didn't need your protection." Sandy slumped against the counter. "Oh, gods! She was gorgeous. Her hands so soft and warm."

"Well, most princesses don't do a lot of work, do they?" Ruth said. "You'd expect them to keep their hands nice."

Sandy scowled at her. "Princess? Not you, too. She was Lady Beryl. Oh, if only I'd asked her surname! Although, it'd just be my luck that her father would be as disagreeable as old Burgermeister Smelt. A lord isn't likely to let his daughter marry someone who isn't rich, is he?"

"Despair not," Drusilla said. "Remember the Oracle of Ring. We are to travel to far-flung places and perform many valorous deeds. That should make us rich. And if not, then I shall reward you from my royal coffers when I regain my family's usurped throne."

"That's very generous of you." Ruth smiled, showing her dimples. "You see, Sandy, it's right what they say about friends being a person's true treasure."

Sandy put a hand across her eyes and groaned. Wasn't there also a saying that went: with friends like Drusilla, who needed enemies?

"Take heart!" Drusilla rose and clapped a hand on Sandy's shoulder. "I have been sorely concerned about your future. But it has just occurred to me that the oracle means that you are not in imminent danger of arrest by the royal guard. If we are to have adventures together, you won't be languishing in irons in the king's deepest, darkest, rattiest dungeon cell for telling the future of the princess. The oracle is infallible."

"That is heartening, isn't it?" Ruth said.

Sandy lowered her hand to cast Ruth a filthy look.

"You know, dear girl," Drusilla said, "if I were not a princess, and had I not just fallen madly in love with a princess, I would seriously consider marrying you."

Ruth blushed. "That's very sweet of you, Drusilla."

"Well, I would," Drusilla said, "if you weren't already in love with someone else."

Ruth's blush deepened and spread down her neck and up to the tips of her ears. "I'd better be getting home."

Ruth bustled out. Sandy frowned at the closing door. She had no idea that Ruth was interested in anyone. Ruth hadn't brought anyone around from next door to introduce to the Blunts. Sandy's mother would love Ruth and whoever it was to have dinner with them. Now that Sandy thought about it, she was curious to meet this mysterious person herself.

Drusilla grabbed the basket that Ruth had forgotten in her hasty departure. "We had best be getting home to Mrs Blunt. The good woman does like us to be washed and punctual for dinner."

"Yeah. I'll be there soon."

After Drusilla left, Sandy slumped at the table and idly shuffled the tarot deck. Beautiful Beryl had sat just there. In less than an hour,

Sandy had found and lost love at first sight. Even quiet, dependable, easily-overlooked Ruth was able to hold onto someone longer than that, apparently.

Sandy listlessly turned over the top tarot card. Death. Sandy quickly stuck it in the middle of the deck and picked another. The Hanged-Man. She had to try eleven times before getting The Lovers.

Sandy turned the page of the spell book and frowned at the list of required ingredients. Three failed dreams? There would be plenty of those floating around this part of town. Heck, there should be hundreds of them crouching in the dusty corners of this emporium. But how did you catch and contain one? A net? Trap? Perhaps you'd use a broken jar to catch a failed dream.

Whipping up some rare enchantments had seemed such a good idea to make some decent money. Sure, the outlay on ingredients could get pretty steep, but the profit margins could be astronomical. But there was the small matter of the skill and talent necessary to pull it all together. Sandy had overlooked that inconvenient point.

The doorbell tinkled. The copious, sagging figure of Mrs Bustlewaite entered. She was Sandy's mother's bridge partner. Sandy forced a smile past the headache of her hangover as she closed the spell book. Her smile grew warm and genuine when she saw the pretty young woman drawn into the shop in Mrs Bustlewaite's wake. She looked about eighteen and had very attractive large brown eyes.

"Good morning, Mrs Bustlewaite," Sandy said as she stared at the young woman. "How may I help you today?"

"You're looking a little peaky, Sandra. I must tell Betty to make sure you get plenty of fresh air. It can't be good for a young person to be stuck in a gloomy place like this all day."

"I have a living to earn," Sandy said. "Hello."

The young woman politely nodded at Sandy, but let her gaze drift away.

Mrs Bustlewaite ran a finger across the counter and tutted at the dust she picked up. "It's not like Betty to not keep on top of the cleaning. Oh. You won't have met my niece, will you, Sandra? Ursula is staying with me until some wretched little megalomaniac in a pointy hat gives up trying to take over her home kingdom. Why is it that the male menopause takes such strange forms? We women just have a few hot flashes and don't bother anyone else."

Sandy tugged her tunic sleeves into place and struck what she hoped was a professional pose behind the counter. "Welcome to the city, Ursula. You'll have to come to dinner with us during your stay."

Ursula murmured noncommittally. Sandy mentally increased the chances that Ursula was straight. Pity.

"Goodness, yes," Mrs Bustlewaite said. "I must take you to meet Betty. That's Mrs Blunt. Sandra's mother. She's my oldest, dearest friend. I've known her since before Sandra here was crawling around chewing the chair legs."

Sandy's smile wilted. "What can I do for you today, Mrs Bustlewaite? Tonic? Unguent? Charm?"

"Oh, yes." Mrs Bustlewaite grabbed two jars of the Startlingly Remarkable Zandibel's Leather-Like-New™ Cream and showed them to Ursula. "Can you get this at home? I swear by it. It's useless on leather, but it works wonders on those embarrassing itches and sweaty spots. Under your b-r-e-a-s-t-s. I remember smoothing some of this on Sandra here when she had nappy rash. Worked a treat on her red little buttocks."

Ursula smiled at Sandy and looked like she barely contained a giggle. Sandy's ego dropped to the floor to mingle with all those failed dreams.

After their departure, Sandy took another hopeless look at the spell book. She wondered if her great-great-grandfather had really been able to whip up half the spells in it. If he had, surely he'd have built a shop on Golden Wand Street instead of Faded Road.

Sandy wandered outside for some fresh air. A few desultory morning shoppers wandered up and down the street. The dung collector waved. Sandy smiled back. She shoved her hands in her breeches pockets and realised that, however lacklustre her career to date, at least she wasn't shovelling shit.

"Sandy!" Drusilla skidded around the corner of the intersection. "Sandy!"

Sandy watched Drusilla's arms and legs pumping as she headed for the shop at a dead run. Who did she think was chasing her this time? Cloud gryphons? Lightning dervishes?

Drusilla frantically waved her arms. She was not carrying her paring knife. Perhaps she had left it lodged between the ribs of a stone troll.

"Sandy!" Drusilla skidded to a halt and flung her arms around Sandy to brake herself. She panted and glanced over her shoulder. "Run... Coming... Soon... We... Must—"

"No, don't tell me." Sandy smiled at Drusilla's sweaty face. "Three dozen invisible assassins are chasing you."

"Sandy...this...is—"

"Four dozen ice monsters who are so clear that I can't see their bodies?"

Drusilla gripped a fistful of Sandy's tunic, struggled to get her breath, and jabbed an arm to point. "Coming!"

Sandy saw flashes of light from metal helmets and spearheads. A detachment of armed men in smart red uniforms marched down the road. Some of the pedestrians had stopped to watch.

"Let me guess," Sandy said. "The king has learned of your noble— sorry, royal lineage and is jealous, so he's sent a troop to arrest—"

"You!" Drusilla shook Sandy. "Run. Now." Drusilla tried to drag Sandy by the grip on her tunic. Sandy dug her heels in and swatted at Drusilla's fists.

"Stop that!" Sandy said. "If you must, you can hide in the storeroom until the danger is past, but—"

"They've got—" Drusilla gulped air. "Mrs Blunt. Ruth."

Sandy sighed. "One of these days, reality is going to smack you so hard on the head that it might—"

"Too late," Drusilla said.

The stomp of marching feet closed around them. The guard formed an untidy arc near the front of the spell emporium.

"Which one of you is Miss Sandra Sybil Blunt the witch?" the sergeant asked.

"I'm—"

"Sybil?" Drusilla smirked.

Sandy shrugged. "I didn't pick it."

"True." Drusilla leaped between Sandy and the sergeant. She whipped out her paring knife. "You will not take us alive!"

"What the hell are you talking about?" Sandy said.

The sergeant eyed Drusilla. "We don't want no trouble. We're just here to arrest a witch. Put that fruit knife away."

"Arrest?" Sandy's gaze snapped around the armed men. "What for?"

Two of the guardsmen grabbed Sandy's arms.

"Wait!" Sandy tried tugging free. "Look, there's been a mistake. I haven't done anything."

The sergeant sniffed. "Got a warrant for your arrest. Right, lads, let's be getting back."

"Wait!" Sandy dug her heels into the ground. "Dru? You're just going to let them take me?"

Drusilla stood to one side thoughtfully scratching a pimple. She had resheathed her knife. "On second thought, I believe the slaughter of these men would serve your cause ill. They are but following orders. I must turn my fertile royal brain to devising a plan for rescue."

Sandy glared. "You've got to be—mmmm."

One of the guards shoved a wad of rag into Sandy's mouth and tied a gag into place. Another deftly roped her wrists together.

"That should keep the witch from blasting us all to a crisp." The sergeant signalled. "Right, lads, let's move it. Look lively. We don't want to be late for tea."

The guards tugged Sandy down the street. She twisted around to see Drusilla still standing near the emporium.

"Fear not!" Drusilla waved. "I'll look after the shop. Be of good cheer while you languish in shackles in darkness with rats nibbling your toes. Drusilla will not forget you. Remember the oracle!"

Sandy had some rather dark thoughts about the bloody oracle and Drusilla.

The heavy wooden door to the dungeon thumped shut. Sandy strained to the right. Her arm pulled the manacle chain to full stretch, but her fingers flailed inches short of the gag on her mouth. Sandy sagged. This couldn't really be happening. Surely. Perhaps there was more to Special Ingredient X in the Prodigiously Incredible Empericus's Cough Balm than brandy. This might all be some hallucination.

"Sheez. Young people these days. Don't know how lucky they are."

Sandy frowned and peered. Across the dimness of the cell, she saw a ghostly pale, thin woman bound to the opposite wall. Unkempt white hair straggled about her head and shoulders.

"Makes me right mad it does," the woman said. "Here am I. Been here years, I have. Years. Hanging around in fraying rope. Look at it. Tatty, it is. The rats have even been at it. What self-respecting prisoner would want to be caught dead in worn old rope?"

Sandy blinked.

"I've shouted abuse at the gaolers and all sorts," the woman said. "You should've heard some of my best taunts. Got them right angry, I can tell you. Especially that chubby guard with the squinty eye. Did it get me chains? Did it, hell. Then in waltz you young things and straightaway you're out of rope and into fancy manacles. Shiny metal links that make those nice clanking noises and everything. You'll be getting an iron mask next, I bet. I don't know what the world's coming to, I don't."

"Mmmm," Sandy said.

"No!" the woman said. "Ermengarde, don't talk to her! You and I are going to ignore the upstart. If you say a word to her, I'll never speak to you again."

Sandy's gaze scoured the dark but she couldn't see or hear anyone else.

"Now, Ermengarde, what were we talking about before she arrived? Oh, yes, weren't we— What? Your new dress. Well, walk up and down to let me see it. Oh, that is lovely. That shade of turquoise really sets off your eyes."

Sandy definitely could see no one else. She eyed her fellow prisoner and hoped that those ropes were sturdy enough to keep the woman safely on her own side of the cell.

"Now, you sit there on that new gold chair so that you don't get your dress dirty. What? Yes, dear, you go ahead and pour the tea. Two spoons of honey. No cake for me, dear. I'm watching my weight. I don't get as much exercise as I ought. Now, Ermengarde, how many times have I told you not to give birth while I'm trying to plait flowers into your hair?"

Oh, no. Sandy closed her eyes and rested her head back against the cold stones of the dungeon wall. If the woman mentioned an oracle, Sandy would scream: gag or no gag.

The door creaked open. A couple of guards stomped in.

"You squint-eyed cow!" the prisoner called.

"Good afternoon, Ermengarde," the squint-eyed guard said. "Now, witch, let's get you up and out."

Sandy watched with soaring relief as the guards fitted big keys to her manacles.

"Hey! What about me! I've been here longer than her! Why don't I get dragged out to the torture room? Seniority! I should be racked first. Those branding irons should be for me, not her!"

Sandy massaged her sore arms. She reached up to her gag, but the guard apologetically tied Sandy's wrists behind her back.

"Out you go." The guard nudged Sandy towards the door.

"What about me!" Ermengarde called. "It's my turn! Break me on the wheel! Hang me in irons. Rip my fingernails off. I've been here longest. It's not fair!"

"Special orders of the king," the guard said.

Sandy caught a last glimpse of the wild-haired Ermengarde looking livid. The door thumped shut.

"King!" Ermengarde shouted. "King! Her? She's only been here hours. I've been here years! And no summons to be dragged in front of the court jester, let alone the bloody king! That's favouritism, that is! Rank favouritism! You're all corrupt!"

The guards smirked and nudged Sandy up a set of broad stairs. For her first visit to the palace, she would have preferred something more along the lines of the triumphant, rich woman image rather than bewildered prisoner. The odds were fairly slender that the people who stopped to stare did so because they were overpowered by her personal charm, physical attractions, and aura of success.

The guards marched her into a hall over-decorated with banners, heraldic crests, and a shade too much gilding to be the work of a truly first-rank interior decorator. Sandy's attention snapped to the paunchy, balding man on the throne. She had imagined the king as much more impressive. The guards clomped to a halt near an officer whose immaculate uniform looked like he'd never even broken into a sweat in it. His breastplate was so shiny it made Sandy's eyes water.

"Your Majesty," the officer said, "this is the witch."

One of the guards pushed Sandy down to her knees. Marble floors looked nice, but, she discovered, they were hell to kneel on.

The king said something, but Sandy's attention had again leaped. She saw Beryl. Her heart soared. The blonde beauty wore a silk gown, lots of sparkly jewels, and a tiara. The tall, unsmiling woman behind her was the one who had come into the shop with Beryl.

"Is this the witch, Pumpkin?" the king said.

Beryl stepped forward. She rested a hand on the arm of the king's throne and gave Sandy a cursory glance. "Yes, Daddy."

*Daddy?* Something cold and hard dropped through the pit of Sandy's stomach. Lady Beryl was really the Princess Maybelle. Drusilla had been right. That did not bode well.

"And she performed a forbidden foretelling of your future for you?" the king said.

*Oh, shit. Did I?*

"She said the nicest things!" Maybelle said. "Oh, Daddy, I don't know why you're being so beastly about it all. Unicorns and pearl earrings. Adoring legions. And how I shouldn't get my hair restyled."

"Now, Pumpkin," the king said. "No pouting. Laws are laws. If we let one person get away with something, where will we be? Now, witch, you are lower-middle-class and therefore clearly guilty. That means that we'll have to cut your head off."

"Mmmm!" Sandy said.

The guard officer signalled to the sergeant of the guards. She cuffed Sandy's ear. "You don't mumble nothing through your gag at the king."

"Now, we are obliged to let you say a few last words," the king said. "Don't get any ideas about casting spells. Or the hostages will suffer."

Sandy's eyes snapped wide. Her mother and Ruth stood amongst more armed guards.

"Sandra! Darling!" Mrs Blunt waved. "Do you have clean underwear on?"

Sandy groaned into her gag.

"Halt these proceedings!" Drusilla called.

Sandy turned and blinked. Drusilla swept into the hall wearing a billowing black robe and an obviously fake bushy white beard.

"Who is that?" the king asked.

"Your Majesty." Drusilla bowed. "I am Sandy Blunt's lawyer."

"Mmmm," Sandy said.

"Lawyer?" the king said.

Drusilla whispered to Sandy: "It is I, Drusilla. In disguise. I'll get you off this. Trust me."

"Mmmm!"

"Your Majesty, I've come to save you from staining your royal justice with an injustice," Drusilla said. "To wit. This witch, Sandra Blunt, whose head you wish to chop off, is not guilty of foretelling the beautiful princess's fortune."

"My daughter said she did," the king said. "Are you calling her a liar?"

"Oh, no, Majesty!" Drusilla said. "I would call her adorable."

Maybelle smiled at Drusilla.

"Mmmm!" Sandy said.

"Then the witch is guilty," the king said. "Call for the executioner!"

"Wait! I have here a record of what my client rashly and eloquently said." Drusilla tugged a crumpled piece of paper out of her pocket. "Hmm. Okay, it doesn't look good. But there's got to be a legal loophole. There always is."

"Mmmm mmmm mmmm!"

"She condemned herself with her own words." The king snapped his fingers impatiently. "Scribe, read out the prophecies."

A young man stepped forward and partially unrolled a scroll. "Item one. That her Royal Highness will be married in one year and one day."

"That was yesterday," Maybelle said. "It's only a year now. Make a note of that."

"Yes," Drusilla said. "That's right, beautiful lady. A year that will seem like a lifetime."

"I hope not," Maybelle said. "Why do I get the feeling we've met before? Aren't you too old to have pimples?"

"Mmmm," Sandy said.

"Item two," the scribe said. "A unicorn from the lands of the frost giants will arrive in the palace so that all can see that its mane is less pale and less pure than her Royal Highness's skin."

"Well, lawyer, your witch predicted this, did she not?" the king said.

Drusilla stroked her false beard. "Yes."

"Mmmm!"

Drusilla turned to Sandy and bent to whisper. "Panic not. I have everything under control. Or I will think of something in the nick of time."

"Mmmm! Mmmm!"

"Item three," the scribe read. "Someone will give to the Princess the legendary talking pearl earring which currently is the property of Her Aquatic Majesty, the Queen Under the Waves. It will tell her Royal Highness that she is fairer than its previous owner."

"Hmm," Drusilla said. "Yes. I remember her saying that, too."

"Mmmm!"

"Item four. An unnamed individual will present to her Royal Highness a polished scale from the neck of a mature dragon for her personal use as a mirror."

"Let us hope that it is not still attached to the dragon," the king said.

"Aha!" Drusilla said. "My client said nothing about the rest of the dragon. Its appearance or otherwise is not her responsibility. Make a note of that. You see, my resourceful, fertile brain is alert to every technicality."

Sandy lowered her head and shook it.

"Item five. An elven princess will visit the court. It will then be seen by one and all that the Princess Maybelle's hair is more golden and lovely than the locks of said elven princess. General acclaim of Princess Maybelle's beauty to follow."

"I should imagine," Drusilla said, "that her Royal Highness's beauty is already the subject of universal acclaim."

Maybelle smiled at Drusilla. Sandy glared at Drusilla.

"Item six. An ogre from the Wildlands will come to lay a flower at her Royal Highness's feet because of her dulcet voice."

Drusilla nodded. "I remember that one, too."

"Mmmm! Mmmm!"

"Item seven. The Green Hermit himself would emerge from his remote hiding place to prostrate himself at the feet of the most gorgeous woman created. Who is her Royal Highness."

The king looked startled. "The Green Hermit?"

"Astonishing, it is not?" Drusilla said. "It was when I heard Sandy say that, that I decided it was time for drastic action. I thought to myself, we're in real trouble now. There's nothing else for it: I'll have to get my trusty paring knife on the job."

Sandy glowered at Drusilla. "Mmmm!"

"You have a paring knife?" Maybelle said.

"I keep it perpetually sharp and ready to take on all evil that assails me," Drusilla said. "Assassins. Trolls. Dragons."

Maybelle's eyes widened. "Oh, really?"

"And it's handy for peeling oranges," Drusilla said. "Perhaps I could show it to you, beautiful lady."

The king cleared his throat and glared at his daughter. Maybelle demurely lowered her lashes.

"Item eight," the scribe read. "Her Royal Highness's wedding veil will be a gossamer cobweb spun by the giant spider of."

"Of what?" the king asked.

"That is all it says, sire," the scribe said.

"We can forget that one, Daddy," Maybelle said. "I hate spiders. Those hairy icky little legs."

"There, there, Pumpkin." The king patted her hand. "Well, lawyer, you agree that the witch predicted all this? Against the law."

"Mmmm!" Sandy shook her head. "Mmmm!"

Drusilla stroked her false beard. "This case looks open and shut, does it not, sire? My poor client looks doomed to the axe. Condemned by her own drunken, libidinous folly. And there is nothing that even a silver-tongued advocate, such as my secret royal self, could possibly say to avert her terrible fate. I did try to warn her. But would she listen to me?"

"Mmmm!"

"Would it work, Majesty, if I flung my secret royal self on the floor, thus? Prostrating myself at your Majesty's feet and begging for your mercy and clemency on behalf of my poor, fatherless client?"

"No," the king said.

"I didn't think so." Drusilla picked herself up and dusted the front of her oversized robe.

"Mmmm!"

"Let her have her last words before dragging her out to chop her head off," the king said.

"Wait!" Drusilla threw both arms in the air. "I've thought of something. Sire, it would be a travesty to hack my client into two pieces when she is only sort of guilty."

"*Sort of* guilty!?" The king thumped the arm of his throne. "But you've just admitted that she prophesied all this stuff!"

"Not prophesied." Drusilla flashed a confident smile at Sandy and lifted a finger with a triumphant flourish: "Promised!"

"Promised?" the king said.

"Promised?" Princess Maybelle said.

"Mmmm?" Sandy said.

"Yes, sire!" Drusilla said. "My client *promised* to bring all these talking earrings, dragon scales, and what-have-you to the ravishingly lovely princess. *Ipso facto soup du jour* legal hair-splitting, etcetera etcetera, that is not foretelling. Surely, royal cousin, you do not want to make a law that forbids anyone from showering your beautiful daughter with tributes worthy of her peerless self?"

"No, Daddy," Maybelle said, "you don't want to do that."

The king stroked his chin. Princess Maybelle smiled at Drusilla. Sandy's mother dabbed her eyes with a handkerchief. Ruth patted Mrs Blunt's arm and looked admiringly at Drusilla. Sandy frowned at them all. If they were going to cut her head off, they could at least let her stand up: her knees were killing her.

"So, you're saying that this witch is going to give all these things to my daughter?" the king said.

"Strike the cruel shackles from my client!"

"Not so fast." The king eyed Sandy and Drusilla suspiciously. "I'm not sure about all this."

"Daddy!" Maybelle said. "I'd really, really like that talking pearl earring."

"I'll tell you what I'll do, then," the king said. "If everything the witch said to my daughter comes true, then you can keep your heads. Both of you."

Sandy blinked.

"Fear not, royal cousin," Drusilla said. "I resent you not for so mean-spirited a judgement against me. You are powerless to make any other decision."

"Mean-spirited?" The king's eyes narrowed to dangerous slits. "Powerless? Me?"

"Yes," Drusilla said. "The infallible Oracle of Ring has foretold that I, Drusilla, will accompany the Great Obtuse Mage on many valorous adventures. All our personages are but pawns in the mysterious workings of the oracle. Had you been inclined to be generous, charitable, noble, and honourable towards my unfortunate client, the oracular powers would have perverted you into acting like such a creep."

The king's scowl deepened. Sandy wanted to bang her head against the floor—and Drusilla's. Really hard.

"Daddy." Maybelle put her hand on the king's sleeve. "I'll need a new mirror to admire myself in when I'm wearing my talking pearl earring. That dragon scale would be nice."

The king patted her hand and his expression softened slightly. "A year and a day, witch. Or heads will roll. Yours and theirs."

Sandy followed his finger to where her mother and Ruth stood. Mrs Blunt rounded on the king. Surprised guards belatedly grabbed her arms to stop her just short of the throne.

"Well, what a nasty thing to do!" Mrs Blunt said. "You ought to be ashamed of yourself. Threatening a respectable taxpayer like me. And a poor, defenceless widow. I'm chairwoman of the Patch Street Ladies' Bridge Club! They'll all hear about this, I can tell you. And they won't be happy. What would your mother say if she could hear you?"

The king jerked back on his throne as if he feared Mrs Blunt might try to cuff his royal ear.

Sandy wanted the marble floor to open and swallow her. She couldn't imagine Drusilla's applause helped their case.

"Daddy." Maybelle tugged her father's sleeve. "It has to be a year, not a year and a day. That's when I'll get married."

"Oh. Right." The king straightened his crown. "Yes. A year. Herald! Have it proclaimed. The witch has a year to make good all those promises or she, and that lunatic oddity in the beard, and her termagant of a mother all die. Oh, yes, and that plain, easily-overlooked young woman there as well."

"Majesty?" The Chief Court Wizard stepped unsteadily forward in a swish of spangly robes. He smelled of mothballs and the Prodigiously Incredible Empericus's Cough Balm. "A witch, sir, might devise—devise magical ways to—*hic*—to rescue the hostages and not—"

"Yes. Yes." The king said irritably. "Tyrone. Stop polishing your damned parade armour. Aren't you always boasting that that sword of yours is anti-magical?"

The immaculate officer bowed. The light bounced blindingly off his shiny cuirass. "Yes, my liege. This priceless magical heirloom was passed down from father to son from my grandfather. It renders the wearer immune to the wiles and trickery of magicky types. So that you can give them a good, old-fashioned slicing."

The Chief Court Wizard fixed the officer with a bleary stare and looked like he wished he were sober enough to turn the captain into an amphibian.

"Right," the king said. "Tyrone, you're in charge of the witch. Make sure she doesn't escape. Or free the hostages."

"Me?" Captain Tyrone glanced down at Sandy. "Would that involve leaving the palace precincts, sire? And getting grimy?"

"You're a soldier, man!" the king shouted. "Wouldn't you die for me?"

"Would that involve quietly and loyally dying in my sleep, sire?" Tyrone asked.

"No! You imbecile. It would involve blood and dirt and little bits of brains and pieces of partially-digested food from inside your guts sprayed all over your new uniform."

Tyrone paled and swayed as if he might faint.

"You have to keep this witch in your sight," the king said. "You go where she goes. And make sure she comes back no later than one year from now. At which time, we'll cut all their heads off if she hasn't made good her promises to my daughter."

No need to thank me," Drusilla said.

"You have no idea, have you, how badly I wish our technological level were high enough to include a flush toilet that I could shove your head into?" Sandy slapped a hand to her forehead. "Oh, shit. What have I done? Mother. Ruth. They could be in chains. In the same dungeon as Ermengarde! What are we going to— Take that stupid beard off."

Drusilla thrust a crumpled piece of paper at Sandy. "Well, I have—"

"If you mention the oracle, I might be tempted to shove your paring knife where the sun doesn't shine." Sandy grabbed the piece of paper. It listed the "promises." "Did I really say all this?"

"You were drunk," Drusilla said. "But still remarkably coherent and inventive. It is curious how alcohol only reduced your instinct for self-preservation, not creativity."

"Land of the frost giants?" Sandy groaned. "What was I thinking?"

"My guess would be that you were thinking of the soft, perfumed delights of having your arms around Princess Maybelle, rather than risking life and limb in the icy fastness at the end of the world. Take heart. The thought of the beauty's charms will armour us with warmth even as our toes are turning black and dropping off with frostbite."

L-J Baker

"You are such a comfort."

"It's something I'm often told."

Blindingly bright flashes of light heralded the approach of Captain Tyrone. He looked extremely neat and extremely unhappy.

"You there," he said. "Witch. And peculiar person with the pimples. Try nothing on me. I am his Majesty's handpicked man. I have my trusty anti-magic sword."

"How can it possibly be anti-magical?" Sandy said. "If it were anti-magical, wouldn't the magic that makes it anti-magical drop off?"

Drusilla removed her beard to reveal a broad grin.

Tyrone's face folded in a deep frown. He dropped a hand to the hilt of his sword. "The blade is etched with *WWI*," he said. "Wizards and Witches Immune. Now, I won't take nothing funny from either of you. You hear? No magic or...or saying slippery magical tongue type things to make me doubt my royal commission."

"No magical slippery tongue things?" Sandy grinned. "You are aware that we're dykes?"

Drusilla laughed. Tyrone blushed scarlet to the roots of his impeccably styled hair.

Sandy made a cup of tea in her mother's spotlessly neat kitchen. Even Tyrone deigned to risk the seat of his breeches on one of the polished chairs.

"I've been thinking," Drusilla said. "We could try to break Mrs Blunt and Ruth out of the dank, dark dungeon where they writhe with suffering and torment. My paring knife and I are willing."

Tyrone's hand dropped to his sword hilt. "You forget the forces of his Majesty."

Drusilla looked at him. "No, I hadn't."

"I don't think that would be a good idea," Sandy said. "And aren't you forgetting the oracle? And all our adventures?"

"We could have those as fugitives on the run from royal justice," Drusilla said. "That would be even more exciting and just the sort of thing that dispossessed princesses in disguise would do. And think of the affecting scene when my beloved Maybelle falls into my arms and her father realises that he has hounded his future daughter-in-law almost to the edges of the earth. I know you won't mind a bit of persecution in the name of romance."

"I'm thinking you might not know me as well as you believe."

Sandy set Drusilla's piece of paper on the dining table and smoothed out the fateful list. "A year. All this stuff shouldn't be that hard, should it? A quick visit to the icy lands of the frost giants. Then a few days on the bottom of the ocean to get the pearl. Nothing could be easier. I'm sure the Green Hermit will only take a chat over a cup of tea to agree to break half a century of self-imposed isolation to come back with us."

"Exactly what I was thinking," Drusilla said. "With your powers of persuasion and my commanding albeit disguised royal presence, we shouldn't have any problems. And if the tin man here gets too annoying, we can let the ogres of the Wildlands eat him."

Tyrone looked up from polishing away an imaginary blemish on his breastplate. "Ogres?"

"Weren't you listening?" Sandy said. "I don't think there's a single unpleasant impossibility that my drunken imagination missed."

Sandy rose and automatically rinsed out her dirty cup, dried it, and replaced it in the cupboard. She went upstairs to her bedroom and stuffed some clean clothes in a bag, including several pairs of underwear. Drusilla waited with her own bulging pack on her back. Captain Tyrone stood outside near his horse. Small children from the neighbourhood stood pointing and staring at him.

Sandy locked the front door and took the key down the street to Mrs Bustlewaite. In Mrs Bustlewaite's front room, Sandy saw the pretty Ursula sitting on the window seat. For the first time in her life, Sandy tried to quell the impulse to approach a pretty woman. Her task was made easier by remembering the axe she was living under. It helped, too, that Ursula barely spared Sandy a glance for eyeing Tyrone.

"Oh, Sandra!" Mrs Bustlewaite enveloped Sandy in a motherly hug and pulled her close to an ample bosom. "You poor, dear child. Having to rescue your mother from our wicked, wicked king! Don't worry, I'm going to start a petition. I'm sure all the bridge club will sign it. Except, perhaps, Mrs Pickering. She's not forgiven Betty for that incident over the ace of spades. But we'll let the king know what he's up against with his tyranny against our dear Betty."

Sandy thought that his Majesty might already have a shrewd idea. There couldn't have been too many prisoners who tried to box the royal ear.

"So, while you're off risking life and limb on your hopeless quest," Mrs Bustlewaite said, "rest assured that we'll be thinking about you as we sit by the cosy fire of an evening and sip our warm milk. And I'll whip a duster around Betty's house once a week. It wouldn't do for her to come home from that dungeon to find dust on the mantelpiece. That would break our Betty's spirit worse than any racking, iron maiden, water torture, or thumbscrews, wouldn't it?"

"Dust?" Tyrone said with disgust. "Madam, nothing could be a greater torment!"

Mrs Bustlewaite smiled approvingly at him. Ursula batted her eyelashes.

Sandy bent under the small sack of meat, cheese, pies, bread, and a pair of Mr Bustlewaite's woolly socks that Mrs Bustlewaite had insisted she take. Tyrone did not offer to tie it to his monogrammed saddlebags.

"Where to now?" Drusilla said.

"North, I suppose," Sandy said. "Isn't that where it's colder? Where the frost giants live?"

The guards on the city gate smirked at Captain Tyrone as he rode past them and out into the countryside ahead of Sandy and Drusilla.

"Plucking the moon from the sky for her," Drusilla said.

Sandy glanced up from wondering how many dusty miles she would have to walk in her boots. And whether or not she should have worn the new ones her mother bought her, despite them giving her a blister. "What?"

"It's a common lover's promise," Drusilla said. "You know. Fair maiden, I would pluck the moon from the sky for a quick kiss and squeeze your tits. That could've been tricky to make happen."

"Quick kiss and squeeze your tits?" Sandy said. "I'm beginning to see that acne alone is not responsible for your lack of girl action."

"You don't have a girlfriend, either, do you?" Drusilla said.

"True," Sandy said. "And it's not as though any woman is likely to throw herself at me while the axe hovers over my neck."

Drusilla shrugged. "As one accustomed to living with perpetual danger, it has been my experience that women can be impressed with a person's constant, indefatigable battle with adversity. Or, perhaps, it's my royalty shining through my disguise."

"Royalty?" Tyrone said.

"It's obvious, isn't it?" Sandy said. "I bet you realised the moment you saw her."

"It's a secret," Drusilla said. "But even I, Drusilla, dispossessed princess of an oppressed people, have difficulties concealing my elevated birth and superior blue blood."

"That's why the assassins and trolls and everyone are always finding you and trying to kill you, isn't it?" Sandy said. "That blue tinge to your skin."

"Assassins?" Tyrone put a hand to his sword hilt and quickly looked around. "Trolls?"

"Fear not." Drusilla whipped out her paring knife. "I am armed and ready."

Tyrone peered at her knife. "That looks very sharp. Great shine. Do you use the Phenomenally Fabulous Dexinon's Multipurpose Armour and Sword Oil?"

Drusilla glanced around as if any of the grazing cows in the fields they walked past might be eavesdropping. "Mrs Blunt's lard."

"Mrs Blunt's lard?" Tyrone said. "Is that some magical substance?"

Sandy stared at him. He looked serious. This was shaping up to be the longest year of her life.

Later in the afternoon, they stopped at a crossroads to share some of Mrs Bustlewaite's apple pie and drink from a stream. Sandy's legs and feet already throbbed, though they had walked less than five miles according to the signpost. She had not heard about famous adventurers getting blisters and aching legs. Certainly not after just a few hours walking. Still, your average hero probably didn't have a sedentary day job in the retail sector.

"I don't suppose either of you know how far we have to go?" Sandy said. "You'd think the icy fastness of Frostheim, where it is always deepest winter, would be more than a couple of days' walk, wouldn't you?"

"There is a very nice inn perhaps six or seven miles hence at Little Hollow," Tyrone said. "The beds have clean straw and no fleas."

"No fleas?" Sandy said. "We won't be able to afford it."

The inn proved well out of Sandy's and Drusilla's price range. Tyrone commanded the services of the laundry maid, a manservant, and the boot boy. Sandy and Drusilla sneaked into the hayloft of the stables and set about wolfing down more of Mrs Bustlewaite's food. With her mouth stuffed with ripe cheese, Sandy made a quick calculation of how much they had eaten today and how much they would eat in a year. The result was considerably more than what remained in the sack.

"We'll need to earn some money or we won't get within spitting distance of the snowy wilderness," Sandy said.

"I have no worries." Drusilla belched and stretched out on the hay bales. "You are a fully fledged witch and I am a person of infinite resource. Between us we can do anything. Besides, the tin man carries a lot of pocket change."

Drusilla pulled a bulging purse from inside her tunic. It bore Tyrone's monogram.

"You picked his pocket!" Sandy said.

"I told you that I am resourceful. I have taken his purse into protective custody. If I hadn't taken it, some cutpurse or other casual criminal would have. I'm sure he'll thank me for keeping it safe for him."

Sandy imagined Tyrone in the morning when it came time to pay the innkeeper. She grinned.

Hay, Sandy quickly learned, sounded a lot more romantic and less prickly than it really was. How you would roll around on the stuff naked and make love without being continually jabbed in soft and inconvenient places defied her imagination. Nor had she truly appreciated how much horses stank. They farted a lot. The nightly soundtrack also included the soft patter of unseen paws.

"This place is crawling with mice," Sandy whispered.

"Be grateful they're not Rats of Unusual Size," Drusilla said. "They'd be hunted by Owls of Unusual Size and Cats of Unusual Size. Which would be a little unnerving in this closed space."

Moonlight slanted in through the window in the roof. Sandy could see a light dusting of stars. For no obvious reason, they made her throat tighten.

"I hope they didn't put mother and Ruth in the same dungeon with mad Ermengarde," Sandy whispered.

"Mad Ermengarde?" Drusilla said.

"You know, going on adventures sounds great. Until you actually do it. I'm not really enjoying this. I feel sore all over. I'd kill to be in my own bed."

"I am more accustomed to hardship and being homesick. But I, too, miss Mrs Blunt's dinner. She makes the best custard. When I am restored to my usurped throne, I shall order the royal chefs to use her recipe."

"Especially on prunes. And the way she does roast potatoes."

"With the crispy outsides and soft middles. That, too, I shall command copied by royal decree."

"My mouth's watering as if I could taste them," Sandy said. "And the way she does cabbage so that it doesn't go all mushy."

"The way Ruth shows her dimples when she smiles."

"Baby peas with—" Sandy twisted her head to frown at Drusilla's dark shape. "Ruth's dimples?"

"They are really very charming. Especially on the dear girl. Don't you think so?"

Sandy's frown deepened. "Does she have dimples?"

"I am so pleased that I am an impoverished princess rather than a slightly clueless heroine. I don't have to choose between the beautiful princess with the golden hair and pearly teeth, or the deserving, practical, loving girl next door."

Sandy scowled.

"And, of course," Drusilla said, "being royal, I can look forward to one day getting my throne back and eating prunes and custard for tea every day."

Sandy rolled her eyes at the dark. "Goes without saying, really, doesn't it? That the desire for prunes and custard is everyone's reason for wanting to overthrow a country's ruling regime?"

"History is littered with people who have done a lot worse for reasons that aren't half as good as a really nice prune custard."

Washing in the horse trough, Sandy discovered, was another of those things that read a lot better than the reality. The water was cold and tasted funny. It had bits of hay floating in it, and green scummy stuff clung to the sides of the trough below the water level. Having forgotten a towel, Sandy dried herself on her tunic. It was imperfectly absorbent and not very clean.

Drusilla used her paring knife to cut them uneven chunks of bread and cheese. As breakfasts went, it would probably sound a lot better in a book than standing in a damp tunic in the stableyard of a busy inn with a mare noisily urinating nearby.

Shouts erupted from the inn. Captain Tyrone's breastplate flashed as he stomped out with the innkeeper close on his shiny-spurred heels. The innkeeper's wife, a maid, the cook, a manservant, the boot boy, and one of the stable lads poured out after the pair. Tyrone gesticulated. The innkeeper threw his arms around more wildly and shouted louder. Tyrone glowered.

Drusilla smiled.

"You'd better give him back his purse," Sandy said. "I have no objections to losing our shadow, but it wouldn't be fair to leave the innkeeper and servants out of pocket. It's always we small business owners who suffer the most from petty crime."

Tyrone managed to look simultaneously relieved and deeply suspicious when Drusilla handed him his purse. He spent most of the morning glaring at her from the saddle and patting his tunic to make sure his purse was still there.

The countryside crawled by. Sandy lost count of the number of villages they passed. Farmers spared them a glance before returning to the much more important task of ploughing. The road, which was often little more than two wheel ruts through overgrown grass, wound an erratic but generally northerly course. In the distance, Sandy spied the smudgy tops of hills.

"Perhaps those mountains will prove to be the ramparts of the terrifyingly enormous home of the frost giants," Drusilla said. "The walls around dangers without number that we must scale."

"Perhaps."

Sandy paused to remove her boot. She shook it upside down to let a disappointingly tiny pebble fall out. It had felt more like a rock as it rubbed her sole for the last couple of miles.

"We will have to valiantly brave not only the giants," Drusilla said, "who will want to make sausages out of us, but also avalanches and rock slides and falling hundreds and hundreds of feet off the side of a mountain to our deaths."

"You missed your calling as a motivational coach," Sandy said. "I've been thinking that we should have bought a map."

"Cartography is not yet a terribly exact science," Drusilla said. "It will take some large advances in geographical exploration and the invention of a reliable clock before much accuracy is possible."

"I'd be happy with something that says 'Here be frost giants,'" Sandy said. "It's not as though we have much idea where—"

"Are you expecting to be followed?" Tyrone said. "Is this some sneaky magical trick you're trying to pull on me?"

Sandy halted and turned around. Drusilla grabbed Sandy's arm and tugged her off-balance. Drusilla pulled her through a hedge. Sandy sprawled on the grass. Drusilla clamped a hand over Sandy's mouth.

"Ssh!" Drusilla whispered. "Trust me. I have much experience at hiding from pursuit. It's probably more assassins after my royal self. The Brotherhood of the Stabbing Blade never gives up. We can wait here, unobserved, until the danger has passed."

Sandy pulled Drusilla's hand away. "Haven't you forgotten Captain Shiny sitting on a big brown horse in the middle of the road? Or do you think no one will notice him?"

Drusilla frowned. Sandy stood. Tyrone sat with his hand on his sword hilt squinting along the road. His horse unconcernedly nibbled the nearest patch of grass.

"I don't see anyone," Sandy said. "How do you know we're being followed?"

"Dust," Tyrone said. "I can smell the stuff from miles off. Someone has been kicking up dust behind us most of the morning."

"That's an unusual ability," Drusilla said. "Are you sure it's not magical?"

Tyrone glared at her. His fingers tightened on his sword hilt. "Magic cannot exist near my anti-magical sword!"

"It could be just some merchant following on his wagon," Sandy said. "Or a farmer taking his produce to whatever town is next. This is hardly a secret road, is it? And, let's face it, who would be following us?"

"I am perpetually shadowed by enemies," Drusilla said.

"Well, okay," Sandy said, "apart from the countless assassins, trolls, dragons, ogres, cyclopses, and other assorted monsters with their own mysterious motives for wanting to track you down and kill you, who would be following us?"

"Do hordes of men perverted into the dark, mindless, and vile forms of orcs count amongst the assorted monsters?" Drusilla asked.

"Yes."

"Oh." Drusilla shrugged. "Then I don't suppose anyone should be following us."

Sandy spent most of the afternoon walk glancing over her shoulder. Despite Tyrone's assurances that there was someone behind them, Sandy saw no one apart from a couple of tinkers and a gloomy journeyman torturer who didn't return their friendly wave as he overtook them with his huge sword, *Terminal angst*, strapped across his back.

Sunset caught them between towns.

"How about those woods?" Sandy pointed. "There should be plenty of firewood and shade from the wind. Real adventurers always whip up a comfy camp in a forest in no time."

After a spirited argument, Captain Tyrone finally realised that neither Drusilla nor Sandy would oblige him by grooming his horse. He muttered unhappily as he removed his shiny cuirass. Drusilla and Sandy set about gathering firewood. They made the discovery that an axe would have been handy.

"I'll have a go with the flint." Sandy held out her hand.

Drusilla looked blank. "I thought you had one."

They both turned to the sulking Tyrone.

"Why would I carry so plebeian an article as a flint?" he said. "The quartermaster sergeant takes care of all that."

Drusilla and Sandy shared a look.

"Then I suppose there's only one thing for it," Sandy said. "I fully expect some sympathy from you both for the splitting headache I'll have."

Sandy knelt on the damp ground and worked through the mind-clearing meditation necessary for lifting up a tiny corner of the curtain to the Elemental Void of Fire. She set her finger on the kindling. Nothing happened. Not so much as an orange spark.

Sandy scowled. "That's odd. I can usually get that one to work. Maybe I'm more tired than I thought."

Drusilla's face was all but lost in the coalescing shadows of encroaching night. "I wonder if the tin man's sword really is anti-magical?"

Sandy turned a disgusted look on Tyrone. "I'd forgotten that. I don't suppose you could take a good, long walk away? And take your sword with you."

"Leave you?" Tyrone looked up from smoothing the front of his tunic. "Against the orders of my king? So that you can work your magicky mischief? What sort of fool do you think I am?"

"Do you really want me to answer that?" Drusilla said.

"Cold food and no fire, it is, then." Sandy groped for her dwindling sack of food.

Two days of walking was more exercise than Sandy normally got in months. She thought she would fall asleep as soon as she lay down, but she had not bargained on the ground being so uncomfortable. Lumpy. Damp leaf litter. And probably crawling with all sorts of insects who would love to curl up snug and warm in her ears. And she was cold. An extra tunic was no substitute for two or three thick woolly blankets that one's mother had lovingly hemmed.

Sandy lay wide awake, dog-tired, shivering, and listening to every crack and snap from the dark woods around her. Tyrone snored loudly enough to wake the dead. But, then, he had a big, thick, fluffy blanket cunningly sewn into a sleeping bag. Only two days into this mess and Sandy felt pessimistic of her chances of saving all their heads. Why couldn't she have promised Princess Maybelle something straightforward like a bunch of roses?

"Are you asleep?" Drusilla whispered.

"Can there be a stupider question anyone could ask?" Sandy said. "Why not ask me if I'm awake?"

"Aren't we grumpy and pedantic tonight?" Drusilla said. "Still, even one as inured to hardship and danger as I, Drusilla, dispossessed princess of an oppressed people, find this uncomfortable."

Sandy sat up. She rubbed her thighs. Her feet felt numb. She wondered if she could steal Tyrone's sleeping bag.

"You know, I'm used to being a second-rate witch," Sandy said, "but I'm rapidly realising that I'm a third- or fourth-rate adventurer. Grob the Brave Barbarian Hero curls up on the ground and sleeps soundly without a problem all night as if outdoors or featherbeds made no difference to him. But it's bloody impossible. I'm freezing."

"I believe that you are the unlikely and endearing type who stumbles through all the plot twists to scrape through in the end," Drusilla said. "And I am your talented sidekick with the special destiny."

"I'd have preferred to be redoubtable and rugged, albeit not terribly bright. Sandy the Brave Barbarian Heroine, who doesn't fret about bugs crawling in her ears and who has to fight off all the women who throw themselves at her. Oh, yeah, and who wins a fortune along the way. I could just about live with that."

"There wasn't much chance of you turning out that way, with your mother," Drusilla said. "Look, my ever-resourceful brain has come up with an idea. We could try to put each other to sleep with stories. I know some very scary ghost ones. About the headless horse."

Sandy might have pointed out the obvious, but she was too cold and weary. Instead, she hugged her knees and told Drusilla to start.

"...and they crouched behind their doors," Drusilla whispered. "The wind whined through the rafters. *Woo. Woo.* Their blood froze in their veins. *Thud.* And their breath lodged in their throats. *Gasp. Wheeze.* As they strained to hear the ghostly *clip-clop-clip* of the headless horse approaching them. *Clip. Clop. Clip.* It searched for warm livers to nibble. Its dead eyes that dripped blood could see through walls and—"

"How could a headless horse have eyes?"

"Oh. Erm. They're sort of floating up there where its eyes should be. Yes, that's it. Same with its teeth, which are really fangs sharp enough to rend—"

"Ssh!" Sandy sat up, ears cocked. "Did you hear that?"

"*Clip-clop-clip*," Drusilla said in her best spooky voice. "It's coming to get—"

"Ssh! I mean it. I heard something."

"It's okay. No need to be afraid. I should never have started this story. I have a Gift. It's one of many. My tale-telling is so authentic that it can scare the spit—"

"Shut up!"

Sandy flung her hands across Drusilla's mouth. Sandy's ears felt as though they strained out from the sides of her head. She heard her own unnaturally loud breathing and Tyrone's snores. The soft creak of an axle. The muffled thud of a hoof hitting hard-packed ground. The hairs on the back of Sandy's neck prickled erect. Her heart hammered as if it wanted to break out of her ribcage and flee. Drusilla stiffened and tugged Sandy's hands from her mouth.

"Oh, no," Drusilla whispered. "My extraordinary powers of eloquence have exceeded even my expectations and summoned the supernatural creature itself. Oh, crap."

Sandy scrambled to her feet and bolted. She blundered through the dark woods, banging into trees, crashing against bushes, and stumbling over roots and fallen branches. Thumps and crashes chased her. Her lungs couldn't suck in enough air as she stumbled and staggered as fast as she could.

Sandy lost her footing on slippery ground.

"Aaarrgh!"

She fell, slid, and splashed into cold water. Drusilla landed on top of her and knocked her breath away.

Sandy sat up. She was waist deep in water, on what felt like soft mud. Drusilla's breathing sounded as laboured and loud as her own.

"Can you hear it?" Sandy whispered. She peered into the darkness. "Did it follow us?"

"Yes!" Drusilla grabbed Sandy's arm. "I hear its undead nostrils quivering with the miasma of death drawn straight from the pits of the underworld and— No. Wait. That was me breathing."

Sandy took the opportunity to secretly urinate in the water before groping and squelching her way back up the streambank. Along with running away, terrified, in the night, that was another thing you never heard of any true adventurers doing.

The stubby little blade of Drusilla's paring knife glinted in the starlight. Sandy wasn't convinced that, as their only weapon against a malevolent equine ghoul, it would prove much use, but she stood close behind Drusilla anyway.

"Captain Tyrone is still back there," Sandy whispered. "Do you think the headless horse hasn't pursued us because it stopped to eat his liver?"

"That is possible. He may have nobly and bravely sacrificed himself so that we may live on to pursue our quest."

"Tyrone?"

"It does seem somewhat unlikely, I agree. And we have not heard the blood-curdling screams of his mortal agony or seen any pale pieces of his ripped innards flung past us."

Sandy couldn't see much or hear anything other than herself and Drusilla. "Do you think we ought to go and check, or should we wait here?"

Drusilla paused to consider this. "Under normal circumstances, we would, of course, sneak back, armed with my paring knife, to surprise and slay the foul foe. However, more is at stake than the quest for personal glory. We must think of Mrs Blunt's head. And Ruth's. What would happen to them in the unlikely event that either or both of us were overcome and rent into small, bloody, meaty chunks by the unkillable creature?"

"Oh, good thinking. Much as we would like to return to battle the fiend, we daren't risk ourselves because of Mother and Ruth."

"Exactly."

Sandy shivered and wrapped her arms around herself. "You know, that was probably the most sensible thing I've ever heard you say. And this was a great time for it to happen."

L-J Baker

andy woke with a jolt. She sat propped against a tree trunk. Drusilla leaned against her, snoring. Sandy felt cold to the core and damp from the night's immersion. But it looked like she still had her liver.

Sandy had to use the tree to straighten and stand. Every part of her felt stiff and sore. She looked around and found that they were on the edge of the woods beside a sluggish brown stream. Cows looked up on the opposite bank from drinking. Sandy eyed one scrawny creature with a pendulous pink udder and imagined a hot, sizzling steak.

"We could milk her," Drusilla said. "For warm, creamy milk."

Sandy's immediate reaction was that they were stealing from a farmer, a fellow small businessman. But she was hungry and shaking with cold. Sandy nodded and started towards the stream. The cows mooed and moved away. Drusilla and Sandy waded across the muddy water and ended up chasing the cows around the field.

Sandy stopped to glare at the scrawny one that seemed to be laughing at her. "You know, we still have some food left. In the bag. If the ghoul horse didn't eat it."

Sandy and Drusilla crept back into the woods. After getting lost, they finally tracked down their campsite by spotting Tyrone's horse through the trees. Tyrone still slept as peacefully as a baby in his snug blanket.

"We could leave him," Drusilla whispered.

"If we did, he'd ride back to the king," Sandy whispered. "Where would that leave Mother and Ruth?"

Tyrone grunted and woke. "Bacon, eggs, kidneys, and sausages. Toast. A pot of tea and honey. Warm the cup for me. Eggs sunny side up. And be quick about it."

Sandy dropped a dry chunk of three-day-old bread on his blanket.

For Sandy, the morning passed in a blur of green fields, hedges, cows, sheep, smoky villages, and a dull headache that gradually spread throughout her whole body. Tyrone's news that they were no longer being followed failed to rouse much interest in her, nor did his later revelation that whoever had been behind them was now in front of

48

them. Sandy fast sank into the first miseries of a really bad cold. Her thoughts, though she would never have admitted them aloud, were for being tucked up in bed with a warmed brick at her feet and her mother fussing and bringing her a nice hot posset.

By late afternoon, Sandy stumbled with weariness and she could barely think. She had to squat behind a hedge to relieve herself. Drusilla and Tyrone argued about something. Sandy sighed and plucked leaves from the hedge. They were coarse and scratchy on her backside. She wondered if real adventurers remembered to carry personal hygiene products. The thought of menstruation did nothing to cheer her. Perhaps getting her head cut off might not be such a bad idea. At least it was quick and you didn't have to worry about washing your hands afterwards.

Sandy peered at the weathered signpost at the crossroads. Neither of the three arms pointed to LAND OF FROST GIANTS FIFTY MILES.

"This way!" Tyrone jabbed his gauntleted hand to the right fork.

"This way leads north." Drusilla pointed to the left. "Perhaps your secret wizardly nature is prompting you with some magic to take a different route?"

Tyrone paled and patted his sword hilt. "WWI. Wizards and Witches Immune. No magicky tricks can exist near me. If you—"

"Look," Sandy said, "why shouldn't we go north?"

"Captain Supernatural Senses," Drusilla said, "swears that the person who was following us passed us in the night and has gone this way."

Tyrone glowered. "The dust trail goes that way. My superior grasp of military tactics says we should therefore take a different route."

Sandy ran a hand through her greasy hair. "Look, how can anyone be following us from in front?"

Drusilla smirked at Tyrone. Sandy trudged off along the left fork. Eventually the other two joined her.

"We ought to plan our halt for the night with more care than last night," Drusilla said. "We don't want the headless horse to find us again."

"Headless horse?" Tyrone said.

"It stalked past the woods where you lay sleeping," Drusilla said. "Do you feel any pains in your guts?"

Tyrone scowled at her. One hand lifted to his breastplate. "Pains? Why?"

"I was thinking that if you had some liver disease," Drusilla said, "that might be the reason that the headless horse didn't eat it out of you last night."

Tyrone paled.

Sandy wrapped her arms around herself to try to control the return of her shivers. She pointed ahead to a hunched cluster of small houses. "Let's see if someone will let us sleep on their floor."

"Floor?" Tyrone said with disgust. "Peasants keep their pigs and goats in their houses with them. They'll be riddled with fleas and all manner of vermin."

"And grime," Drusilla said. "Forget not the steaming heaps of filth everywhere."

"This is intolerable," Tyrone said. "We must continue on to find a reputable hostelry."

"You can," Sandy said. "But Dru and I are broke."

Sandy began haggling with a grimy, pinch-faced woman for the rent of a piece of her not very clean floor near a hearth when Tyrone guided his horse into view. The peasant woman sucked in breath through the gaps in her teeth.

"Soldier!" the woman shouted. "Rape! Torture! Hide your sheep! Hide your daughters!"

"No, wait," Sandy said. "We aren't—"

The woman slammed her door in Sandy's face. All the hovel doors slammed.

Sandy turned to glare at Tyrone. He looked unconcerned and urged his horse on down the road with the airy comment that there was bound to be a nice inn in a mile or two.

Drusilla eyed him with hostility. "One day, he shall feel the wrath of the paring knife of Drusilla."

"One day, I shall cheer you on. But not today. Think of Mother's head."

"And Ruth's."

Sandy trudged on along the road in the wake of Tyrone's horse. The Fat Sow and Piglet Inn failed to meet Captain Tyrone's exacting standards. Drusilla and Sandy ignored his entreaties to continue on to find an establishment where the innkeeper had clean fingernails.

Sandy woke the next morning to a thunderous sneeze that felt like it tried to shove her brains out of her nostrils. She shivered, and could eat nothing for breakfast, though Drusilla tucked into a mysteriously acquired bowl of steamy porridge drizzled with honey. Sandy stumbled along the road north and began to sweat even as she felt chilled to the core.

"You're not looking so good," Drusilla said. "Even less than normal, I mean."

"Thanks." Sandy sneezed.

"And those grey clouds look ready to dump gallons and gallons of cold wet rain on us," Drusilla said. "We ought to stop. And— And make a fire or something equally caring and soothing."

Oddly, Tyrone agreed.

"You did buy a flint and tinder at that last town?" Drusilla said to him.

"I?" Tyrone said. "As an officer, I do not concern myself with—"

"You're the one with money, tin man," Drusilla said. "You just wait until I have my throne back and am married to the Princess Maybelle. I'm going to have a word to two to say about you to the king. I can tell you that I won't be honey-coating it if my dear friend Sandy, the Great Obtuse Mage mentioned by the infallible Oracle of Ring, dies a horrible and protracted death of pneumonia huddled in a roadside hedge because you were too miserly to provide us with the means to start a fire."

"I say!" Tyrone said. "It's not my fault she spent the night in a stream. If you—"

"Beg an ember," Sandy said.

Tyrone and Drusilla looked at her.

"From a house," Sandy said. "Ask if they'll let you have an ember. Then we can start a fire."

"Oh, that is good thinking, fearless leader," Drusilla said. "The tin man here can get on his horse and—"

"Ware!" Tyrone's hand dropped to his sword hilt. "They're coming. I can feel that dust. It's clogging every pore."

"What dust?" Drusilla said.

"From the person who has been following us. I warned you that the vile fiend was following us from ahead."

Big, fat, wet drops of rain hurled down about Sandy's head and shoulders. The road here wound through scrubby uncultivated rocky hills dotted with the occasional sheep but nothing in the way of a tavern, hovel, or even derelict barn.

"There's as much dust about," Drusilla said, "as there are houses crammed with glowing embers. Unless you mean that cute little lamb over there is kicking up great gouts of ugly, smothering, hateful dust from its hoofikins."

"You are not amusing," Tyrone said. "And sheep can be dangerous under the wrong circumstances."

Drusilla smirked at him. "Know a lot of sheep, do you?"

Sandy tugged her tunic collar up, chafed her hands, and walked away from their squabble.

"Warmth," Sandy croaked to herself. "A roaring fire. Hot brick. Blankets. Snug. Hot soup. Gentle—"

Tyrone shrieked. Sandy could imagine him frantically wiping at the glassy beads of rust-bringing water clinging to his precious breast-plate.

"Gentle hands soothing me," Sandy continued.

"Are we imagining?" Drusilla fell in step with Sandy. "That, too, is one of the Gifts that bounteous nature endowed my royal self with."

"In abundance," Sandy agreed.

"Crackling logs," Drusilla said. "Leaping flames. Orange glow of warmth seeping all around us. Mrs Blunt's hot milk."

"Wriggling your toes in fluffy dry socks that don't have holes in them."

Tyrone guided his horse alongside them. He wiped his breastplate with a rag. "We must find shelter! It's raining."

"It's all that military training," Drusilla said. "Nothing gets past him, does it? I feel so much safer with him along."

A tearing cough snuffed Sandy's grin.

"Rust!" Tyrone said. "And dust! I hope my liege lord realises the extraordinary dangers I have been forced to endure in his service."

"Sitting in Mrs Blunt's kitchen," Drusilla said, "with an empty dish of prunes and custard in front of me. My tummy stretched full. And Mrs Blunt offering me the last morsel of dessert."

"Bed." Sandy wiped rain and sweat from her forehead with an icy cold hand that felt like it belonged to a dead person. "Not having to walk. Sleeping. Dry. Something hot to eat. Anything."

Drusilla put an arm around Sandy's shoulders. "We will find somewhere to shelter. Take heart. The infallible Oracle of Ring said nothing about your miserable death. Or me having to drag your corpse around with me when I have my valorous adventures. Although, on the other hand, it did not say that you were not to suffer a little bit along the way."

"You're a great comfort," Sandy said.

"Aaah!" Tyrone stopped his horse and pointed ahead. "Ware!"

"Oh, no!" Drusilla said. "The infamous evil dust monster."

"Yes! I can sense—"

"Panic not, tin man." Drusilla whipped out a rumpled handkerchief. "I haven't lived in Mrs Betty Blunt's house for several weeks without learning a thing or two about combat dusting. Leave this to me! Me and my trusty rag will give this dust monster a gruesome and agonising end. A wipe here. A dab there. A quick—"

"That's not funny," Tyrone said.

Sandy was too weary and too miserable to stop them bickering. She stumbled on into the rain.

Drusilla jogged to catch her. "You know what we need?"

L-J Baker

"A tavern?" Sandy said. "A lot of money? A big hole in the ground to drop you two in?"

"Actually, that nice, cosy, well set-out campsite just ahead in those trees looks great." Drusilla put an arm around Sandy's shoulders and steered her to the left. "With a welcoming fire. A camp kettle of hearty stew bubbling hot and ready. A roomy, waterproof tent. Dry blankets inside. A change of clean clothes waiting for us in the morning. And a sensible, pleasant young woman to welcome us and ready with a dose of some chest tonic for you."

Sandy sniffed and spared her a watery glance. "You really do live in a world unhindered by mundane reality, don't you? If only—"

"Hello, Ruth," Drusilla said. "I hope you haven't been waiting too long, dear girl."

"Hello, Drusilla," Ruth said. "Hello, Sandy."

Sandy stopped to blink. Ruth rose from beneath the awning of a sturdy blue tent and stepped around a fire over which a tin kettle hung. A mouth-watering meaty smell pervaded the damp air. A tethered pony munched grass near a sturdy two-wheeled cart.

"You're wet," Ruth said. "Come closer to the fire. The stew is ready."

Drusilla tugged Sandy towards the tent. "Our fearless leader has a wicked head cold, dear girl. I trust you know how to care for her."

"I suppose you've all been wearing damp socks," Ruth said.

Sandy soon found herself tucked up snug in warm woolly blankets and with Ruth kneeling beside her encouraging her to sip a warm posset. The rum quickly floated Sandy's already fuddled wits loose.

"I dreamed this," Sandy said.

Ruth smiled and took the empty cup. Sandy sank into the bedding. Ruth tucked the blankets up around her.

"She was right," Sandy muttered. "You do have dimples."

Ruth quickly departed the tent.

Sandy looked sharply at Ruth. "My mother did?"

"Mrs Blunt can be a formidable woman," Drusilla said. "Even I, Drusilla, quail at the prospect of refusing when she offers me a second helping of seed cake."

Sandy caught her next sneeze in her already damp handkerchief. "My mother convinced the king to set you free and give you this pony, cart, equipment, and supplies? And only keep her as hostage? I thought he wanted to cut her head off."

"Oh, yes," Ruth said. "Now more than ever, I think. But your mother pointed out to him how unfair he was being in expecting you to walk all over the known and unknown worlds. From his Majesty's expression, it was clear that he had not previously given any thought to how you might be able to carry enough pairs of clean underwear to last a whole year. Nor how badly his actions would go down with the mothers in his realm. And the PR disaster of her being a defenceless widow."

Drusilla grinned as she cleaned the last of the porridge out of the kettle. "I feel sorry for my hapless father-in-law to be. He knew not what power he pitted himself against when he callously ordered Mrs Blunt arrested. Wait until he receives the petition from the ladies' bridge club. Perhaps then he will repent of his hasty nastiness in condemning us all to death."

Sandy considered her sense of unreality completely justified during the time she didn't spend dozing on the seat of the pony cart. One wasn't given to thinking of one's mother as a heroine who would brave a king's wrath for the sake of protecting her child. Anyone less like the protective she-bear or lioness of legend was hard to imagine than homely, round-faced Elizabeth Blunt who wielded no more dangerous implement than a wooden spoon—or her tongue.

Sandy's thinking and dozing was enhanced by wearing clean, dry clothes and being wrapped in a thick, new cloak. The fine drizzle that misted the morning on and off harmlessly beaded her exterior. Drusilla and Ruth took turns in driving and walking, though Drusilla chivalrously did more than her share of the walking. Captain Tyrone meekly and quietly brought up the rear. He had grumbled about his armour, rust, and the prospect of rain, only to be brought up short by Ruth's sensible advice to not wear his armour. His cuirass, safely oiled, clanked in the back of the pony trap inside one of Tyrone's monogrammed leather sacks.

Sandy jerked out of sleep. They had stopped near a leaning signpost.

"We were going to the land of frost giants first," Drusilla said. "For the unicorn."

"They live in the icy fastnesses to the north," Tyrone said. "That way."

"Do unicorns really live in a cold climate?" Ruth asked.

Drusilla scratched a pimple on her nose. "They must. That's what Sandy said. Oh, beautiful lady, blah blah blah skin paler than mane of a unicorn that lives in the lands of perpetual snow. Or something to that effect. She really does have a way with words that even I, Drusilla, with all my Gifts, cannot emulate."

"Considering where it has landed all of us," Ruth said, "you're probably safer that way."

"True, dear girl," Drusilla said. "We wouldn't want to have our heads cut off a second time because of me. How would they stick them back on after the first time?"

Sandy sneezed. Ruth handed her a clean handkerchief.

"We were wondering, fearless yet dozy leader," Drusilla said, "which way to go."

"I don't suppose there's a map in all those supplies you brought?" Sandy said.

"You don't know where you're going?" Ruth said.

Sandy shrugged and blew her nose. "How hard can it be to find unicorns? They're blindingly white big horse-things with spiral horns on their heads. Now, correct me if I'm wrong, but that's hardly the shape you'd take if you wanted to be inconspicuous. And everyone knows they live in snow. Makes sense. It— It camouflages them. When they hunt. And stuff."

Drusilla nodded. "If I were a unicorn, I'd pick somewhere white to gallop around in. Then everyone would see that my mane was whiter than the snow, if not paler than the skin of extraordinarily beautiful princesses."

"Only sneaky, cowardly peasant types camouflage themselves," Tyrone said. "We learn that in military training. Noble men, and creatures, meet each other in gallant hand-to-hand combat. In the open. None of this hiding."

Drusilla stared up at him. "So, are you agreeing or disagreeing?"

Tyrone frowned. "Yes."

Ruth turned to Sandy. "You don't know where you're going?"

Sandy shifted uncomfortably. "Well, I wouldn't put it quite like that. Cold and stuff is north."

"And you don't have a map," Ruth said.

"Fear not, dear girl," Drusilla said. "I have an innate sense of direction. It is another of those Gifts, with a capital G, that Mother Nature bestowed on me with such a lavish hand. Were I not so humble, it would be embarrassing how well endowed I am. North is that way. I, Drusilla, the human compass, know this."

Sandy might have commented on this, but Ruth continued to watch her with that unnervingly sensible look of hers. She decided that it was time to change the subject.

"What— What is the pony's name?" Sandy said.

"Bill, of course," Ruth said. "I've promised him that he won't be abandoned should we go into a mine. Perhaps we could ask directions."

Sandy shared a look with Drusilla and Tyrone. She had the sneakiest suspicion that real adventurers knew where they were going. She had never read in any book about Grob the Brave Barbarian Hero stopping at a roadside fruitstand to ask which way the battle for the world was. On the other hand, maybe Ruth had a point.

"Hypothetically," Sandy said "if we were to want to ask someone where unicorns live and how to get there, who would be best?"

"The land's wisest man," Tyrone said.

"At some point, a band of ill-assorted heroes will pass us," Drusilla said. "They will recognise my royalty, which will be inconvenient, but I should be able to use it to overawe them into telling us all they know."

"How about the Sword of Power, Helm of Invincibility, Ring of Greatness, and Staff of Ineffable Magic Tavern?" Ruth said.

"What's that?" Sandy asked.

"The place where adventurers and other miscellaneous heroes go to take a rest between deeds, quests, and wars," Ruth said. "We should find it in three or four days if we take that road."

"How do you know?" Sandy said.

"I asked."

Drusilla smirked.

"This large man in armour with an improbably enormous battle axe and a pet hamster told me all about it," Ruth said. "Trevor was on his way there to look for work. He told me that he hadn't seen you three on the road. So, I knew I'd overtaken you accidentally in the night and decided to wait. He invited me to have a drink with him at the tavern."

Trevor? Sandy frowned for the next mile or two of jolting, muddy path as she considered Ruth and this warrior bloke. Her frown deepened when she remembered Drusilla's remark about Ruth being in love with someone. Ruth with some enormous slab of beefcake? For a reason that Sandy couldn't put her mental finger on, she didn't like that idea.

An hour before sunset, they selected a suitable spot to make camp. Drusilla and Sandy wrestled with the tent, while Ruth rubbed down Bill the pony. Tyrone approached her.

"You have a goodly manner with horses," Tyrone said. "I've hobbled mine over there. You can use this brush on him."

"Bill is quite happy with this brush," Ruth said. "Now, don't take too long over your horse, we have a fire to light and food to prepare."

Drusilla and Sandy smiled at Tyrone. He saw them, realised how foolish he must look, and stomped off to care for his horse himself.

Drusilla searched for firewood. Ruth made Sandy sit down and keep warm. Sandy would rather have dragged branches than drink a generous measure of Grandmother Blunt's Ague Remedy.

Ruth efficiently wielded flint and tinder to start a fire. Tyrone strode over to it and dropped onto one of the collapsible canvas stools thoughtfully provided by his Royal Majesty's palace stores. The captain began smoothing his hands over some wrinkles in his breeches. He was busy with this when Ruth returned from the back of the cart with the tin kettle, some potatoes, a cabbage, a couple of carrots, and some smoked rabbit meat.

"Ah!" Tyrone rubbed his hands together. "This is more like it. A woman's touch. And you are a capital cook. This might not be such a terrible duty if— What?"

Sandy grinned. Ruth had deposited the kettle at Tyrone's feet and handed him a cooking knife.

"What am I supposed to do with this?" Tyrone asked.

"The vegetables cook better if they're cut up," Ruth said. "Here's Drusilla with some water. Now, mind you don't slice yourself on that knife. It's very sharp."

"But—" Tyrone held the knife up in protest. "Me? Tyrone, Captain of His Majesty's Own Bodyguard? You can't seriously expect me to— to cut up vegetables."

"They won't cook faster whole for you, will they?" Ruth asked. "They don't for me."

Sandy stifled a giggle. Drusilla smiled.

"But— Cook?" Tyrone said. "Me? Oh, no. This is woman's work."

"Is eating woman's work, too?" Sandy said.

Tyrone chewed his moustache and looked between the three women. "I have never performed such menial tasks before."

"There's a first time for everything," Ruth said. "It won't kill you. I promise."

Tyrone glowered and grabbed a carrot to hack his frustrations out on it.

Ruth gently guided him through the process of preparing their
stew while she busied herself with darning a couple of pairs of socks
for Drusilla and Sandy. Drusilla provided the firewood and fetched
more water. Sandy felt perfectly useless. Her sole contribution to the
evening was several painful sneezes and a couple of handkerchiefs full
of sticky green mucus.

At bedtime, Tyrone vanished into his own small tent. He was still
muttering and grumbling to himself. Ruth wished him a pleasant
good night as she took the lantern off towards the stream for a wash.
Sandy and Drusilla piled into the women's tent. Last night, Sandy
had been too ill to take much notice of the arrangements. Now she
saw the blanket hanging across the inside to divide it into two com-
partments. She and Drusilla stripped and climbed into thick, warm
blankets on sacks of soft straw. Sandy frowned at the divider that she
could barely see in the gathering dark. Ruth must sleep on the other
side of it.

"Dru?" Sandy whispered. "I never guessed that Ruth was straight."

"You've given her that much thought, have you?"

Sandy scowled. "What she said about that big warrior inviting her
for a drink. Trevor. I wouldn't have thought muscle-heads were her
type."

"Who do you think is her type?"

Sandy coughed so hard that it felt like she ejected pieces of her
lungs. She considered Ruth as she lay gasping for breath. "I'm not
sure. But I'd bet everything that Tyrone won't be throwing himself at
her feet any time soon."

Drusilla chuckled. "Poor Captain Shiny. His military training has
left him woefully ill-prepared to deal with common sense."

That must be the place," Sandy said.

About a mile away, down the gentle slope, a huge wood and brick building stood at the centre of a cluster of smaller buildings, tents, shacks, and corrals. The arrhythmic banging of smiths' hammers carried on the wind to them. Four roads running towards the cardinal compass points quartered the tiny town.

They passed shop after shack after stall selling adventurers' supplies. Armour that might not be protective but which looked impressive enough to make even jaded maidens swoon. Large, impractical weapons with fancy names that carried warnings, in fine etchings, that they were for show only. Chests for storing booty that were mysteriously larger on the inside than the outside. Special belts to store those handy-dandy instantly restorative health and mana potions, with patented quick-release tabs so that you could glug them down when near death in the middle of a fight.

All four roads converged at the Sword of Power, Helm of Invincibility, Ring of Greatness, and Staff of Ineffable Magic Tavern. The swinging doors looked well-scratched, probably by the passage of men in spiky armour being thrown out through them.

"Perhaps you ought to wait outside with Bill," Sandy said to Tyrone.

"Me?" His breastplate flashed blindingly as he turned from looking in vain for some passing stable lad to take his horse. "And let you three women walk into that place alone? Without male protection? I'll have you know that it sounds like it is full of ordinary soldiers and the like. Drinking. And gambling. Such low fellows have strong inclinations to be impolite and—and use intemperate language."

"Well, yes," Sandy said. "That's why I thought you'd be better off outside."

Tyrone scowled.

"Who is more likely to get picked on in there?" Sandy asked, "Three women who look utterly harmless, or a bloke in shiny armour without a scratch on it who likes bossing everyone around and impressing people with his superiority?"

"If you prattled on about that Tyrone, Captain of the King's Own Tin Men Corps stuff," Drusilla said, "I'm thinking they'd take it as a challenge. And want to dent you. A lot."

Tyrone bristled. "Are you impugning my courage?"

"It will be terribly grimy," Ruth said. "I bet they don't sweep the floors very often."

The three women entered the tavern while Tyrone guarded the horse and cart.

Sandy paused inside the swinging doors. The room was enormous with a bar running along the back wall. Sturdy wooden tables and benches filled the insides apart from an open area the size of a wrestling ring in the middle. The air was all but visible with the thick mixture of stale beer fumes, rancid sweat, old socks, armour oil, yesterday's vomit, and lanolin. Ruth had guessed right about the floor. It was littered with dirty clumps of straw, spilled ale, bits of broken armour, tufts of hair, and human teeth.

Sandy studied the patrons. To her left, the benches and tables were dwarfed by enormous, muscular men in armour. They bristled with swords and axes. She had never seen as many shaved heads or tattoos in one place before.

"The Eighteen-bar-one-hundred Club," Drusilla said. "No self-respecting adventuring party would be complete without one."

"Hello." A weary, middle-aged barmaid, with a beer-stained apron and hair spilling out of her plait, looked the three women up and down. "Hmm. The pimply one looks like a dispossessed princess in disguise. You other two aren't in need of rescuing, are you? Wicked step-parent persecuting you? The easily overlooked one in the skirt might be looking for a hero to help her fight off the advances of an evil half-brother. But you're just a clueless dyke witch, aren't you?"

Drusilla grinned. Ruth's profile showed a dimple. Sandy might have taken exception, but she noticed that the tavern was now deathly silent apart from the creak of badly oiled leather armour or chest harnesses. All the men had broken off their talk, laughter, and arm-wrestling contests in favour of leaning to hear what the newcomers wanted.

"Well?" the barmaid said. "You looking for someone for a job? Warriors, fighters, and berserkers for hire over there. Barbarians at the back with the furry loincloths. No knights or paladins seeking noble quests in today, I'm afraid. Rangers, bowmen, and half-elven archers near the bar. Thieves at the tables closest to the gentlemen's toilet. Assassins in the shadowy corner over— Oops. Make that *an* assassin. Mages, wizards, sorcerers, and enchanters near the hat stand and cane rack. Bards and troubadours normally sit near the end of the bar. You're better off coming back on a karaoke night if you want one of them. Assortment of young men who have been chosen for special but as yet unrevealed destinies, that table there. Not to be confused with the lads reared on farms or in manual-labouring households but who will turn out to be heirs to kingdoms, they're near the window. Nondescript spear-carriers for banging in tent-pegs and being the first to die horribly are out the back in the patio area. What is it to be?"

"Erm," Sandy said. "How about a drink? Two half pints of light ale and a glass of port and lemon, please."

The barmaid sniffed. The creaking reached deafening proportions as the men turned away, disappointed, and resumed their drinking, gambling, and boasting.

"Ladies' lounge over there." The barmaid pointed and bustled off to deliver several umbrella drinks to the table of wizards.

The table she indicated looked just like the others except that it had a dead flower in a vase sitting in the middle. Its sole occupant was a strapping woman sipping a glass of dry sherry. The Amazon had flaming red hair and breasts barely restrained in a skimpy leather bra with aggressive conical metal points over her nipples. The way she sat on the bench showed strong, muscular thighs thrusting from the leg holes of a pair of utterly inadequate chain mail panties.

"Psst!" Someone tugged Sandy's sleeve.

Sandy turned. A bent old man with a flowing grubby white beard, a dirty white robe, and bristly eyebrows smiled toothlessly up at her.

"Prophecies," he said. "Prolix is your man."

"No thanks," Sandy said. "I can screw those up all on my own."

"Arcane languages." His bony fingers dug into her forearm when she tried to pull away. "Dead languages that no one else can read. Mysterious scripts suddenly unearthed in unlikely places. Scrolls tucked away on dusty back shelves of libraries. Rusty chests in the castle attic. The book that everyone was forbidden to ever read. I can do the lot."

"No, thanks. Really."

"Magical lettering. Ominous squiggles that no one in the world can make head nor tail of. Prolix is your man. I can interpret them exactly how you want. Delivered in ringing, authentic tones that carry the conviction of a centuries' old prophecy so that everyone will implicitly believe it."

"I'm sure you're very good," Sandy said. "But I really don't need—"

"Twelve silvers per day with board and lodging. Plus the standard surcharge if there are one or two sceptics who need extra persuasion. Double if they're close blood relatives of yours who will stand to lose all their power and property to you once the prophecy comes true. Some clients offer to throw in a performance bonus."

"No. Really, I don't have any need for—"

"Okay, I'll waive the travel allowance just for you, because I'm having a slow month. And because your pimply friend there is a princess in disguise. Can't say fairer than that, can I?"

"Erm. No. That all sounds very reasonable," Sandy said. "But I don't need—"

"Take my business bit of wood. Keep me in mind. If I'm not here, ask around and they'll tell you where to find me. Prolix, remember?"

"Right you are. Prolix. Thanks."

Sandy accepted the roughly shaped piece of wood. A splinter jabbed into her palm. The spidery writing, burned onto the wood, read: PROLIX THE OFF-WHITE. *Purveyor of Fine Prophecies. No script too old: no claims too big or small. Approximation to Authenticity Guaranteed. Reasonable rates.*

Drusilla and Ruth already sat with the Amazon. Sandy nodded politely to her and sat beside Ruth.

"Anax'athelia," Drusilla said, "this is Sandy Blunt, the Great Obtuse Mage."

"Anax—?" Sandy said.

"The gratuitous apostrophe is a bitch, I know," Anax'athelia said. "But I don't get any work without it. My real name is Mavis Green."

Sandy couldn't help noticing that the vast amount of attractively tanned, taut flesh, which Mavis displayed between her fiercely riveted bracers and her barely adequate leather bra, was covered with goosebumps. Sandy's gaze snagged on the necklace hanging low enough to highlight Mavis's superb cleavage. The leather thong supported twenty-seven white bones about the size of cow molars carved into tiny skulls. A further six skulls on one end were dyed a deep red. The necklace and accompanying cleavage shifted as Mavis sat back to stare between Sandy and Drusilla.

"You two are dykes, aren't you?" Mavis said.

"Oh. Erm. Sorry." Sandy blushed and made a great show of looking around to catch the overworked barmaid's eye.

"I was— I was admiring your necklace," Drusilla said.

"It's great, isn't it?" Ruth said. "I suppose, if you don't wear clothes with pockets, you need something like that to keep track of your periods."

Mavis smiled. "Men think it's a cute way for a girl to try to look fierce. This game is all about appearance, I can tell you. There aren't many kingdoms that have rules about equal opportunity employment or gender balance in the composition of adventuring parties. I'm thinking of starting a union. But it's not easy. The blokes tell you to stop interfering and go back to waiting in towers to be rescued where you belong. As if one female in a party would kill them. Or mysteriously make them less masculine."

"Do you really think that enforced tokenism is the answer?" Ruth asked.

"Of course not." Mavis leaned forward to plant her fists on the table. "We need to address the core issue of men's stranglehold on the definition of sex roles. Biological destiny, traditional families, and all that other bollocks they use to oppress us into the kitchens and nurseries while they do the waged and salaried jobs and have meaningful careers that society values. But you have to start somewhere, don't you? Get a booted toe in the door."

"Or in the loincloth," Sandy said.

Mavis grinned. "I like the way dykes think. But, I tell you, when you do finally get hired on a dragon hunt or quest, guess who ends up doing the cooking, washing, and looking after the rescued princesses? Some of those spoiled little rich girls need a good spanking. I've lost count of the number of times I've given one a shake and told her to stop whining and plan her own rescue. Stand on her own feet. Go and have it out with her wicked stepmother herself, not meekly munch the poisoned apple and wait for some handsome dork to come and kiss her into lifelong domestic passivity and subservience."

"Do many take your excellent advice?" Drusilla asked.

Mavis gestured airy despair.

Sandy volunteered to go to the bar to fetch drinks herself, including a sherry for Mavis, since the barmaid didn't look like she was coming this way any time this side of autumn. When she returned, Ruth had said something to make Mavis frown down at herself.

"I know," Mavis said. "I continually get colds and a touch of exposure. Winters are hell. I have permanently hard nipples. But there's nothing I can do about it. If I don't dress like this, men won't look twice at me. It's not just Amazonian fighters. Those poor little sorceresses have to show a lot of thigh and tits, too, no matter if they could fry a bloke as soon as look at him."

"But men wear tunics and proper armour," Drusilla said.

"Oh, yeah," Mavis said. "You won't catch those big, strong blokes risking a chill by exposing a bit of skin, or having their all-important dangly bits shrink in the cold. Until, of course, they get within spitting distance of the pretty, rich, young women in distress. Then it's all padded loincloths and stripping off shirts to show oiled torsos. Thanks for the drink. Your health. So, what are three dykes doing in here?"

"Do you know a warrior called Trevor?" Ruth asked.

"Trev? Oh, yeah. He has the cutest pet hamster. Flaming fag. One of the nicest blokes you'll meet who owns a Lochaber axe. He has a way with rabbit kebabs to die for after a long day hacking and slashing through a dungeon. And he lets a girl wear a decent cloak and trousers. Why? You looking for him?"

"He suggested that this was a good place to ask for information," Ruth said.

"Oh, right." Mavis sipped her sherry. "You lost?"

Sandy was conscious of Ruth and Drusilla looking at her. She put her tankard on the table and cleared her throat.

"Not lost, *per se*," Sandy said. "We were wondering... Erm. I don't suppose you know where unicorns live?"

"Unicorns?" Mavis said. "The other side of the Wildlands."

"Oh," Sandy said. "Really? Is that where the icy home of the frost giants is? The Wildlands is where ogres come from, right?"

"Ogres, yes," Mavis said. "But frost giants live way, way off yonder. Or somewhere like that. Where it's cold. As you'd expect. Where it frosts a lot."

"So, the unicorns live with the ogres?" Drusilla said.

"No," Mavis said. "Ogres here where my right fist is. Unicorns there under the vase."

Sandy frowned. "So, where are we?"

"My left breast," Mavis said.

"And the frost giants?" Drusilla asked.

"The sensible, cute one's right breast," Mavis said.

Ruth faintly flushed.

"So," Sandy said, "we still have quite a long way to go, but not as far as Drusilla's sleeve. Are there many dangers we have to face?"

"You mean apart from the ogres?" Mavis said. "And the roaming packs of cutthroat brigands, wolves, rogue sorcerers, the occasional army of an evil overlord raping and pillaging everything in its path, and the ever-present possibility of food poisoning at wayside inns?"

"Dear lady," Drusilla said, "we are not deterred by the thought of constant mortal struggle on our way to getting our heads cut off."

"We're not?" Sandy said.

"Remember the infallible Oracle of Ring," Drusilla said. "We are to complete valorous deeds together."

"Of course," Ruth said. "I'd forgotten the oracle. That is comforting."

Sandy glared at Ruth and received a dimpled smile in return.

"Look," Mavis said. "I don't suppose you'd like to hire someone to help out with the rough stuff? I'm currently between jobs, as they say. I reckon I could cut you a pretty good deal, seeing as you're all women."

"I think it would be an excellent idea to add your sword, javelin, and bow," Drusilla said, "to our already formidable arsenal of my wickedly sharp paring knife."

"But no touching," Mavis said. "That's my rule with all my hires. It's not just because you're dykes."

"We understand," Sandy said. "Erm. I'm not sure we could afford you, to be honest. We had to leave town in a hurry, without the benefit of a quick whip-around or anything. We have the threat of execution hanging over our heads."

"Necks," Drusilla said. "My father-in-law-to-be has threatened to chop off all our heads, and that of Sandy's mother, Mrs Betty Blunt, widow and distinguished chairwoman of the Patch Street Ladies' Bridge Club, if we don't make all these improbable events happen in a year and a day minus eight days."

"Charity?" Mavis thoughtfully stroked her bracer. "I don't do—"

"In case you hadn't guessed," Drusilla said, "I'm a princess in disguise. When I regain my throne, I'll be able to reward you handsomely. Name your price, dear lady."

Mavis's eyes lit up. "Seriously? How about a royal decree about the rights of female adventurers to protective clothing at all times? And equal sharing of camp duties? And a Royal Commission of Enquiry into Employment Rights for Women? Daycare provisions for working mothers? Affirmative action in—"

"Look," Sandy said. "About Dru being a princess. Well, it's like this, you see—"

"Oh, yes." Drusilla looked around and lowered her voice. "It's supposed to be a secret."

"I can see that," Mavis said. "You learn to recognise types in my business. The acne is a good touch. Not many go that far. Even princesses in disguise tend to be a bit flighty and vain. Sad, really."

"But—" Sandy looked to Ruth for help.

"We can do the royal decrees about equality and gender nondiscrimination," Drusilla said. "And I'm open to other feminist ideas you might have along the way."

Mavis smiled and extended a strong hand to Drusilla. Drusilla shook it, but then pointed to Sandy.

"Sandy is our fearless if occasionally bewildered leader," Drusilla said.

Sandy did feel somewhat bemused by the turn of events. Not that the offer of Mavis's company held any negatives apart from reinforcing Drusilla's delusions about herself.

"I'm glad that's settled," Ruth said. "Now, Anax'athelia, I'm sure we can find you some warm, comfortable clothing to wear."

"Mavis, please," Mavis said. "I'll be glad to be rid of the wretched apostrophe for a while."

"Me and Dru are too short for our clothes to fit Mavis," Sandy said.

"True," Ruth agreed. "But Captain Tyrone is about the right height. And his clothes are of the best quality."

Sandy smiled. Drusilla burst out laughing and sprayed a mouthful of light ale across the table.

Mavis stood and gathered her weapons. "I like you," she said to Ruth. "A lot. So, which one of these two are you sleeping with?"

Ruth turned scarlet. "I—I'm not."

Mavis shrugged her muscular shoulders. "Straight women are hopeless at guessing about dykes, aren't they? I'm not sure I ever really came to grips with butch and femme. But, then, why would two women want to emulate male and female roles? Surely a negotiated relationship freed of controlling and restrictive stereotypes would be the way to build a truly sharing, equal, and mutually supportive partnership irrespective of the genders of the participants."

As they walked out, one of the young men with a special but as yet unrevealed destiny muttered: "Lezzies."

Drusilla and Sandy opened their mouths to retort, but Mavis spoke first.

"Well done," Mavis said. "Three out of four is three better than anyone of your IQ normally guesses right. It's worms like you, limp dick, who make women like me think becoming a dyke is a great idea."

Sandy and Drusilla shared an approving nod that included Mavis Green the Amazon.

# Chapter Five

Sandy peered in the direction that Mavis pointed. She saw dark forest blanketing undulating hills that looked indistinguishable from the dark forest blanketing undulating hills that they had spent the last two weeks slogging and sweating their way through.

"Are you sure?" Tyrone said. "It looks the same."

"Of course I'm sure, you steel-coated imbecile!" Mavis said. "Ogres over there. Ogres not back there. Is that too hard for you? I hate working with amateurs!"

Mavis stomped back down the hill to where Ruth waited with the pony cart. Sandy and Drusilla shared a look.

"Well, I say," Tyrone said. "Aren't we cranky this morning? I was only asking a civil question. It's not as though there's a big sign over there that says: CAUTION, YOU ARE NOW ENTERING OGRE-INFESTED WILDLANDS. Is there?"

"No, you're right," Sandy said. "But it probably pays to use a lot more tact if you're going to point it out to a radical feminist Amazonian warrior woman when she's on the rag."

Tyrone looked blankly at her. "On the rag?"

"Didn't you notice that her necklace is showing the first red skull?" Sandy said.

"I've noticed that her hair isn't as red as it was," he said.

"She's menstruating," Drusilla said. "Having her period. Aunt Flo is visiting her. She's got a twat full of clots. Bleeding like—"

"Aaarrgh!" Tyrone clamped his hands on his ears. "I can't hear you. Can't hear a thing. Not listening."

Sandy and Drusilla shared a smile before they followed Tyrone's hasty retreat down the hill.

In camp that evening, Tyrone showed that he'd developed a thin smear of instinct for self-preservation by unusually making no comment on Ruth making something special that he wasn't offered. Mavis drank her raspberry-leaf tea and dragged her hunched self into the tent for an early night of lying in a misery of cramps.

"I'm betting that's another thing that female adventurers and heroines don't get a lot of sympathy or credit for," Sandy said. "Yet let Grob the Brave Barbarian Hero take a cut on the finger or something and women have to swoon at his endurance and manliness. I'd like to see Grob walking all day, let alone having a pitched battle, while his insides felt like they were constantly twisting and trying to drop down through his arsehole."

Sandy swatted at the sharp stinging on the side of her neck. Her hand came away with a black insect squashed on it in a smear of her own blood. She imagined that her neck must be covered with red welts from the feast the biting flies were having off her.

"The insects bothering you?" Mavis said. Her long muscular legs, attractively encased in a snug-fitting pair of Tyrone's breeches, made short work of wading through the tall grasses. "It's the river. You always get clouds of them near water. But it's safer than going through the woods. Better teeny little flies nibbling on you than seven-foot ogres. And we can get the cart through this way."

"I'm being eaten alive," Sandy said.

"Every dyke's dream," Drusilla said.

Sandy grinned.

Mavis rolled her eyes. "You're a witch, aren't you? Can't you zap them? Or travel in some protective bubble of power? Come to think of it, I haven't seen you do any hocus-pocus."

Sandy nodded along the bank to where Tyrone rode ahead as their shiny pathfinder—a potentially dangerous task that just happened to keep him safely out of earshot of the women's banter.

"I'm not a very good witch in the conventional sense," Sandy said. "Straight C student at magical school. My talents aren't of the sort that gain traditional academic recognition. However, Captain Rust-Free has an anti-magical sword that, unexpectedly, seems to work."

"No magic? Because of him?" Mavis frowned as she wiped sweat from her face. "Bloody typical. Men are always trying to negate women's power with their phallic symbols. Why don't we take it away from him? Emasculate him for a change."

Drusilla smiled and patted her paring knife. "You have but to say the word, dear lady, and I, Drusilla, will aid you with my trusty clitoris symbol."

Sandy frowned at Tyrone's back. "I'd be happier without the damned thing. But I'm not so sure it wouldn't be more trouble than it's worth. He's bound to take the loss of his sword very badly. If he sulked and rode off back to the king, that might mean Mother's head."

"Not if we tied him up in the back of the cart," Mavis said. She slapped at the side of her neck.

"Here." Ruth halted the cart near them and offered a bottle. "The Mildly Surprising Blunt's Patented Insect Repellent."

Mavis shook out a large dollop of the thick pink liquid onto her hand and passed the bottle on to Drusilla. "Hey, this stuff smells nice. A great improvement on slathering yourself with horse dung."

"It's also an effective moisturiser," Ruth said.

"No kidding?" Mavis said. "Wow. You're right. It feels good already. And not greasy. Is this Blunt any relation of yours?"

Sandy worked the lotion into her forehead and cheeks. "Erm. Yes. My dad. He wasn't a conventional wizard, either. Spent most of his working life searching for the elixir of life and the sorcerer's stone. But he only produced shelves full of this sort of stuff. If he hadn't been such a nice bloke who didn't let anything get him down, I'd have said he died a disappointed man."

"What?" Mavis stared down at Sandy. "Disappointed? But the person who made this stuff must have been worth a fortune."

"Dad? Oh, no. He had to give up his hobby of weekend gryphon-watching expeditions so that he could save the money to put me through magic school." Sandy frowned at the bottle. "Fortune? From this stuff?"

"Do you know how hard it is to get good skin-care products?" Mavis said. "Especially at frontier outposts or in towns that have been nearly deserted by people fleeing invasions or malevolent magical manifestations."

Sandy scowled. "Aren't cosmetics and stuff incompatible with your feminist principles?"

"Tarting myself up as something I'm not for the sake of some man would be a betrayal of my self," Mavis said. "It's bad enough that I have to do it to earn a living. But there's nothing wrong with me liking my body and wanting to take care of it. Self-love, not prostrating myself for the sake of someone else."

"For what it's worth, dear lady," Drusilla said, "I cannot imagine you on your back for anyone's sake save your own."

Mavis flashed her a smile.

Sandy handed the bottle of insect repellent back to Ruth for storage on the cart. "A fortune? I still don't see it."

"Imagine day after day of trekking through ominous forests, noisome bogs, snake-infested deserts, or dripping dungeons," Mavis said, "and getting splashed with toxins or acidic blood from the scores of kobolds, sprites, vampire bats, or were-ferrets you slash your way through. Your skin goes to hell, I can tell you. Not to mention the sunburn and armour chafing. Trust me, I'd pay good silver, gold, or electrum pieces for a decent moisturiser and cold cream."

"And shampoo?" Ruth said.

"Oh, yes!" Mavis said. "You wouldn't believe the split ends after wearing a helmet all day. And I'd kill for an effective conditioner. That red dye can leave my hair so dull and lifeless. Look. It's horrible to run your fingers through. Oh, and the absolute nightmare after using caustic lice soap. Brittle? Sister, you don't know the meaning of the word."

Sandy chewed her lip as she considered this. She had never paid much attention to Dad's "failures", though she hadn't had the heart to throw them out. They were all still crammed on the shelves, gathering dust, in his workroom.

"A life of adventure is full of countless hidden pitfalls," Drusilla said. "A few determined assassins are just the tip of the iceberg."

"Most women in my trade end up using saddle grease on themselves because there's nothing better," Mavis said. "Not that it really does much for damaged and dry skin. Or your sex life. Men can be so superficial and riddled with double standards. They're happy to reek like a troll's armpit and will scream about their precious masculinity if you suggest they splash on a little cologne. You're supposed to gag and bear with their manly stench as they grunt away on top of you. Yet let them get one whiff of saddle grease on your breast and you can forget your jollies, girlfriend."

Sandy frowned to herself as she continued on in Mavis's wake through the long grasses and reeds. Could she be on to something? Part of the spell emporium could remain stocked with remedies and charms, but she could devote part to selling cosmetics, perfumes, and skin-care products. It sounded a bit dodgy. But, then, most successful ideas started out with lots of people laughing at them. Just look at that bloke who had the idea of strapping a miniature sundial to his wrist so that he could tell the time wherever he was.

"Hey, fearless leader." Drusilla jabbed a finger in Sandy's back. "That stuff really does work. The insects aren't touching me. And my hands feel great. I don't suppose Mildly Surprising Blunt Senior concocted anything for acne?"

Sandy heard the singing and turned. Ruth had plucked some of the wilting wildflowers that dotted the riverbank and stuck some in Bill's mane and her own hair. They might be deep in the trackless Wildlands crammed with bloodthirsty ogres lying in wait to ambush them and rend them limb from limb, but it also happened to be a gloriously warm, sunny day with just a few fluffy clouds in the sky. Ruth's voice was neither strong nor steady, but she was smiling and enjoying herself. Even her dull brown hair showed some interesting highlights from the sun and seven or eight days without being washed. Sandy found herself smiling and glancing over her shoulder as she walked. As companions for a venture into the unknown to perform improbable deeds went, she could have done a lot worse than Ruth. Who else would have thought to bring soap?

"Aaarrgh!"

Sandy jerked to a halt. Her gaze snapped ahead just in time to see a blinding flash as Tyrone fell off his horse. The horse bolted. Mavis and Drusilla ran towards Tyrone. Sandy hesitated, then followed.

Mavis helped Tyrone up from the ground. Spear in hand, she looked capable and professional—in stark contrast to Tyrone, who wailed about the dirt on his clothes, and Drusilla whose paring knife looked a little inadequate beside Mavis's long weapon.

"Ware!" Tyrone said. "My breeches! Look. Dirt on the knees. This is a disaster."

"What spooked your horse?" Sandy said. "Surely not a few grains of mud on its—"

"A skeleton." Mavis pointed.

Sandy left Tyrone dusting at himself and stepped across to stand very close to the tall Amazon. Mavis frowned at a bleached skeleton hanging from a tree branch. The bones gently knocked together as it swayed.

"Is— Is it human?" Sandy whispered.

"It's supposed to be," Mavis said. "As is that rotting head."

Sandy turned and gasped. A grotesquely black, eyeless mass of pulpy, picked-over flesh stood rammed on the top of a crude spike at about shoulder-height. The breeze riffled its straggly hair and black beard.

Sandy dragged her gaze from the hideous spectacle to frantically scan the trees. It looked dark and brooding in there. The undergrowth looked like it wanted to grab her with twiggy fingers and never let her go. The shadows were watchful. Did that tree blink at her with black, evil, knotty eyes? Sandy shuddered.

"I, Drusilla, dispossessed princess of an oppressed people, am no stranger to dangers," Drusilla whispered hoarsely. "I sense something unwelcoming."

"You're meant to be so scared that you'll wet yourself, drop your weapons, and run away," Mavis said. "This must be ogre handiwork."

"Ogres?" Tyrone broke off brushing dirt from his elbow. "Here? Now?"

"This looks more elven than human." Mavis stepped over to a pair of skeletal arms arranged in a forbidding X-shape across what looked like a well-trodden path from the riverbank into the trees. "You can tell by the material of the sleeves. That shimmer even though it's unwashed and frayed. And the dirt under the fingernails. Whoever did this was a real artist. Great attention to detail."

Sandy frowned and straightened from her defensive, ready-to-run-away hunch. "Artist?" she whispered. "What are you talking about?"

"Look at that." Mavis waved her spear at the skeleton. "Do you have any idea how long it must've taken to string all the bones together like that? Many a long winter's evening by the fire, I can tell you."

"String them together?" Drusilla said. "Dear lady, what do you mean?"

"And a grass stain!" Tyrone said.

"If someone had been hanged here," Mavis said, "there'd be nothing left by now but an untidy pile of bones. Arms and legs and other body bits would have fallen as the muscles and sinews rotted away. Most of the little bones from the hands and feet would be missing thanks to scavengers."

"Oh." Sandy forced herself to look at the gruesome rotting head again. "That's not real, either, is it?"

"No," Mavis said. "But isn't it great? Almost had me fooled. In poor lighting, if I were tired, it would've worked."

"Where did my wretched horse go?" Tyrone stomped away. "I simply must find my lint brush."

"My natural Gift for sensing danger with my secret royal corpuscles," Drusilla said, "still warns me to keep my paring knife handy. But did anyone else just smell roses?"

"Roses?" Sandy said. "Here? In the untamed wilderness? Of course not. Perhaps your royal nostrils aren't as Gifted as your royal corpuscles. So, Mavis, have we stumbled into some outdoor ogre art gallery? Or civic beautification project?"

"It's odd." Mavis rubbed her bracer. "Every ogre I've ever heard about rips your arms and legs off and laughs at you as it snacks on them. They like catching people. I've not heard of one who tries to frighten dinner away."

"Aaarrgh!" Tyrone screamed.

Neither Mavis, Sandy, nor Drusilla looked around to see what was the matter with him.

"Perhaps it's a vegan ogre," Sandy said. "Do ogres—"

"Sandy!" Ruth shouted. "Help!"

Sandy spun around. Bill the pony ran away with the cart bouncing behind him. Ruth was not on the driver's seat. A flash of light from Tyrone's breastplate quenched in the trees.

"Ruth!" Sandy ran.

Mavis quickly overtook Sandy and loped to the spot where they'd last seen Tyrone. The cart had overturned and dragged Bill to a halt. Their baggage lay strewn on the riverbank. Sandy skidded to a stop near Mavis. Drusilla collided with Sandy and came close to removing one of Sandy's kidneys with her paring knife.

"What—" Sandy clamped her mouth shut at Mavis's curt shake of her spear.

Mavis made some complicated gestures and bent to stalk into the trees. Sandy and Drusilla exchanged a look and followed the Amazon. Mavis stopped, turned around, and repeated her hand signals.

Drusilla looked as mystified as Sandy felt.

Mavis sighed. She repeated her gestures slowly, as if to backward children, and whispered a translation. "You two. Stay here. Go and secure the cart. Wait for me. You'd only get in my way. I'll go and track Tyrone and Ruth. But if you hear me screaming, come running. Okay? You got that?"

Sandy and Drusilla nodded. Mavis impatiently waved them back.

Sandy and Drusilla strolled away to where poor Bill the pony now stood looking as shamefaced as equine physiognomy would allow. They began freeing him from the harness.

"I got most of it, of course." Drusilla made a complicated gesture. "Everyone knows that means: 'But if you hear me screaming, come running.'"

"Yeah. Of course," Sandy said. "It was the twiddly thing she did with one finger that meant Tyrone that I didn't understand."

Drusilla coaxed Bill free of the traces. Sandy bent to examine the trap. She found a crushed flower caught near the driver's seat. Sandy straightened with the flower in her hand and frowned at the trees.

"She'll be all right," Drusilla said. "I'd wager half the kingdom that will one day be mine on Mavis in any contest with some wimpy, iron-deficient vegan ogre."

"She didn't say that there were any vegetarian ogres. She said they chewed your arms and legs off and made you watch as it ate them."

Drusilla stepped across to put a hand on Sandy's shoulder. "Well, if that's the case, then Tyrone is going to give it chronic indigestion long before our dear girl is in any peril. And with a spot of luck, it'll forget to peel Captain Shiny before it eats him. The metal will choke it to death for sure."

"There is that, I suppose," Sandy said.

Drusilla and Sandy finished emptying the cart before they attempted to right it. Both paused frequently to listen.

"Shouldn't she be back by now?" Sandy said. "It's been ages. And I feel like the trees are about to spring upon us."

Drusilla pointed to Bill, who grazed unconcernedly nearby. Sandy shrugged and took her place to heave on the side of the cart.

"Even were we all to meet bloody, painful, protracted ends as ogre sushi," Drusilla said, "I will at least have the rosy satisfaction of having seen you finally waking up a bit where our dear girl is concerned."

"Ruth?" Sandy frowned. "Of course I'm concerned. Can you imagine the rest of my life if my mother learned that we let Ruth get eaten by an ogre? I might as well let the king cut my head off. She—"

"Did you hear that?" Drusilla whipped out her paring knife. The deadly, if small, blade flashed in the sunlight.

"Mavis!" Sandy patted herself, discovered she had no weapons, and grabbed the first branch she found.

Sandy followed close on Drusilla's heels. They crouched as they ran, dodging from tree trunk to tree trunk. Sandy's heart pounded so hard that she was surprised Drusilla didn't ask her to keep the noise down.

Drusilla darted across to crouch behind a tree. Sandy peered around at the suspicious undergrowth, which could be sheltering hundreds of ogres if they all squatted low enough. Drusilla signalled. Sandy crouch-ran to join her. They both peered into the leaves and shadows ahead. It was amazing how comforting Drusilla's paring knife had become now that it was their only weapon against a slow, agonising death. Sandy shifted her sweaty grip on her highly inadequate bit of branch. The gigantic ogre of her imagination would probably use it as a toothpick.

"Can you see anything?" Sandy whispered.

"No," Drusilla whispered.

"This undergrowth is a bitch," Sandy said. "How do you think real adventurers know where they're going?"

"They probably do what we're doing and follow the path. Although, I am wondering if we should continue to hurtle straight into the den of the monster who must be quite something if it has overpowered

Mavis. Keen as I am to grapple with the beast, as one of our valorous deeds that will impress my beloved Maybelle no end, we must still bear in mind Mrs Blunt's head."

"What if we tried to sneak…" Sandy sniffed. "You know, I do smell roses."

"And a trace of lilies, perhaps. And a jonquil or two."

"Doesn't that strike you as odd? Wouldn't you think ogre lairs would be littered with the bones of their hapless victims that they've broken and sucked the marrow out of? Bits of rotting flesh? And other miscellaneous decaying things that add to a general air of unpleasantness?"

Drusilla wrinkled her nose. "I think I just caught a whiff of compost. Does that count?"

Tyrone screamed.

Sandy started and stared at Drusilla. "We— We'd better go and try to help."

A deep bass howl, issued from no human throat, tore through the forest. Sandy and Drusilla hunched and grabbed each other's sleeves.

"Shit," Sandy whispered. "It— It's eating him."

"We should trust the infallible Oracle of Ring," Drusilla whispered. "And face the foe."

"Does— Does it say anything about Captain Tyrone getting his legs and arms ripped off?"

"Well, no. But it's quite comforting where we're concerned."

"Right." Sandy resolutely gripped her branch. "Mother, forgive me."

Sandy and Drusilla quickly shared a hug before they stood and ran down the path, shoulder to shoulder, weapons held before them, and shrieking at the tops of their lungs.

Sandy hurtled around the bend in the path and skidded to a halt. The trees opened out to give way to several landscaped acres of flowers. Red, white, lavender, and yellow blooms spilled from raised beds, along paths, and around the bases of birdbaths, rustic benches, sundials, and glassy skull-shaped gazing balls. Bees happily buzzed amongst the pale blue flowers of a low hedge of semi-upright rosemary. A melange of sweet scents perfumed the air.

Tyrone screamed. Sandy's gaze jerked across the knot garden to a gazebo half smothered in honeysuckle. Tyrone dangled upside down near some smashed clay pots. Enormous yellow-brown claws held Tyrone's booted ankles. Sandy's mouth dried as her gaze slowly rolled along muscular arms as thick as tree branches. The ogre stood seven feet tall. His bulky shoulders were as broad as Sandy was high. His head was a strange bulbous shape with a tuft of coarse green hairs sprouting from the pointy top. Had the creature not been shaking Captain Tyrone, Sandy might have mistaken him for a lightning-blasted stump of an ancient tree surmounted by a large onion.

The ogre roared. Sandy's knees weakened. The ogre shook Tyrone. Tyrone shrieked. Drusilla yelled, flashed her paring knife, and lunged along the path. Sandy dove for Drusilla's legs and tackled her to the ground. They sprawled on the chamomile lawn.

"You'll never kill it with your paring knife!" Sandy said to Drusilla. "It's bloody enormous."

"The oracle," Drusilla said.

"Sod the oracle," Sandy said. "Look at that thing!"

The ogre's basso bellow reverberated through the garden. "My *Gladiolus recurvus 'Purpurea Auratum'*! Do you have any idea how long I've been propagating them? They were about to flower!"

"Can't we re-pot them?" Ruth said.

Drusilla stopped struggling and exchanged a look with Sandy. They both sat up. Ruth straightened, holding one of the shattered pots in one hand and a shooting bulb in the other. Mavis leaned her spear against the side of the gazebo and strode across to a large wooden potting shed.

The ogre grunted, but the shake he gave Tyrone looked half-hearted. His thick neck bulged with muscles as he flicked his attention between Ruth and Mavis.

"The roots look undamaged," Ruth said.

Mavis emerged holding a pot. "This looks—"

"No!" The ogre shook Tyrone. Tyrone shrieked. "Not the blue glazed, shallow pot. That's for my bonsai. Humans! Do you savages know nothing about horticulture? You blunder around, trampling my flower beds, vandalising everything, and upset—"

"Are these aphids?" Ruth said.

"*Aphids?*" The ogre dropped Tyrone. He snatched the bulb from Ruth's hands and held it close to a huge black eye. His thick eyebrows joined over the bridge of his broad nose as he frowned intently at the emerging green gladiolus spikes.

"No!" The ogre shook a massive fist at the sky. "They are! Pests, pests, pests. I'm plagued by them. Aphids and humans in one day! Dread God of the Claw, why do you punish me this way?"

Drusilla and Sandy shared a perplexed glance.

"Look, you vile, evil beast." Tyrone's sword flashed as he whipped it out of his scabbard with a steely whisper. "Not only do you soil my clothes, but you insult these ladies. As a man of honour, there is only one course open to me."

"No!" Sandy and Drusilla shouted together.

They raced across the chamomile lawn, around the birdbath, and vaulted the thyme bench. They were too late. Tyrone advanced on the ogre, sword at the ready. The ogre turned around and held a large meaty index finger against Tyrone's breastplate. That stopped him in his tracks. Tyrone flailed and slashed his sword, but the ogre's reach advantage meant the point flashed harmlessly across his front without so much as dislodging his pruning shears from the pocket in his leather jerkin. The ogre's irritated gaze flicked past Tyrone to where Drusilla and Sandy had skidded to a halt.

"More of you," the ogre said. "If you trample my *Heliotropium arborescens*, I'll turn you all into mulch."

Sandy and Drusilla looked down. They stood near several patches of plants. Sandy carefully picked her way across to the nearest pebbled path.

"And you needn't think that you can willy-nilly help yourself to a bouquet while you're here," the ogre said.

Drusilla quickly tucked her paring knife away.

The ogre sighed and shook his head. "Why didn't you all run away from my scare-humans? Hours and hours I took to make them. They usually work a treat."

"If it's any consolation," Mavis said, "we did admire the workmanship of them. True artistry."

"Yeah?" the ogre said.

"You brute!" Tyrone grunted with the effort of still vigourously swinging his sword. "Creature of dirt and other vilenesses."

"There's nothing nicer than a rich compost," the ogre said.

"There." Ruth held up a pot with three strong gladiolus spikes sticking up out of it. "I'm sure it will blossom beautifully."

The ogre frowned down at her. Slowly, he nodded his oddly-shaped head. "That looks okay. But what about the others? If any of them die, he'll suffer. And there are still the aphids. I might kill you all just because the aphids have put me in a bad mood. We ogres do things like that, you know. Very moody. Violent. And arbitrary. It's why you should keep away from us."

"Fight like a real man," Tyrone said. "Are you too afraid of Tyrone, Captain of the King's Own Bodyguard? You monstrous creature. Feel the bite of my steel!"

Mavis stepped around Ruth and through the gazebo to emerge behind Tyrone. She grabbed him by the neck of his back-plate and hauled him backwards.

"That's it!" Tyrone said. "Together, we shall—"

"Can it, tin man," Mavis said. "Unless you want to become fertiliser for a patch of crocuses."

Tyrone's sword drooped in his hand and he stopped his futile struggles to free himself from Mavis's restraint. The ogre let his arm fall and looked at Mavis. His thick eyebrows twitched upwards as he studied her.

"Beast!" Tyrone called. "You are fortunate that—"

Mavis clamped a hand across his mouth.

"Beast?" The ogre's eyebrows scrunched together again. He shook the bulb in his hand at Tyrone. "You did this. And aphids! Have you any idea how irritated I become at the sight of tiny little bugs sucking the life out of my precious plants?"

"Sandy!" Ruth called.

Sandy was horribly conscious of the ogre's gaze flicking to her, but Ruth beckoned urgently. Sandy skirted around the path, giving the ogre as wide a berth as the raised beds and artificial banks would allow.

Ruth grabbed Sandy's sleeve with a hand dirty with potting mix. "In the cart. A bottle of your father's non-systemic insecticide for use on indoor and outdoor plants."

Sandy blinked at her.

Ruth gave her a push. "Please hurry. Before Captain Tyrone provokes the ogre into bending his armour into a novelty watering can."

Sandy ran back along the path to the river. Tyrone's horse had returned to graze near Bill the pony. Sandy felt more than normally bewildered as she rummaged through a large collection of bottles. Insecticides for plants? Her father had made some strange stuff. Strangely useful stuff, it was turning out. Now, that really *was* surprising.

As Sandy jogged back to the ogre's garden, she noticed the daffodils lining the path that she had missed before. And the bird feeders hanging from the trees.

When Sandy handed Ruth the bottle, she saw that Mavis and Drusilla sat on Tyrone. The captain's anti-magical sword lay on a patch of prostrate thyme, several feet safely out of his reach.

The ogre looked sceptical as Ruth demonstrated the use of the insecticide. Sandy still felt utterly unreal not long afterwards while she and Drusilla, at Ruth's prompting, fetched the kettle and brewed tea for all of them. Mavis finally let Tyrone up when they settled for a drink in the gazebo. The ogre stood outside peering at his pots. His deep, ferocious scowl looked as if he were deciding which one of them to rip into bits first.

"It's working." His eyebrows lifted and he looked at Ruth. "They're dying. Those nasty little aphids. Dropping off. Stone dead. I've never seen anything like it. The efficiency. And it doesn't seem to have affected the plant. No brown spots on the foliage."

The ogre set his pots aside to pluck the bottle out of a tunic pocket. "The Mildly Surprising Blunt's All-Purpose Plant Insecticide. I've never heard of this Blunt. Yet he must be a god to gardeners all over the world. How could I not know the name? I'd like to shake his claw. Is he an ogre-mage?"

"I'm afraid not," Ruth said. "Sadly, he has passed on. But Sandy is his daughter."

The ogre peered at Sandy. "You're not what I would've pictured from the child of so magnificent a wizard. Do you take after your mother?"

Sandy cleared her throat. "Erm. I've been told that I have her nose."

"And green fingers," Ruth said.

Sandy glanced at her. Ruth showed her dimples.

A massive ogre claw thrust at Sandy. She flinched, her heart jumped, and she closed her eyes. The ogre grabbed her hand and shook it. He squeezed down on the bench beside her and nearly knocked Drusilla onto the ground-cover.

"Here." The ogre offered Sandy a pot with one of his gladioli in it. "In thanks. I haven't given one of my babies away before. But, a cure for aphids! That's something special, that is. Who would've thought such mighty magics existed in the world, eh?"

"Oh." Sandy eyed the pot with misgivings, but decided that one did not look a gift bulb in the shoot—especially not when a seven-foot-tall ogre was offering it to you. "Thanks. That's— That's just what I always wanted. It— It'll come in real handy on our trek around the world."

"Make sure you don't overwater it," he said.

"I— I will," Sandy said.

"Now," the ogre said, "what do you want in exchange for a lifetime's supply of the insecticide? How about I spare all your lives and throw in a small bag of gold?"

"Erm." Sandy cast an enquiring glance at Ruth. "Do we carry much of the stuff?"

"And how about a fungicide?" the ogre said. "I'm sure your magnificent father must've whipped up an easily-applied multipurpose fungicide."

"Oh. It's possible, I suppose," Sandy said. "He was a very talented man, I'm belatedly realising."

"A lifetime's supply of both," the ogre said. "Name your price."

"I don't think— Oof!" Sandy broke off when Ruth elbowed her in the ribs. Sandy couldn't read the look Ruth was giving her. "What?"

"Your father's recipes are all at home," Ruth said.

Sandy frowned. "I knew that. So?"

"I, Drusilla, dispossessed princess of an oppressed people, would dearly like one of your beautiful blooms," Drusilla said. "Any chance my secret royal self could purchase one, oh noble gardening ogre? It would make the perfect gift for my bride-to-be, the Princess Maybelle."

"Oh!" Sandy stared down at the pot in her hands. "Of course! You're a dread ogre of the Wildlands. And this is a flower. I don't suppose—? Erm. Look, how about this for a deal. I'll supply you with as much plant stuff as you can carry—for free, but you'll have to fetch it yourself. And, maybe, while you were in town, you might just happen to visit the palace and tell the princess how melodic her voice is. What do you say?"

The ogre frowned and scratched his chin. "Leave my garden? When there is so much to do? Pruning. Weeding. Mulching. I don't know."

"I can't be certain," Ruth said, "but I think Mr Blunt also concocted a fast-acting liquid fertiliser concentrate."

The ogre's black eyes flashed with greed. He ran a grey tongue over his lips and thrust an enormous claw at Sandy. "Throw in a few hundred bottles of that and we have a deal. Bob's your ogre."

Sandy found her hand again enveloped in a slightly scaly claw with lots of humus rather than human under the talons. "Bob?"

"It's short for something Ogrish that you'd never be able to pronounce," Bob said. "I bet you'd taken it for granted that I just happen to speak fluent, grammatically correct, unaccented English that requires no lexical tricks or annoying made-up dialect to represent in written form. You blithely assumed that you'd never have to face a language barrier wherever you went, didn't you? Whereas, in fact, you're incredibly fortunate that I'm bilingual. Or I'd have eaten you long ago, because I wouldn't have understood a word you said. Then I'd never have learned about the fabulous magical feats of your peerless father. And wouldn't that have been a tragedy?"

"Exactly what I was thinking," Sandy said.

Doesn't— Doesn't it make you nervous?"
Tyrone said. "I mean, it's an ogre."

Sandy looked ahead to where Mavis and
Bob strode at the head of their group. They
looked like they were deep in conversation about
trees.

"What a pity," Drusilla said, "that your anti-
magical sword is not also anti-ogre. That
would've got Bob's knees knocking. Since it
looked like your military training let you down
somewhat. Still, I don't suppose you have the
chance to devote much time to combat exercises
near bedding plants."

Sandy smirked.

Tyrone sniffed and turned his horse. Sandy
didn't think he'd get much sympathy from Ruth,
who brought up the rear in the pony cart.

Bob and Mavis selected a campsite. Sandy
and Drusilla fetched wood. Mavis helped Ruth
set up the tent. Tyrone groomed his horse and
Bill. Bob crashed back through the undergrowth
carrying a sack full of berries, roots, shoots, and
edible fungi. He volunteered to cook, much to
Tyrone's disgust. Sandy and Drusilla went to the
river to bathe after Tyrone returned. Mavis and
Ruth went off together when they got back. Bob
sat stirring the kettle.

"That smells good," Sandy said. "I thought it
was Mavis's turn to cook."

"I volunteered," Bob said. "Since I found the ingredients for my speciality: root and shoot stew."

Drusilla turned to Sandy to mouth: "Vegetarian."

Ruth and Mavis returned with towels wrapped around them and hung up their wet clothes to dry. Both had washed their hair and left it loose. Sandy had not seen Ruth with her hair unplaited before. It was longer than she imagined, and with a slight wave. Drusilla nudged Sandy. Bob was staring, as if entranced, at Mavis's long, brown—with a lingering trace of red dye—hair. Oblivious, Mavis dropped onto one of the royal canvas stools. Ruth stepped behind her with a pair of scissors.

"Are you sure?" Ruth said.

"Do it," Mavis said. "I don't even care if you make me look like a dyke. It will be so much easier to manage."

Ruth snipped great handfuls of Mavis's hair off. When she finished, Mavis had a stylish new hairdo that would be practical under a helmet and easy to run a lice comb through, yet which suited her face admirably. Mavis ran a hand through her hair.

"It feels so much lighter," Mavis said. "And cooler. The back of my neck feels exposed."

"It looks great," Sandy said.

"I agree." Drusilla said. "Not that we're judging you on your physical attractiveness and thereby discounting your innate worth as a human being."

Mavis smiled, stood, and took the scissors from Ruth. Sandy felt a strange pang as she watched Mavis hack off Ruth's hair. Mavis didn't do nearly as nice a job with the styling. Bits of Ruth's hair stuck out at odd angles and the ends were very uneven. Ruth, though, seemed very pleased.

Bob's vegan stew tasted great. Everyone told him so, even, reluctantly, Captain Tyrone.

"You know, Bob," Sandy said, "I didn't believe that ogres were anything like onions, but your head is."

Bob put a hand to his tufty green hair. "Yes. I don't like to boast, but I do have an unusually handsome head. I took it as the Dread God of the Claw's way of telling me to grow vegetables. I'm so glad it's not shaped like a potato. Or a yam. Who would ever take a yam-headed ogre seriously?"

"Or a bean," Tyrone said. "That would look very strange."

Bob stared at him. Tyrone hastily excused himself and disappeared into his tent.

"I thought ogres were supposed to be green," Drusilla said.

"Only unripe ones." Bob chuckled. "That was a gardening ogre joke. Seriously, the green skin is just the make-up we wear in amateur theatrical performances."

Sandy straightened, with her hands in the small of her back, and glared down at her wet shirt plastered to a rock on the riverbank. "I don't think I'll ever get the hang of this."

Drusilla sent up a spray of water that splashed Sandy. Sandy was so wet she didn't care. At least she hit the rock with her washing. Drusilla's attempts were more miss than hit.

Tyrone glared at Drusilla's back and lifted his wet underwear clear of the water. "I hope his Majesty realises the sacrifices I make in his service. Washing! This is what young, ill-educated women who work for low wages at inns are for."

"Don't let Mavis hear you speak like that," Sandy said. "You'll be peeling yourself off a rock."

"I, too, wish this task were being performed by someone proficient at it," Drusilla said, "and who isn't me. When I regain my throne, with my beautiful Maybelle at my side, I shall engage plenty of washerwomen and at a reasonable living wage."

"And provide childcare facilities," Sandy said.

Tyrone grunted as he examined one of his shirts. "This used to be white. How low have I sunk to even think of being seen in such a grubby garment?"

L-J Baker

"Considering that the rest of us are a lot grimier than you," Sandy said, "I don't see what you're complaining about. Here. Use the last of the soap."

"Last?" Tyrone juggled the slippery bar. "You jest? How can I possibly reach any semblance of cleanliness without soap?"

"What a pity that anti-magical sword isn't also anti-dirt," Drusilla said.

Tyrone looked up sharply. "Anti-dirt? Magic could do that?"

"I didn't think you held with magic?" Sandy said. "That tricksy, nasty, slippery stuff."

"Well, naturally, I don't," he said. "On principle. My family is famed for its staunch stand as the foe of wayward sorceries. But— But maybe it isn't all bad. It might have one or two practical applications."

Sandy smiled and lifted her hands. She twiddled her fingers at him. "All right, then, you chuck away your sword and we'll see what I can do."

"No!" Tyrone dodged across to where he'd left his sword on the bank. "I have my royal commission to eliminate all your dire arts."

Sandy shrugged. "Have it your way. Do you really think you look good in beige?"

Sandy wiped the rain from her face for the zillionth time and wondered why she bothered. Rain kept hurling down from a sullen grey sky. It pelted the canopy, which quickly funnelled the trickles and fat, wet drops downwards. Dampness had soaked through her woollen cloak and into her tunic and shirt underneath. Water dribbled from her hood. Her feet squelched in mud-caked boots. She was cold, wet, miserable, and tired, and had been all morning and most of the afternoon.

After a conference between Mavis and Bob, they were cutting across the Wildlands to get to the land of unicorns. This had meant long, painfully slow days of hacking a path through the undergrowth wide enough for the pony trap. The roughness of the ground meant that Ruth had to spend more time walking than driving and Sandy had lost count of the number of times they'd had to unload the cart completely to get it past some rocks, streams, or simply uneven ground that might have broken a wheel or axle. Even Sandy, inexperienced adventurer—third-grade—realised that they were approaching the point where they would be better off abandoning the cart. But she wasn't looking forward to the weight of her share of the baggage. Some days, she was barely able to drag one foot in front of the other as it was. The blisters on her hands from hacking at the undergrowth had developed blisters of their own and bled. Not even the Mildly Surprising Blunt's Medicated Blister Balm had done much good. Just when Sandy thought adventuring couldn't get any worse, the rain had started.

Drusilla stopped to wring out the bottom of her cloak. Water streamed from it.

"With my naturally optimistic nature augmented by a Gift for always seeing the bright side," Drusilla said, "I suppose we can look on this as practice for when we have to voyage to the bottom of the ocean to steal away the unique talking pearl earring from the Queen Under the Waves."

"I've figured out why you never read about Grob the Brave Barbarian Hero slogging his way through ankle-deep mud in continuous rain to only make a deeply depressing three or four miles a day," Sandy said.

"Because no one would want to read it?" Drusilla said. "People read primarily for escapism, so they don't want gritty, wet, sweaty reality? And so authors skip over the dull, mundane bits to concentrate on the fast-paced, dramatic scenes like dragonslaying, sex, horse chases, more sex, etcetera etcetera."

"Oh, yeah. Good point. I was thinking that it had something to do with the fact that Grob wanted to gloss over the bits that didn't show him in such an heroic light. But maybe you're right."

Mavis squelched to a stop beside them and offered them each a damp ration of leftover from last night's not completely successful experiment with flourless pancakes.

"Don't underestimate author ignorance and inadequate research," Mavis said. "How many tale-tellers do you think have actually got their bums off their padded seats and know how unpleasant and hard it really is to slog through virgin forest? Or even spent two days walking, getting bitten by insects, blisters on their feet, aching shoulders from carrying a pack, eyes inflamed from smoky campfires, dog-tired from not getting enough sleep from lying on hard ground in a cold tent, and having to squat behind some bushes while constipated from badly cooked food and a monotonous diet?"

"You could have a point, too," Sandy said. She sucked water off her tunic sleeve to wash down the gluey pancake. The rainwater tasted of wool. "Bleh. Whatever it is, I wish we could skip forward to the time when we get to the land of the unicorns."

The land of the unicorns." Mavis pointed.

Beyond the ridge they stood on, golden sunshine caressed rolling lands of emerald-green grass and clumps of trees arranged into easily navigated, pleasant-looking woods that looked spaced at just the right intervals for foraging for firewood. Even the occasional fluffy white clouds drifting lazily above the land looked hand-crafted to lend themselves easily to the spotting of dog's heads and other interesting shapes.

Sandy turned around. The way they had come, dark, damp, brooding forest stretched further than she could see. Grey skirts of rain swept over vast tracts of it. She could still smell the sucking, sticky mud and wet decaying leaf litter that had shrouded and dogged them for week after week.

"It looks perfect," Tyrone said. "Neat and clean."

"Were I to choose the kingdom from which I was dispossessed," Drusilla said, "I think I'd like this place. The woods-to-arable-land ratio looks just about bang on to yield the agricultural surpluses necessary to support a reasonable population of artisans and other non-food producing individuals in towns and cities. And yet, there is sufficient forest to provide habitats for abundant game for hunting."

"Think of the gardens you could grow," Bob said. "What vistas. Imagine the hedge-lines. Vast parterres. And those lakes there would make terrific water features."

"Doesn't it look too perfect?" Sandy said. "Too... Too fairy tale-ish."

"Where else would you expect magical creatures like unicorns to live?" Mavis said.

"Even if it is suspiciously unreal," Ruth said, "it must be preferable to a land of perpetual snow and ice filled with frost giants."

Sandy glared at her. Ruth flashed her dimples and turned to scramble down to where Bill patiently waited.

A road?" Sandy said.

"Most convenient and civilised," Tyrone said. "And the surface hard-packed but not too dry that it throws up lots of dust."

"Makes life a lot easier, doesn't it?" Mavis said.

"Very nice on the claws," Bob said. "Wow. Look at that *Castanea sativa*. What a beauty. You don't see single specimens like that every day."

Sandy saw only a big, perfectly-shaped chestnut tree. Her frown quickly snapped back to the improbable road. It was smooth and broad. The wheels of the pony trap rolled easily over it with only minimal jolting and bumping. It was exactly the sort of road you'd like to have stretching into the heart of the land of unicorns. For mile after uneventful mile, the road cut across broad, grassy plains with an occasional foray around low hills to provide relief from mundane flatness and afford an elevated vista of breathtaking beauty and, once or twice, a really nice waterfall. Woods crowded the road now and then to provide an alternate variation to the scenery and the delight of cool shade with flashes of the plumage of brightly coloured birds and air musically filled with cheery, chirpy, tweeting song. The road forded a river at about the right time for them to take a rest and have a refreshing drink. Bob only had to put his claws into the water and he came out with a big, silvery fish. Colourful butterflies darted and flitted everywhere. Drusilla plucked two handfuls of the gaily-coloured wildflowers and presented a bunch each to Mavis and Ruth.

When they resumed walking, Drusilla tied her tunic around her waist by knotting the arms. She rolled up her grubby shirt sleeves as she fell in step beside Sandy.

"I can imagine why you frown so, oh fearless and sceptical leader," Drusilla said. "Even my fertile and free-ranging imagination has had to admit defeat in this idyllic land and let me experience the reality that is beyond even my wildest dreams."

"It's so right that it's wrong," Sandy said. "Look. Even the rain clouds look artistic. And over there. We've been in this place for three days and it hasn't rained on us once, yet everywhere looks as if it receives just the right amount of rainfall. Not too much, not too little."

"It's the kind of place you'd want to invent if you had to travel through somewhere on an improbable quest, isn't it? There's always just enough dry firewood within easy foraging distance of our camp-sites. Nice places to dig toilet holes in soft soil amongst decorative shrubs that form perfect privacy screens and with soft, absorbent leaves. What more could you ask for? Save, perhaps, my Maybelle being here so that we could skip hand in hand through the meadows full of flowers. And a nice soundtrack, perhaps. With violins."

"And that grass is another thing." Sandy pointed to the grass bordering the road. "It's short and springy. Not all wild, tough, raggedy, and mixed in with weeds, shrubs, and brambles."

Drusilla shrugged. "Perhaps the unicorns crop it."

"What unicorns?" Sandy spread her arms wide. "We haven't seen a single one. Nor a horse, cattle beast, or deer. The only other person we've seen was that girl with the yappy little dog running away from the flying monkeys. Apart from that, zip. No villages. No farms. Not even a lone traveller and his faithful companion or a knight asking the way to the closest grail store. It's like we have the whole place to ourselves. And that it's been made just for us. Like in a not-very good story where everything is unrealistically perfect."

Drusilla shrugged. "Beats the Wildlands, doesn't it?"

"I suppose so." Sandy scowled and jammed her hands in the pockets of her now ragged and patched breeches. "But, if we just happen to come across three little pigs in straw houses, or a couple of children leaving a trail of crumbs behind them, I'm going to scream."

"Personally, oh fearless and grumpy leader," Drusilla said, "I'd not complain at stumbling across a gingerbread house. Mavis could persuade any disagreeable old witch that she ought to rethink her child-care strategy, Ruth could point out that her ovens needed a really good clean before she baked anything else in them, and Bob could tear us all off a piece of the house. I could really go for a chunk of spicy, sweet guttering with a hot cup of tea."

"We've nearly run out of tea," Ruth said from the seat of the pony cart behind them. "But Bob is keeping a look out for *Camellia sinensis*."

"In this hokey place," Sandy said, "I wouldn't be surprised if we just happened to come across whole woods full of tea bushes."

"Do you need a dose of the Mildly Surprising Blunt's Gripe Water?" Ruth said.

Drusilla grinned. "It's not her stomach that's playing up, dear girl. Our fearless and deeply dubious leader isn't enjoying this pleasant if lamentably common improbable fictional landscape."

"Or is she on the Flo?" Tyrone said.

"On the rag," Drusilla said.

Sandy glared at them all.

"I have deep misgivings about this place, too." Mavis frowned and rubbed her bracer. "Every time we crest a rise, I expect to see a tall, solitary tower or a fire-girt rock with some poor young woman imprisoned inside who has been brain-washed into believing that her highest purpose in life is to be the passive object that will reward some male for his quest to prove his manhood."

So," Sandy said, "our clothes are all dropping to bits. We stink. We've run out of tea, soap, salt, and would've starved to death if not for Bob's superb horticultural knowledge and a profusion of berry bushes, wild crops of cabbages and potatoes, and fruit and nut trees that all just happen to be unseasonably ripe at the same time."

"My boots are dropping to bits." Drusilla wiggled a toe to show the hole in her left boot. "Who would have thought that being ill-shod would be more of a danger to reclaiming my usurped throne than a whole guild of assassins?"

"My horse has thrown a shoe," Tyrone said. "I need a farrier."

"We need a trading post," Mavis said.

"And we still haven't seen hide nor horn of a unicorn," Sandy said. "Aren't they supposed to gallop about the place in blindingly bright white herds? You'd think that would be reasonably easy to spot."

"Given that we've already established that your unicorn lore is somewhat less than comprehensive," Drusilla said, "perhaps we're looking in the wrong place."

Sandy could hardly refute that. "Okay. Anyone got any suggestions?"

"Is that one?" Bob pointed.

Between the trees of the nearest bluebell-carpeted copse, Sandy caught a flash of luminous white. It looked as if a piece of a bright new moon flitted between the trees.

"Yes!" Tyrone shouted. "I see it! I see it! Tally ho! Let's go!"

"Wait!" Sandy called.

Bob grabbed Tyrone as he kicked his horse into motion and plucked him from the saddle.

"But we must hurry," Tyrone said as he dangled from Bob's claw. "Before the elusive beast gets away."

"Perhaps we might be better off employing a little more subtlety," Sandy said.

"I'll get the unforeshadowed coil of rope from the back of the cart," Mavis said.

Bob set Tyrone down. "And I shall quickly knot together some sturdy vines into a net."

"Good thinking," Sandy said. "If we're to capture the equivalent of a wild stallion with a spike on its head, we're going to need something reasonably strong."

"You hadn't forgotten," Drusilla said to Tyrone, "that it is a creature of legend and very possibly magical?"

Tyrone's jaw tightened. He patted his sword. "*WWI*. Wizards and Witches Immune. That goes for any tricksy magical quadrupeds, too. No one and nothing can overpower Tyrone with nasty, underhanded tricks."

"Which might turn out to be rather unfortunate to our chances of catching a unicorn," Sandy said. "A spot of even my magic might've come in handy about now."

"Perhaps we might try to get closer to it," Ruth said, "and then assess what to do about capturing it?"

"You always inject a dose of much-needed common sense into every situation," Mavis said. "I really do like you a lot. If I were a dyke, I'd be tempted to marry you."

Ruth's cheeks pinked as she clambered down from the cart.

Sandy barely breathed as she tiptoed closer to the copse. She waded through tightly packed bluebells that looked far too picturesque to be convincing. She paused behind the cover of a broad trunk.

"*Cornus stolonifera*," Bob whispered.

Sandy stared at him. His bulky body, with his deftly whipped-up vine net slung over one shoulder, crouched behind the neighbouring tree.

"Dogwood," he said. "This species has bright red—"

Sandy put a finger to her mouth. "Ssh!"

Bob raised his claws in apology and mouthed: "Sorry. Got a bit carried away. I'm focussed again now. Unicorns. Bob's your ogre."

Sandy frowned as she peered to catch another glimpse of the astonishingly white creature.

"Psst!" Drusilla waved from several yards away. She gesticulated wildly.

Sandy looked. She saw the flash of whiter-than-whiteness. Her breath caught in her throat. The legendary unicorn. Luminous coat. Fiercely proud spirit. Flashing silver hooves. Never had their backs been broken to the saddle from time immemorial. The light of the glade changed as the unicorn moved: as if the golden shafts piercing the canopy deferentially bent aside from the unicorn's own magical glow. Sandy swallowed hard down a drying throat. She heard a gentle snapping of twigs as the unicorn moved closer. The way the light bent around the tree trunk cast a faint, shimmering rainbow between Sandy and Bob. Sandy saw the ogre's big eyes wide with wonder as he watched entranced by the approaching creature.

"Get your net ready," Sandy mouthed.

Oblivious, Bob continued to stare as if he were caught in a waking dream.

Sandy tried wiggling her fingers to attract his attention, but stopped when she saw a whiter-than-white muzzle limned in pure white radiance. The unicorn nosed amongst the bluebells. The tip of a spiral horn bobbed as it moved its head. Sandy froze, hardly breathing. Her eyes felt like they bulged out to twice their size. Slowly, inch by inch, whisker by whisker, the unicorn edged into the gap between Sandy and Bob.

Sandy blinked. And blinked again. It was hard to see properly through the funny white light, but the creature at the centre looked about the size of small goat. "Shit."

The unicorn's head snapped up. Bob jerked out of his trance. He hurled his net. Sandy dove forward. The unicorn bolted. The heavy vine netting landed on Sandy. She tangled in it when she tried to rise.

"Oops." Bob hurried across to help Sandy. "Sorry, I didn't mean—"

"Get it!" Sandy called. "The unicorn. Forget me. Run!"

Sandy watched from inside irregular squares of vine as Bob, Mavis, Tyrone, and Drusilla crashed futilely through the copse. Ruth strode towards Sandy and began helping her get free.

"Did you see how small it was?" Sandy said.

"Perhaps it was a young one," Ruth said.

"Or perhaps I got even that bit of unicorn lore wrong."

"Yes, that's possible." Ruth handed Sandy an armload of netting. "I'll go and make tea."

Sandy sweated to drag the net back to the side of the road where Ruth lit a fire and set out the camp chairs. By the time the other hunters returned, sweaty, scratched, and empty-handed, Ruth had brewed the tea.

"Perhaps we need to refine our strategy," Sandy said.

"Do we have one?" Drusilla asked. "I must've missed that."

Sandy ignored her. "Any suggestions?"

"If it's a boy unicorn, couldn't we lure it with a girl unicorn?" Tyrone said. He nervously glanced at Mavis. "Or vice versa. There's no reason it couldn't be a girl unicorn. In which case we'd use a boy to attract it."

"What if it's a gay unicorn?" Drusilla said.

Tyrone stared at her. "Then... Then we use another gay unicorn. Of the same gender. Whichever it happens to be. Boy or girl. You see. You mock my military training, but—"

"If we had a unicorn of whatever gender or sexual orientation that we could use as bait," Sandy said, "why would we need to bother with another one?"

"There's that incredibly stupid legend about virgins being able to tame unicorns," Mavis said. "How could some equine know whether or not a human being had had sexual intercourse? I ask you, does that make any kind of sense?"

"I believe that it's metaphorical," Ruth said. "Or figurative."

"Is figurative sex the illustrations you get in books of etchings?" Tyrone said. "I may or may not have one in my saddlebags that we could use as a lure."

"No, that's pornography," Mavis said. "The nastiest, most blatant method of degrading women and feeding men's dangerous fallacies about women as sexual objects for their enjoyment."

"Oh." Tyrone edged to the side as if he wanted to hide behind Bob. "Then— Then I definitely don't have any of that. No. Not at all."

"Leaving aside for now the thorny philosophical and psycho-analytical questions," Sandy said, "will this virgin idea work? Can we use it to catch a unicorn? Should we have Bob carry an oversized fishing rod with a virgin dangling on the end and when a unicorn darts from hiding to snatch the bait we all jump it?"

"If I understand the matter correctly," Bob said, "notwithstanding Mavis's excellent logical point, a virgin should be able to walk up to the unicorn and it will let her put a noose around its glowing neck. And it will follow her anywhere."

"Or him," Mavis said. "Virgin is a gender-neutral term. You shouldn't assume that it applies to one sex or the other."

"Of course," Bob said. "That's what I meant. Follow her or him anywhere."

"That simple?" Sandy said. "Are you sure?"

"It's not personal experience, you understand," Bob said. "I've not had many unicorns wander into my garden asking for cuttings. It must be racial memory. Or I read about it in a book. There are a lot of clever people out there who write books."

"Sadly," Sandy said, "there are a lot of unclever ones, too."

"Do you read a lot about unicorns?" Mavis said. "I'd have thought you'd be into gardening books and seed catalogues."

Bob shrugged and looked strangely shy. "I have a secret weakness for romance novels."

Mavis stiffened. Sandy shared a glance with Drusilla, who also looked like she was wondering what pulverised ogre would look like.

"Romance?" Mavis said. "What, exactly, do you mean by that? Not stories where women ultimately subordinate themselves to some man, and abandon their life aspirations, all in the so-called name of love? A term that has become a trap for women."

Bob lifted his massive claws defensively. "I like a good love story. They make me cry. Happy tears. Like when I eat a really good, fiery radish fresh from my garden. I keep a stack of novels in the potting shed. But only the ones with strong female protagonists. Not the ones where the males are dominating and domineering, and which usually carry the insidious unwritten subtext about natural male superiority and a woman's secret desire to be overpowered. Pah. Trash. Not worth composting."

Aggression bled from Mavis's expression. "Are you just saying that? Or do you have a genuine interest in women's rights and equality of the sexes?"

"Why would anyone want to oppress another merely because of slight biological differences in form?" Bob said. "I always thought it would be nice to have a mate who could help me with the potting and pruning. Together. Sure, we have different roles in pollination and fruit production, but matched spades in the potting shed. His and hers hoes." He sighed. "Sadly, not many ogresses are interested in long nights sitting in the gazebo under the stars, smelling the night-scented irises, sipping blackcurrant wine, and discussing the deeper questions of the universe as two equal minds."

Mavis frowned at him.

"What do ogresses do, then, to while away the evenings?" Drusilla said.

Bob shrugged. "Rip hapless elves and humans apart. Or play bridge."

"A good, exciting game of cards," Tyrone said. "Now you're talking. It would be terribly boring to just sit there talking. I need to do things. But, then, I'm a man of action."

Sandy stared at him. "Correct me if I'm wrong, but we have already established that you haven't a strong grip on romance or dealing with women?"

"Isn't that the unicorn?" Ruth said.

Everyone turned around. The luminous white glow showed through the trees.

Through frantic, and oft repeated, hand signals, Sandy got them all to shut up and creep towards the woods. Mavis carried the rope.

Sandy paused on the other side of the copse, behind one of the last trees before the grassland. The little unicorn grazed out in the open. No chance of sneaking up on it. The way the direct sunlight bent around it made it look a lot bigger than it really was. Like a magnificent stallion standing about seventeen and a half hands, solid muscle, and with a horn the length of Sandy's forearm. But, squinting and tilting her head to the side, Sandy could see through the bendy brightness to the little white animal itself.

"What do we do now?" Drusilla whispered. "I believe that it would be inappropriate of me to bring my paring knife to bear on this problem. Although that magical pelt might make a truly splendid hearth rug, and a conversation piece second to none, that probably wouldn't do our quest much good."

Sandy turned to Mavis. "Can you tie a noose in that thing so that we can use it as a halter?"

Mavis deftly tied it and offered the coil of rope to Sandy.

"Right," Sandy said. "Who wants to give it a go? I can't. I don't have the right qualification."

Drusilla shook her head.

"Nor me," Mavis said.

"Sorry," Bob said. "Youthful indiscretion. Sowing my *Avena fatua*." Sandy turned to Ruth.

"I can give it a try." Ruth took the rope and began slowly walking towards the unicorn.

"That explains a few things that have been perplexing me about her," Mavis whispered.

"There's probably something else about the dear girl that you may not have guessed," Drusilla whispered. "I'll tell you later."

"You mean Ruth carrying a torch for you-know-who?" Mavis whispered.

"You've guessed that, have you, dear lady?" Drusilla whispered.

"It's as obvious as the nipple on your tit," Mavis whispered.

"Not to you-know-who," Drusilla whispered.

"Well, you'd have to be blind not to see that you-know-who can be a bit dense sometimes. If she'd—"

"Ssh!" Sandy hissed.

Mavis and Drusilla shared a collusive look that Sandy pointedly turned away from. She watched Ruth inching closer to the unicorn. The unicorn jerked its head up. Ruth stopped. Sandy held her breath. The unicorn sniffed the air. Its ears pointed forward.

"Nice unicorn," Ruth said. "Easy, boy. Or girl. Or whatever gender you are. I won't hurt you. I promise. You can ask Bill. Or Nameless. That's Tyrone's horse."

The unicorn shifted uneasily. Ruth took another step forward. Sandy gripped the tree trunk.

"Careful," Sandy whispered, though Ruth had no chance of hearing.

"Good unicorn." Ruth slowly lifted her hand. "Nice unicorn. Are you going to let me slip this over your handsome head?"

The unicorn trembled, but stood its ground. Sandy willed it to remain still. Ruth slowly, carefully, and gently lifted the noose around—

The unicorn leaped backwards and bolted.

Sandy stared in disbelief. Ruth had been so close.

"Shit," Mavis said for them all.

Ruth returned with the rope.

"Take heart, dear girl," Drusilla said. "It almost worked."

"It seems that I have been mistaken about something," Ruth said. "I hadn't thought *that* counted as sex. I'm sorry. Perhaps someone else could give it a try."

Sandy came within half a breath of asking the question that she also saw on Mavis's and Drusilla's faces. Instead, she accepted the rope back and frowned. "All right. Who?"

Sandy ran through a swift mental elimination process and turned to Tyrone. He blushed violently and shrugged in a miserably unconvincing attempt at nonchalance.

"Too busy with your military training?" Drusilla asked.

"Too busy admiring yourself in your shiny armour?" Mavis said.

"I've been saving myself for the right woman," he said. He snatched the rope out of Sandy's hand and stalked away. Without making any attempt to quieten the creature, Tyrone strode straight up to the unicorn and looped the rope around its neck. Oddly, but mercifully, this quenched much of the supernatural light around it. The miniature white horse with the horn meekly trotted at Tyrone's booted heels as he led it back to them.

"There's something about such complete and illogical submission that makes me deeply uneasy," Mavis said.

"Not nearly as uneasy as losing my head will make me," Sandy said. "I promise that we'll let it go once I've taken it to the palace."

Sandy went to meet Tyrone.

"Well done," she said. "That'll be something to boast about in the officers' mess when we get back."

Tyrone's expression brightened. "You're right. Overpowered the mighty brute, I did. Barehanded, no less."

"It's magical, too," Drusilla said. "That's how the amazing wild stallion has shrunk down to the size of an athletic sheep. Don't forget that. And sheep can be dangerous when cornered, so I'm told."

"Of course!" he said. "My anti-magical sword! That was the real key to my success! Not any—any other reason. We— Hey! Stop licking my boots."

Tyrone leaped and dodged to evade the long tongue of the unicorn which had taken a liking to the taste of the very last of his boot blacking. "Stop! No. Get away! Not my boots!"

"What does it say?" Sandy called from the cart seat beside Ruth.

Mavis peered at the canted signpost and pointed north. "Dragons that way."

"That's handy," Sandy said.

"There's some fine print," Bob said. "It reads: *Taking this road may invalidate your life insurance cover and health policies. Which would be a shame, because there's nowhere else in the world that you'd need them more.*"

"I could've lived without knowing that," Sandy said.

Within the space of a few hours, the road had deteriorated to a rough pair of wheel ruts. The cart rolled and jounced. It was likely to get worse soon, by the look of the rising hills ahead and the dark, jagged peaks beyond. Tyrone had been reduced to walking, since his nameless horse had thrown a shoe. The unicorn trotted behind him on its improvised leading rein. It would move for no one but Tyrone. Even if Ruth held the end of the rope, the unicorn would not budge.

Sandy noticed Ruth watching the unicorn. "It's an odd little thing, isn't it?"

"Not quite what we expected," Ruth agreed. "But it is so very white."

"Blindingly white," Sandy said. "In full sunlight, it makes your eyes hurt to look at it. At least I got that bit right."

Ruth frowned. "I wonder... I can't remember exactly... She is very beautiful, of course. With a flawless complexion. It's no wonder, really, that she would attract many compliments. But is the Princess Maybelle's skin really paler and purer than the unicorn's mane?"

Sandy turned back to the unicorn and scowled. The little equine was trying to nibble Tyrone's spurs as he walked. Its mane was whiter than white. Much whiter, purer, and paler than Sandy's own grimy, weather-beaten hands and forearms. But what about Maybelle? Sandy tried very hard to conjure up a picture of that divinely beautiful woman. The lips. The hair. The eyes. The cleavage. But what about the skin? She couldn't exactly remember. She saw Ruth watching her.

"I'm not perfectly sure," Sandy said. "But— She is sublimely beautiful. The most gorgeous woman I've ever seen. And I'm still madly in love with her, of course."

"Of course," Ruth said.

"But it doesn't seem likely that anyone could have skin whiter than that, does it?"

"No," Ruth said. "At least, not anyone still alive."

"That little discovery is not going to go down at all well in the palace." Sandy twisted around to rummage through their pathetically diminished belongings to find the crate of her father's strange bottles. "I don't suppose..."

"The Mildly Surprising Blunt's Blonde Rinse," Ruth said. "That should tone down the bright whiteness. We can rub some in before we take it to the palace."

"I don't know what I'd do without you."

Ruth developed a wistful look before the cart wheel hit a rock and jolted Sandy off the seat.

Sandy panted as she trudged the last few steps up the trail. Far below, hidden from view by the intervening folds and ridges of the hills, the pony cart sat forlornly abandoned with its broken wheel. Ruth smiled at Sandy as she led Bill the pony up the hill. Bill walked with a spring in his hooves, despite the steepness of the climb. The load from the broken cart had been distributed between Bill, Nameless, and the bipeds. Where Sandy wilted under the weight of the women's tent, Bob barely broke into a sweat carrying as much as the horse. Although the ogre had put his claw down when Tyrone tried to get him to carry his armour.

Behind, Sandy caught a last glimpse of the fairy-tale perfection of the land of unicorns. Ahead, the countryside spreading greyly from the skirt of the hills looked grimmer, bleaker, and more likely to wear holes in their clothes.

"Look!" Drusilla pointed. "Do you think that is where dragons live?"

Sandy edged forward and shaded her eyes to peer to the west. The afternoon sun shone down on a bank of black, impenetrable cloud. Really black. Not just the sort of black—which is actually dark grey—used to give the impression of thunderclouds; or even the black that is still a very, very dark grey to describe, for emphasis, the disgustingly smelly smoke from a neighbour's annoying bonfire. This was black that actually and literally meant black. It sucked in the afternoon sunlight from above and let nothing through. The ground beneath it lay in permanent, lightless shadow. A faint, erratic flickering looked like flashes of lightning. Sandy felt a bone-deep foreboding.

"There must be a hell of a lot more dragons in the world than even I imagined to create so much air pollution," Drusilla said. "Or your average dragon does a lot more smoking than a pack-a-day habit."

"If that's made by dragons," Bob said, "they must have some serious lung problems. Those clouds or smoke or whatever it is looks worse than the time Uncle Ted's homemade distillery exploded and burned half the forest."

"It looks like the land of the dead," Sandy said.

"Oh, yeah," Drusilla said. "The place where superstitious people believe that people who have not led lives of exemplary goodness—as they define it, which means most of us don't have a chance of making the good list—go when they die. And where their ghosts will be tormented until the end of time by demons with fiery whips and all sorts of gruesome and infernal tortures. That could be quite a challenge for my paring knife."

Sandy stared at her. "Whatever happened to your Gift for sunny optimism?"

"You have seen those hundreds of square miles of unnatural darkness?" Drusilla frowned as she scratched a pimple on her jaw. "Erm. Let my secret, fertile, and nimble royal imagination wrestle with— Yes! I have it. On the bright side, if we do meet horrible and protracted deaths in that dread netherworld, our ghosts won't have far to travel to get tormented. And I'll be in the right place to have a pithy word or two to whichever mischievous shade posed as the spirit guide who fed wrong and misleading information to the otherwise infallible Oracle of Ring."

"Have you ever considered a career writing real-estate advertisements?" Sandy said.

"I did interview, once," Drusilla said. "But they don't like to hire princesses. They knew I couldn't commit to a long-term contract, since I'd be looking to reclaim my usurped throne. And the constant threat of assassins leaping at me when I was trying to explain all the mod cons of the recently renovated outdoor privy might have been a little off-putting to clients."

"That black stuff could be magical," Mavis said.

"Aha!" Tyrone said. "Then fear not, fellow travellers. Tyrone and his anti-magical sword will lead a path of life and truth through that grim land which reeks of evil."

"I'm thinking," Sandy said, "that your sword would have to be a lot bigger than it is to make much of a dent in all that."

Mavis put a hand on Sandy's shoulder. "You're never going to get a man to believe that his phallic symbol is too small for any job."

"Perhaps we can ask about the black cloud land and dragons at that crossroads tavern down there," Ruth said.

# Promises, Promises

The VACANCY sign hanging outside the Abandon All Hope Inn squeaked as it swung gently in the breeze.

"That's lucky," Drusilla said. "Can you imagine travelling all this way and finding the place full?"

Sandy raked her gaze around the bleak countryside, with the ominous blackness as a smudge on the horizon, and failed to imagine any circumstances which might draw so many people that they would seriously challenge the accommodation capacity of a cottage, let alone the large two-storey inn and adjacent bunkhouse. The sign advertising "hourly rates" looked wildly optimistic.

Sandy stepped inside. As she had expected, the place was not standing room only. Behind the bar, a burly man with an eyepatch and a missing ear looked up from polishing a pewter tankard. A couple of elderly patrons played a desultory game of darts using a board made from a squashed wizard's hat, and one man hunched in a corner beneath a NO CHEQUES ACCEPTED UNLESS WITH PRIOR APPROVAL sign.

"Hello," Sandy said. "We'd like rooms for the night. Stabling for a pony, horse, and a unicorn. And two halves of light, a dry sherry, a port and lemon, a vodka martini—shaken, not stirred—and a gallon of wee heavy, please."

The barman scowled past her. "We don't serve ogres."

"Then it's a good job we brought our own," Sandy said. "Any table do?"

Mavis glared at the barman, clasped Bob's claw, and tugged him to the table Sandy chose.

"I would've waited outside if it'd cause less trouble," Bob said.

"No, you would not," Mavis said. "Prejudice! Maybe I've been wrong to confine myself to the dismayingly enormous fight for equality of the sexes. There are so many species in the world who are disadvantaged by rampant, bigoted human-centrism."

"Well, thank you for sticking up for me," Bob said.

"I'd have done the same for anyone," Mavis said. "Anyone and everyone. That's the point."

"Oh." Bob looked disappointed.

A barmaid brought a tray of drinks. She was followed by a skinny youth who rolled a keg across the dusty wooden floor towards Bob and nervously handed the ogre a straw. The barmaid sniffed her disapproval as Sandy opted to charge the drinks to their rooms, which meant no tip for her.

"Even Tom the leper leaves me a little something." The barmaid stomped away.

"Not exactly a welcoming place, is it?" Sandy twisted around to the man in the corner. He stared at his fingers as if expecting bits to drop off as he watched. He wore a silvery-white ring that would've looked a lot more impressive etched with elvish script or magical runes of power. "Hello? Tom, is it? Are you a local? We're looking for dragons. Do you know where we might find them?"

"I don't believe in you," Tom the leper said. "None of this is real. This isn't happening to me."

"Oh, right." Sandy turned back to Drusilla. "He believes in nothing, and you believe in everything. You'd better not get too close to him. You two might cancel each other out, like matter and antimatter."

"Personally, I much prefer someone who enjoys even those aspects of life that don't exist," Ruth said, "to someone who perpetually whines that things aren't as he wants them to be. Anyone care to join me in some shopping at the trading post?"

The man in the adjacent trading post looked like the barman's brother, only with more ears and eyes but fewer arms.

"Lost it on a dragon hunt." He held up his stump. "I was a ninth-level dual-class warrior-cook. The experience I got for this scar gave me enough points to earn promotion to tenth-level cook. Not that it was easy to use a spatula and mixing bowl afterwards. Everyone calls me Stumpy. Or Five-Fingered Pete. Or Lucky Pete. I'm not sure why, because my name is Nigel."

"Did your hand get bitten off?" Drusilla asked.

"A dragon's talon cleave through your arm?" Tyrone said.

"The beast's tail lash you in two?" Bob said.

"I cut my finger chopping potatoes," Stumpy said. "It got infected. Lousy way to learn that medical science has a ways to go yet before the discovery of antiseptic techniques. Next thing you know, gangrene. Nothing for it then, but a quick whack above the elbow with the meat cleaver. Now, from the look of you, I'm thinking that you'll be interested in our ready-made, off-the-rack adventure wear. Ladies' boutique section over there; gentlemen's outfitters here."

"Do you carry extra-large sizes?" Bob asked.

"Our Fashions for the Fuller-Figured Humanoid range is near the sword rack," Stumpy said. "You might like to check out the bargain bins, too. We're having an end-of-season clear-out."

Mavis sorted through the bin, grunting unhappily as she discarded set after set of leather and metal-enhanced bikinis. Sandy watched Drusilla and Ruth head for opposite ends of the women's section.

"Goodness." Ruth pulled a dress off the rack and held it against herself. It was velvet and silk, and heavily embroidered across the bodice. "I wouldn't have thought a demi-train terribly practical unless riding sidesaddle and travelling with a large retinue of servants."

"That's our Precious Princess line," Stumpy said. "Beautiful workmanship. Just the thing to wear to catch the eye of an adventurer if you want to be rescued."

"You probably don't want to say that quite so loud," Sandy said, "if you want to keep your other arm."

Stumpy followed her gaze to where Mavis still rummaged amongst the marked-down items.

"Oh," he said. "That's not Anax'athelia, Amazonian warrior, deadly with spear, short sword, and equal-rights petitions, is it?"

Sandy nodded.

"Oh, shit," he whispered. "Thanks for the warning. I'd better go and close the curtain to the Adults Only Etching and Sex Toys corner before she sees it."

"Now this is what a princess should wear." Drusilla held against herself a brocade jacket and a pair of silk knee britches. "A lesbian one, anyway. Pity they're a size too small."

"You'd look a right prat in that get-up," Sandy said. "Besides, remember how you have to beat it against a rock to wash it."

"You know," Drusilla said, "people who are always practical can be every bit as annoying as those who are always right."

"Oh, dear, do you think so?" Ruth said.

"Not you, dear girl," Drusilla said. "Now that dress will look charming on you. That shade of brown really matches your eyes. Don't you think so, Sandy?"

"Uh?" Sandy said.

"Actually," Ruth said, "I chose it because the material will be hard-wearing and the colour won't show the dirt. And it isn't very expensive."

Sandy watched Ruth bustle away to the changing room. Drusilla shook her head at Sandy.

"Sometimes," Drusilla said, "I find it very hard to believe that you are the same Sandy Blunt who once climbed up a vine beneath the balcony outside Ms Julie Smelt's bedroom to tell her that the skin of her throat is whiter than the purest snow to fall upon the mountain in the garden of the Goddess of Loveliness. Or that your extravagant way with complimenting lovely young women is what has resulted in us being on the edge of the known world in search of a dragon."

"I thought that I was supposed to have learned my lesson," Sandy said. "Character development and all that."

"One can't help thinking that, between getting us all under threat of execution by lusting after the wrong woman and wandering through life oblivious to the qualities of every woman, there is a happy medium."

Before Sandy could point out that Drusilla was the world's unlikeliest person to be advocating moderation, Drusilla walked off to examine the men's clothes.

Later, Sandy set her four new shirts, two pairs of breeches, five pairs of underwear, eight pairs of thick, woolly socks, two tunics, and sturdy pair of Never-Blister™ boots on the counter. The others had already piled up a small mountain of clothes. Sandy glanced at some of the dangling price tags and wondered if even the bag of gold that Bob had given her would cover it all, not to mention the new packs, blankets, soap, salt, cooking supplies, and untold stuff that Ruth had laden Mavis's, Drusilla's, and Bob's arms with. Tyrone excused himself from general shopping on the grounds of not wanting to get his new clothes dirty. He stood near the counter smoothing out imaginary creases in his new breeches and shirt.

"I never imagined I'd find a Manly Man-labelled garment in such a dismal place," Tyrone said. "It has heartened me for our continuing adventure even more than new bottles of metal polish and boot blacking. My armour will look great with these breeches, don't you think?"

Without waiting for a reply, he strode away to admire his reflection in a shiny suit of full-plate armour.

"All up, it comes to twenty-five gold pieces, fourteen silvers, forty-eight coppers, and half an egg," Stumpy said. "But I'll let you off the egg for buying bulk. You know, I've seen some ill-assorted bunches of questing heroes in my time, but you lot are one of the queerest."

"Two of us are." Sandy counted out the coins. "With a question mark over Ruth."

"That bloke is a strange one. Is he bent?"

"Tyrone? No. He's just incredibly vain. The only person he's ever loved is his own image. And he's got a unicorn to prove it. Only he would shop for adventure wear based on label. There. I think that's right."

Stumpy scooped the coins across the counter and chuckled. "Look. Between us. That Manly Man stuff is a cheap knockoff. A group of seven dwarf women have a sweatshop near here. They churn this clothing out as a way of supporting themselves and their kids since their husbands ran off to shack up with some young tart."

Sandy grinned.

"Here's your receipt." Stumpy bit a piece of wood until he'd left the required number of tooth indentations in it. "And here's your Abandon All Hope Trading Post coupon booklet, with some discount vouchers in the back on the off chance that you live long enough to ever come this way again. Now, let's see. You have an ogre and a unicorn, so that's two plot coupons we can stick in for you. Do you have many more to go?"

"We need to find a mature dragon. I don't suppose you could point us in the right direction?"

"Oh!" He shook his head. "I hope you've left your loved ones amply provided for with a family trust. If you haven't yet made one, we have these Quick-n-Painless Plain Language Will Kits, no lawyer required. Ten silvers, plus two silvers for my fee as a witness. They're one of our best-selling items."

"No, thanks. I don't plan on dying."

"I didn't plan on losing my arm, but look who they call Stumpy now. Mature dragons. Very, very nasty. They'll roast you as soon as look at you. Well, the red ones will. You did know that dragons come in handy-dandy colour coding? Red ones breathe fire. Green, poison. Black, acid. And so on. That's really rather thoughtful of Mother Nature, don't you think? Takes the guesswork out of what sort of agonising end you'll reach."

Sandy accepted the waterskin from Drusilla. They stood on a low rise overlooking an uninviting landscape of pale grasses, rocks, and tight, stunted shrubs. This made the country they had left around the tavern five days ago seem lush and inviting.

"We can't be above the snowline," Sandy said. "Yet where are the trees?"

"Were I to make an educated guess," Bob said, "I would say that there is no species of tree that has yet evolved which can survive frequent fire-blasting by dragons. Unlike the flora we see. If you look carefully, you'll notice a high proportion of plants that are traditionally first colonisers of fresh ground."

"What baffles me," Drusilla said, "is why you never hear any stories about Grob the Brave Barbarian Botanist. Our horticulturalist has proved the most valuable member of our party. Bob's knowledge about plants is about a billion times more useful to our survival than the ability to knock a kobold over at ten paces with a war cry and bad breath."

Bob blushed self-consciously.

"I think it comes back to the sexiness," Sandy said. "Practical survival can be boring stuff, unless you're the one actually doing the surviving. People like hearing about Grob doing the flashy, spangly heroics rather than the stuff of real utility."

"A man of action," Tyrone said. "Dash. Style. Verve. And with a suitably handsome profile. And a decent wardrobe."

"It's not that easy to buy clothes when you're seven feet tall and have a head shaped like an onion," Bob said.

"Only superficial people place any value on appearances," Mavis said.

Bob smiled at her.

"Need we remind you, Captain Shiny," Drusilla said, "that we asked Bob to come along with us? We got stuck with you."

"Look here," Tyrone said. "If—"

"Is that a dragon?" Ruth said.

Sandy's heart thudded. Everyone hunched defensively and turned to scan the cloudy sky for the shape of an enormous, flying reptile.

"Where?" Sandy said.

"I must have been mistaken," Ruth said. "Sorry. Shall we continue?"

Sandy looked suspiciously at Ruth. Ruth showed her dimples before turning away to lead Bill down the slope.

Shit." Sandy frowned at the teeming valley. "What is that?"

Drusilla finished crawling up beside Sandy and peered down over the rocky ledge.

"There must be hundreds of them down there," Mavis said.

"They're awfully small and upright to be dragons," Drusilla said. "And those rustic but tidy little stone houses look far too small to hold hoards of wealth beyond your wildest dreams. Well, my dreams run to something a lot more substantial when I think of dragons basking on beds of gold, silver, gems, etcetera etcetera."

"And gardens," Bob said. "Those are vegetable plots, or I'm not an ogre. And a fruit orchard. Looks like someone's a dab hand with pruning and espaliering. You don't hear about a lot of dragons doing that. Not in any gardening magazines I've read, anyway."

"Have you noticed that we've been getting closer to that land of the big black cloud?" Mavis said. "You don't think these are connected with that rather than dragons?"

Sandy frowned. "Did we ever remember to ask at the tavern what the cloud and stuff was?"

"No," Drusilla said. "And considering how unhappy they were with the modest size of the gratuity you left, they probably wouldn't have told if you had asked."

"My bath water was tepid," Sandy said. "I wouldn't have minded so much, but we had to pay extra for heating and tip each of the maids who carried in the buckets of boiled water."

"This trip is really changing you, isn't it?" Drusilla said. "I used to hope, as your mother did, that you'd settle down a bit, but this is knocking the romantic soul out of you. The Great Obtuse Mage has become a penny-pincher. Perhaps we should encourage you to write poetry again. In the evenings. Around the campfire. That should be pretty harmless. And I could copy the best ones to repeat to my darling Maybelle."

"You know, there's poetry in every tree," Bob said. "Each swelling tomato that ripens in the sun. And the smell of well-rotted compost gently steaming in a heap on a crisp autumn morning."

"That's surprisingly beautiful," Mavis said. "Do you write much poetry?"

Bob shrugged modestly. "I dabble in haiku now and then. Purely for my own entertainment, of course. I doubt that I could ever reach the lyrical heights of getting myself condemned to death for it. Though I did have a poem once printed in the reader's section of the *Vegetable Growers' Monthly*."

"Wow," Mavis said. "That's pretty impressive. You're an ogre of many talents."

Bob blushed.

"Does anyone else hear drumming?" Sandy said. "I think we ought to get out of here, give the place a wide berth, and continue on into the heart of dragon country. We don't need to get sidetracked by episodes of dubious drama on our way to near-certain death."

Sandy wriggled backwards from the edge of the ledge. Bob and Mavis began moving to join her. When she was several feet from the ledge, Sandy stood and dusted off her front. Mavis was right, the edge of that black cloud hung darkly on the near horizon. Sandy had been so busy watching for dragons that she hadn't noticed that before.

"Isn't that Ruth down there surrounded by the unidentified creatures?" Drusilla said.

"It doesn't work when you say things like that," Sandy said. "Only when Ruth does."

"No, I'm serious," Drusilla said. "That's Ruth and Bill the pony down there near the entrance to the valley."

Sandy shot a frown at her. "Ruth? Are you—"

"Aaarrgh!"

Sandy jumped. A dozen dark shapes leaped up as if they sprang from the rocky ground itself. Half-crouching, half-bent, the humanoid figures surrounded them. Grotesque brown-black faces looked partially melted. Red eyes stared from slitted sockets. Fangs showed past twisted lips. Oversized gnarled hands and claws gripped clubs and gardening implements. Sandy's heart pounded as her stare flicked from one hideous monster to the next. Demonspawn corrupted by black magics! They were going to die. Horribly.

"Aaarrgh," Bob said.

"Fear not!" Drusilla said. "I have my paring knife. We—"

"Might I ask you to put that away?" Bob said. "You're making them nervous. They think you want to peel their zucchinis."

Sandy blinked and looked between the ogre and the monsters. The clubs did, in fact, look very like marrows. "You can speak to them?"

"I did say that I had a knack with languages," Bob said. "Besides, gardeners the world over understand one another. Aaarrgh. Ugh. Grrr."

"Grrr?" The one with the largest marrow straightened and pointed in the direction of the valley. "Hrrrl. Ugh. Ugh."

"They say that we've missed the roadside veggie stand," Bob said. "It's that way. They'll escort us to it."

Sandy saw the unreality she felt reflected on Drusilla's face and Mavis's. Bob chatted to the big marrow boy all the way around and down to the cleft between the hills which led into the valley. Sandy couldn't help eyeing their escort. Even if the demonspawn shambling beside her did carry a large asparagus spear instead of a sword, and the necklace around his neck was made of dried beans rather than bones, the creature looked like it had walked out of her nightmares.

Wind chimes tinkled from the sides of a large fruit and veggie stall. A couple of female creatures wearing crude tie-dyed dresses rearranged large stacks of bright orange pumpkins, crates of chubby pea pods, sacks of red apples, and bulging bags of pears. A black chicken with blood-red comb that seemed straight from an evil sacrificial rite pecked at the ground near where a pair of naked, misshapen children played a game with stones. One large female stood at the front of the stall and it looked like she was trying to stuff a person in a brown dress into a sack.

"Ruth!" Sandy broke into a run.

The demonspawn woman turned. Sandy skidded to a halt. She saw that the woman's talons gripped a sack that Ruth was filling with carefully selected potatoes. Sandy felt foolish.

Ruth looked up from the tuber in her hand and showed her dimples. "I'm so glad they found you. We might not get the opportunity to barter for fresh fruit and vegetables again for some time."

"Are they organically grown?" Bob asked.

Drusilla patted Sandy on the shoulder. "Much better. Eight out of ten. There's hope for you yet. Next time, grab my paring knife, if you like. Oh, that sweet, ripe smell. Don't peaches make your mouth water? Bob, do we have enough money for some? I'll repay you a thousandfold when I regain my lost kingdom."

"Wow," Mavis said. "Those cucumbers are huge."

The creatures who had escorted them drifted away. One bent to play with the children. Another sidled around the back of the stall to talk with the female. The rest settled on the ground in a rough circle and started passing around pipes that gave off suspiciously sweet smoke.

"Where is Tyrone?" Sandy asked in an attempt to regain some control over the situation.

"He's waiting back there." Ruth pointed with a leek. "The unicorn refused to come any closer."

Sandy frowned at the demonspawn. "The unicorn didn't like being near them? That's worrying in a creature who responds positively only to beings of supposed purity. Of a kind. Bob? Can you ask in a non-threatening manner who or what these creatures are?"

Bob engaged in a prolonged grunting session with the woman filling the potato sack. Talons and claws got shaken in all sorts of indecipherable gestures.

"Their fathers and mothers were born from magical underground vats," Bob translated. "Their race was created from dark magic that blended foulest mud and bits of flesh from murdered, sacrificial victims of many species in a bid to produce a race of mindless warriors intent only on killing for their master."

Sandy stared uneasily at the demonspawn, who—she quickly calculated—outnumbered them by three to one. "Produced? Dark magic? Mindless warriors? Correct me if I'm wrong, but this would indicate that we're not in a good position right now."

"I suppose that depends on how much they want to charge for their onions," Ruth said.

Sandy stared at her.

"They have migrated from the subterranean caverns near Castle Abyss, on the other side of the Great Bog of Slime, in the Land of Black Doom," Bob said. "Where the Evil Overlord, a sorcerer perverted by the love of power, toiled night after night working his filthy magic and wicked arts to bring forth vileness beyond imagination that would one day march to his command and spread death, destruction, terror, and decay across the whole world. His power corrupted even the clouds and plunged the land into perpetual darkness. No light shone anywhere. The Evil Overlord toiled to produce the forces of chaos and darkness that would take over the whole world for him."

"Why?" Sandy asked.

Bob looked blank and engaged in a rapid exchange with the woman. She shrugged her shoulders and called out to the men. They shook their heads or shrugged.

"No one knows," Bob said. "Perhaps because he could. You know, like people who climb mountains or bungee jump off bridges."

"Actually," Mavis said, "believe it or not, lots of people think that evil for evil's sake is reason enough."

"Or he has some deeply-seated, unresolved psychological issues from his childhood," Drusilla said. "That sort of thing can really screw some people up when they hit adulthood."

Sandy refrained from the obvious comment. "Okay. Evil Overlord. Take over the world. Army of perverted monsters. Black magic, etcetera etcetera. So, why hasn't he done it? Why are these creatures sitting around smoking pot and selling fruit instead of taking over the world in a bloodbath of fear, terror, and general nastiness?"

"Apparently," Bob translated, "it all came to nothing in the end. Dark arts are terrific for producing numberless armies of mindless warriors, and impress the hell out of casual onlookers, but the Evil Overlord overlooked the tiny point that he needed to produce enormous quantities of meat, veggies, and ale to feed these thousands upon thousands of troops. They ran out of food. The black cloud meant no sunlight. Which meant no crops could grow, even if the Evil Overlord did belatedly try to knock out some farmers and casual labourers from his magical vats. Cannibalism can only get you so far. Lots of them gave up and went in search of work as extras in movies. This lot threw down their swords and sneaked away to start their own commune. They assure me that they have no inclinations to take over the world or anything. Live and let live. Which is why they caution us against continuing in a northerly direction, as that is where dragons live. And we're bound to die horribly."

"Coming from creatures designed for murder, rapine, death, and war," Sandy said, "that's not a lot of comfort, is it?"

"We're going to eat well on the way," Ruth said.

"Eat, drink, and be merry," Drusilla said, "for tomorrow we may fry."

Ruth flashed her dimples at Drusilla, handed Mavis an armload of marrows, and led the way back to where Tyrone and the unicorn waited.

Sandy frowned. That wasn't how it was supposed to go: Ruth was supposed to flash her dimples at Sandy, not Drusilla or anyone else.

"ere I to take a wild stab in the dark,"
Sandy said, "I'd guess we were in the
right place."

"Those enormous cave openings in the sides
of the hills are a bit of a giveaway, aren't they?"
Mavis said.

"Not to mention the piles of broken and
bleached bones, dear lady," Drusilla said.

"And the general air of crouching watchful-
ness," Bob said. "As if all of the few living creatures perpetually exist in expectation of daily
death swooping from the sky and snatching
them up in scaly talons."

"That was a nice bit of description." Mavis
said. "Good adjectives."

Bob smiled.

"Ah, the strong whiff of dragon pooh," Tyrone
said. "It's as though I've been drawn towards it
all my life—though not so drawn that I won't
watch where I tread. Is there a man born who
does not dream of slaying one of the creatures in
the ultimate test of manhood and valour?"

Bob raised a claw. "Me. I've never given it a
thought."

"Test of manhood?" Mavis said. "To pit yourself single-handed against a creature the size of
a small castle? What, exactly, do you think you're

proving? That you have the innate stupidity not to realise that you're committing suicide the hard way?"

Tyrone bristled.

"We don't actually need to kill one," Ruth said. "Sandy just needs a scale that the Princess Maybelle can use as a mirror. Perhaps we'll find one lying on the ground."

"Women," Tyrone said. "You don't understand guy stuff at all, do you? Pick it up off the ground. Pah. Where is the glory in that? The honour?"

"Well, all right, then," Sandy said. "Off you go. We'll wait here. Bring us back a scale or two after you kill one. Don't forget to wipe the blood off yourself afterwards."

"How about that one?" Drusilla pointed up at the sky. "Or is that too little to be a real challenge? It only looks the size of a row of shops."

Tyrone looked up. All the colour drained from his face and his Adam's apple bobbed up and down. "Perhaps— Perhaps it would be unfair on the creature to—to slay it just for one scale. If— If we wanted a whole foot, say, or a wing, then maybe it would be worth my while to kill it."

Sandy might have grinned at his discomfiture if she had not been too busy trembling with fear as she watched the giant winged lizard soaring off over the hills. Those things were unbelievably huge. She shuddered as if a cold shadow had fallen across her.

"Were we to resort to anachronistic democratic processes for our group decision-making," Drusilla said, "I—"

"With full women's suffrage," Mavis said.

"Yes, of course, dear lady," Drusilla said. "Democratic processes with enfranchisement of men, women, and sentient non-humans, then my vote would be for Ruth's idea. Dragons are bound to shed, aren't they? Or at least lose a scale or two now and then."

"Has anyone else just got a strong whiff of phosphorus?" Bob said.

"And that wheezy noise uncannily like deep breathing," Tyrone said. "That sounds like it's coming from about twenty feet above us."

"Bill has run away. And the unicorn. I'll go and—" Ruth turned and froze.

"Perhaps we ought to back off and plan how to find—" Sandy stopped when Ruth grabbed her arm. "What?"

"Found it," Ruth whispered.

Mavis turned around. "Oh, crap."

Sandy turned. Her eyes widened until they hurt. And still she saw only a small fraction of an endless expanse of red-scaled body that gently moved to gargantuan breathing. Sandy's knees wobbled as if they wanted to flee regardless of what the rest of her chose to do.

"Unless I am greatly mistaken," Drusilla whispered hoarsely, "I, Drusilla, dispossessed princess of an oppressed people, am standing a little closer to a mature fire dragon than health and safety authorities would recommend."

"At least you haven't confused me with a dolphin." The dragon's deep bass voice rumbled up from deep within his huge body.

"I shall never grow another dahlia," Bob said.

"Now— Now's your chance, Tyrone," Sandy whispered. "Tyrone?"

Tyrone's eyes rolled up in his head and he toppled backwards. He landed with a crash of his armour against the rocky ground and lay lifeless without so much as a whimper about the scratches.

"Oh, goody," the dragon said. "I haven't had a chance to play with my food for months."

Sandy saw the massive talons swooping down towards them. She pushed Ruth with all her might. Ruth's eyes flew wide with surprise as she fell. Before Sandy could fling herself to the ground, talons clamped around her. She found herself squashed between Drusilla, Bob, and a warm, scaly palm. The world lurched sickeningly. Wind battered her face. Someone screamed. Perhaps it was all three of them. The dragon held them below its gigantic underbelly as it flew off towards the hills. Sandy caught a last glimpse of Tyrone lying prone and Mavis and Ruth scrambling to their feet. Bill, Nameless, and the white unicorn formed an equine triangle fleeing south. It wasn't often Sandy envied a horse.

The dragon flew straight at the side of a mountain. Sandy squeezed her eyes shut and wondered if Ruth would make up some comforting story about how she had died peacefully in her sleeping bag so that her mother need never know the terror of the last minutes of her only child's life.

The dragon landed with an inelegant thump on the rocky ledge outside an enormous cave. His claws scratched the rock as he waddled inside. The gloomy air reeked of some pungent, overpowering smell that must be the dragon equivalent of sweaty feet.

The dragon whisked the three captives through the air and dropped them. Sandy landed on her backside on a hard but shifting surface. Drusilla landed on her and knocked the wind out of her. Bob splatted beside them and sprayed them with glinting, hard stuff that Sandy belatedly realised was gold and silver coins, bits of bullion, gemstones, and jewellery. The dragon sighed and threw himself down onto his bedding. His massive weight triggered a wave that nearly buried Sandy, Drusilla, and Bob in the world's most expensive surf.

Bob helped Drusilla and Sandy pull themselves free. He plucked a sparkling diamond necklace from where it was caught on the back of Sandy's tunic. "I bet Mavis would look beautiful in this."

Sandy and Drusilla exchanged a look, before both turned to look at the ogre. Bob shrugged and hastily tucked the necklace into his pocket.

"I was only saying," Bob said. "What about that tiara there for the Princess Maybelle you're going to marry, Dru? And don't you think that pair of earrings would suit Ruth?"

"Ruth?" Sandy said.

Drusilla put a hand on Bob's arm. "Not so fast, oh green-clawed one. We're making slow progress with our fearless if moderately clueless leader, but it wouldn't do to push it at this stage."

"I have no idea what you two are talking about," Sandy said, "but in case the terrors of the last few minutes have blotted out your short-term memories, we're about to be eaten by that."

The dragon lay on his front watching them. Each nostril was large enough for Bob to have walked in without bumping the top of his head. His phosphorus-tinged exhalations riffled Sandy's hair. The dragon reached out a claw to tap Sandy with an enormous talon. The playful buffeting knocked her backwards and left her wondering if she'd cracked a couple of ribs.

"I'm used to canned food," the dragon said. "Ready peeled is fine by me. Although, I'm wondering if I should tie you all together to make a presentation snack pack for her. Would food soften her hard heart?"

The dragon peeled back his lips to reveal a mouth full of fangs all larger than Sandy. He idly picked his teeth with a talon.

"Although," he said, "it's hard to believe that a paltry gift of food would prove more efficacious than a sonnet."

*Sonnet?* Sandy glanced at the others and saw similar surprise on their faces.

"Maybe I was a little hasty in eating that Harper," the dragon said. "But he just wouldn't stop asking me stupid questions about didn't I want to find an adolescent human with whom I could form a lifelong mental link. As if any dragon, even one fresh from the egg, would be charmed to enter lifelong servitude to some arrogant little human. Fly me here, fly me there. Oh, goody. I wonder why no dragon I know ever thought of so wonderful a scheme."

Sandy shifted and plucked a dented gold crown from under her left buttock. She eyed the distance to the cave entrance and wondered if those stories about amazing bursts of improbable strength and speed *in extremis* were true. To be safe, she'd only need to be able to run at a hundred miles an hour for the rest of the afternoon.

"Here, I'll take that." Drusilla claimed the crown from Sandy's hand and tucked it inside the front of her tunic. "I was wondering where I was going to get one from. Not every store carries them."

The dragon sighed. The breeze blasted Sandy, Drusilla, and Bob flat.

"Oh, Chlamydia," he said. "*Sweet art thy arching neck, sharp flashing art thy claws, my love is like a red, red smear of blood, I beg thee for a soft thingamud.*"

"Thingamud?" Sandy said.

The dragon's eyes slitted. "Thingamud. Haven't you heard of it? Ignorant being. Why would I expect humans to know anything about poetry and the finer feelings of a sensitive nature?"

"Poetry?" Drusilla said. "Oh, large and terrifying lizard, Sandy Blunt, the Great Obtuse Mage, has a skill with words second to none. Wooing maidens is her speciality. And Bob the ogre is a dab hand with haiku. He's had one published in—"

"Dru!" Sandy grabbed Drusilla's tunic. "What are you doing?"

"Published?" the dragon said. "Really? To my great bewilderment and annoyance, I have only ever garnered rejections. Me. Would you believe it? A wordsmith of my calibre. I'd like one of those editors to tell me to my face that my poetry is not right for their magazine."

"I bet they're all jealous," Drusilla said. "And, recognising your superiority to their own pitiful talents, they reject you out of spite."

The dragon's pupil widened. "Do you think so? It sounds about right, doesn't it? My poems were not really just like ones they already have, or not quite right for their readership. They were simply too good. Yes."

Drusilla smiled at Sandy. "Trust me. This is one situation where my superior powers of imagination might save us from becoming little pats of dragon dung. And don't forget the Oracle of Ring."

"I was afraid you were going to say that," Sandy said.

"But if my poetry is so sublime," the dragon said, "why does the fair Chlamydia not respond to my wordly charm?"

"Well, I'm sure this dragoness of yours is a superior specimen," Drusilla said. "But even she might not be able to appreciate poetry that was so very much better than anything anyone has ever written before."

"Hmm. Yes. Much better than anyone else has written. You make a good point, little bite-sized one. But if my poetry is too elevated, how am I ever going to get invited for a cuddle in her nest?"

"Easy," Drusilla said. "You dumb it down."

"What are you suggesting?" The dragon's pupil narrowed to a dangerous slit. "That my towering talents could be in any way diminished to produce inferior work?"

"Of course not!" Drusilla said. "I know your peerless genius would be incapable of that. Which is why you might like to consider the services of Blunt and Bob's Doggerel Company Inc."

Sandy opened her mouth to speak, but Drusilla clamped a hand over it.

"I have an uneasy feeling about this," Bob said.

"Combine their lesser talents with a smidgeon of your genius, oh gifted draconis," Drusilla said, "and Chlamydia will be yours."

"Anything is worth a try." The dragon shifted and produced an enormous book with pages made from the whole hides of cows sewn together. "I might even let you live if this works."

"Actually," Drusilla said, "the price of our aid will be our lives and our freedom."

The dragon's eyes slitted and his lids dropped halfway. "Do you presume to bargain with me?"

"Do you dream of making little dragon eggs in Chlamydia's nest?" Drusilla said.

Sandy squeezed her eyes shut and hoped that she didn't feel more than the first bite.

"All right then, I'll let you go if Chlamydia likes the poem," the dragon said. "But only if she does. Now, let me read you what I have so far, and maybe you could finish it off with your appeal to a lower common denominator. What page was it on..."

Sandy glared at Drusilla. Drusilla smiled. Bob planted a claw on Drusilla's shoulder.

"You and I are going to have to have a little talk about when it is and is not appropriate to loose your unrestrained creative impulses," he whispered, "if we get out of this alive."

"If we get out of this alive," Drusilla said, "you can thank me all you like, oh rhymester of the potting shed."

"Ahem," the dragon said. *"My love is like a dragoness with shiny wings,*

*"With scales and talons and other things.*

*"Something something something else,*

*"And roses and moonlight and bouquets of bones.*

*"Oh, Chlamydia, thou sweet morsel,*

*"Let's you and I have a good old snorsel."*

Sandy winced and shared a pained look with Bob. Drusilla smirked at the diamond-crusted belt between her boots.

The dragon let his book fall. "Well, what do you think?"

"Did— Did you just make up 'snorsel' because it rhymes?" Sandy asked.

*"What?"* the dragon said. "You don't know what a snorsel is? What use is such glaring ignorance to me?"

"Remember, oh sublime winged-one," Drusilla said, "that the whole idea is to somewhat dilute your powerful and overpowering intellect."

"Oh. Right, little finger food." The dragon sniffed. "I will allow myself to be mollified this once."

"Maybe— Maybe we could move to prose," Sandy said. "Stuff that doesn't rhyme. Perhaps you could woo her with a few well-chosen compliments. That might—might make her feel less inferior. And more in tune with you. Less intimidated."

The dragon scratched the inside of a cavernous nostril. "It's worth a try, I suppose. But such beauty as the way she rips whole stags in two deserves poetry, I would've thought."

"Let's— Let's give my way a try," Sandy said. "If it fails, then Bob can give you some haiku lessons."

"I don't suppose Bob gets much of choice in that," Bob said.

"Not unless Bob wants to be a kebab," Sandy said. "Now, dragon, let's start with her eyes. What colour are they?"

"Oh, a dazzling crimson. The exact shade of arterial blood when you eat a human by biting his head off first." The dragon sighed.

"Right," Sandy said. "Well, how about her scales? What if you were to say something like... Oh, Chlamydia, my fair one, your scales are more brilliant than the shiniest armour of any..."

"Any what?" the dragon said.

"Erm." Sandy chewed her lip. Her mind had gone utterly blank.

"What's the matter?" Drusilla whispered.

"I can't think of anything." Sandy made futile gestures with her empty hands. "It's not flowing."

"Perhaps because you're thinking about a dragon," Bob said. "And it's blocking you. Why don't you pretend you're saying this about some pretty woman?"

"Brilliant!" Drusilla said.

Sandy tried to ignore the large dragon who impatiently tapped his talons. She closed her eyes and tried to think of Princess Maybelle. Eyes. Mouth. Throat. Brow. Hair. Cleavage. "Oh, shit. It's— It's not working. Dru, I can't remember what she looks like. How could I have forgotten Maybelle's beauty? She's the most gorgeous woman I've ever seen and is our reason for all these death-defying scrapes!"

"That is a complete mystery to me," Drusilla said, "as I, the woman who intends to spend the rest of my life with her, have every perfect feature etched in my memory."

Sandy frowned at her. "Do you really?"

"Well... More or less. I'll certainly recognise her again when we see her."

"Think of someone else," Bob said. "Your first girlfriend."

"Irene Boggs?" Sandy said. "She jilted me for a travelling knife-grinder. A very ugly one, too. That scarred me for years."

Bob spread his claws. "Any woman will do, won't she? From what I've heard, you can get worked up about any pretty face and nice pair of—"

"I'm getting impatient," the dragon said. "And when I'm impatient, I tend to snack."

"Every woman I've ever met has vanished from my head." Sandy looked her despair at Drusilla. "Who? Who?"

"Ruth," Drusilla said.

Bob put a claw on Drusilla's shoulder. "I thought we were supposed to be going easy on—"

"There are times when subtle relationship guidance must take second place to saving our arses," Drusilla said. "Or would you rather be eaten?"

"Good point," Bob said.

Ruth? Sandy squeezed her eyes shut. Ruth's face sprang easily to mind.

"You— Your smile is like the warmth of opening the door to home after a long, cold day at work and smelling freshly baked bread. Your dimples— Your dimples are—are really cute. I hadn't noticed that before."

"Dimples?" the dragon said.

"You're doing great." Drusilla put a hand on Sandy's arm. "Really great. But now imagine Ruth with wings. And a tail. And scaly skin."

"When you take flight, oh lizardly female perfection, your wings spread a shadow of beautiful dread over desolate lands," Sandy said. "Your mirror-bright scales flash back glints more searing than the sun that shines in the garden of the Goddess of Fire."

"Oh, that was good," Drusilla said. "Don't stop now. Are you scratching this all down, oh dread scaly one?"

"...Goddess of Fire. Got it. More."

Sandy covered fangs, eye ridges, muzzle, tail—twice, talons, and poison breath. The dragon avidly scratched it all into his book. Drusilla kept patting Sandy and encouraging her to greater flights of terrible eloquence. Bob looked on with frank admiration.

"It's not poetry," the dragon said. "But it's worth a try."

He snapped his book shut, which nearly deafened his guests, and surged up onto his hind legs. He hummed to himself and reached something down from a ledge high up in the darkness of the cave. He rubbed it into one armpit, then the other. He gargled, rinsed his mouth, and spat a few hundred gallons of grey-black liquid at the cave entrance.

"Oh, I'm a handsome, handsome dragon," he said. "I can't understand why she doesn't swoon at the sight of me. Now, let's see if this will work."

The dragon scooped up his book. "Ahem. Poison more noisome than the vent at the bottom of the Abyss of Toxic Waste. How could any chick resist that?"

He waddled and scrunched across the priceless treasure of his nest towards the cave entrance.

"Dragon!" Sandy called. "Sir! Wait. What about us?"

"You?" The dragon's eyelids flicked up. "If I'm at Chlamydia's long enough for you to get away, then you can keep your miserable lives. If your non-poetry doesn't get my claw in the door, then I'll be back very soon and very annoyed to tear, rend, and chew you."

"That's fair," Bob said. "Good luck. Hey, why not take this."

Bob waded through the shifting treasure until he got to a huge two-handed sword that was as tall as himself. It was encased in a gaudy scabbard with sapphires and rubies encrusted all over it. The blue gems picked out the words: *Excalibur—if found, please return to nearest body of water. Do not ram into stones.*

"Girls like it when you give them little presents," Bob said. "I bet Chlamydia would like this toothpick."

The dragon snatched it up and carried it out.

"Oh, that was a great touch," Sandy said.

"Why, thanks," Bob said. "I'm in awe of your way with words, actually. Perhaps you could give me a few tips on—"

"Perhaps we could postpone this meeting of the mutual admiration society," Drusilla said, "until we're outside the dragon's lair?"

Sandy scrambled to her feet, paused long enough to quickly fill her pockets, and waded after Drusilla and Bob. Drusilla also bent to scoop up something from the dragon's hoard on her way out.

The ledge of the dragon's lair stood several hundred feet above a meandering grey river. The skirts of the mountain sloped away in a mixture of scree patches and tussock grass.

"We're never going to make it down in time unless we drop," Bob said.

"A rope would've been nice," Drusilla said. "I don't suppose there'd be any silver or gold ones back there?"

"Hang on," Sandy said. "I might actually be able to do something useful. Tyrone should be miles away. Bob, hold on to me and make sure I don't fall if I black out."

"Black out?" Bob said.

Sandy squeezed her eyes shut. She imagined the new coil of rope that Ruth had very sensibly purchased from the Abandon All Hope Trading Post. She concentrated hard to fill in the details of the picture in her mind's eye. Brown. Twisted strands. It had been stuffed in the bottom of the pack that Sandy carried. Next to some of the bottles of her father's oddly useful concoctions. She imagined the coarse feel of the rope in her hands. The weight—

Bang! Magic smashed Sandy between the eyes as hard as if Bob had punched her. Sandy rocked back. The ogre's strong claws held her. Sandy felt something in her hands. Through the shock of the slamming headache, she quickly closed her fingers on…a bottle.

Sandy peeled open her eyes to squint.

"The Mildly Surprising Blunt's Bruise Ointment," Drusilla said. "Not exactly what I had in mind. Oh, well, this might just have to be one of those desperate times where we have to do something unlikely which will sound vastly heroic when we tell it with suitable editing and embellishment to our grandchildren. Meet you at the bottom."

Drusilla leaped off the ledge, rolled as she landed a few feet below, and with a combination of skidding, sliding, and screaming, she hurtled down the scree slope.

Sandy and Bob shared a look.

"Please don't break that bottle," Bob said. "We're going to need it."

Sandy watched him fall, roll, and disappear in an ogre-sized cloud of dust that hurtled towards the bottom. Her spiking headache actually made leaping off a mountainside an attractive thing to do. Why couldn't she be the sort of witch who only had to wiggle her nose to make stuff happen? Still, if she were, she'd get stuck with a really dorky spouse. She tucked the bottle inside her shirt and jumped.

Chapter Nine

"You jumped?" Mavis said. "Off that mountain?"

Sandy winced as Ruth dabbed bruise ointment on her shoulder. "It was that or get eaten."

"And we knew we had the bruise ointment," Bob said.

Mavis frowned and snatched the bottle from Ruth. She angrily shook a large dollop of the thick liquid onto her hand and began vigorously slathering it on Bob's scratched head. Bob looked like he was gritting his teeth.

"Of all the idiotic things to do," Mavis said. "Take your shirt off. Let me see what sort of mess you've made of yourself. Honestly, Ruth, can you believe these three?"

Ruth silently took the bottle from Mavis's hand, shook some onto a rag, and handed the bottle back.

"Look at that!" Mavis said. "Bruises and bumps. You're lucky you didn't break bones. Sit down."

Bob meekly sat. Drusilla and Sandy shared an amused look, until Ruth found a very sensitive bruise on Sandy's upper arm.

Mavis worked a liberal coating of the ointment on the ogre's back. "I know that pair can be a bit irresponsible, but I expected better from you."

"Really?" Bob said. "We—"

139

L-J Baker

"Why couldn't you have waited?" Mavis said. "We were coming. Tyrone tracked you from the dust you threw up. We have ropes. I have climbing experience, and I once slept with a mountain rescue guide."

Bob might have interrupted her continuing tirade at several points to offer a defence, but he sat and took it all without a murmur.

"I'm only sorry that we arrived too late to tackle the beast," Tyrone said.

"You fainted, Captain Courageous," Drusilla said.

"My blood sugar was low," he said. "That's all. Now I'm raring to go."

"And that's another thing," Mavis said. "You great onion-headed turnip-grower, you pushed me!"

Bob looked up from tying the lacing on his jerkin. "I— I didn't want the dragon to take you."

Mavis's eyes narrowed dangerously. "You think I'm less able to take care of myself than you are?"

"Oh, no!" Bob held up his claws. "Of course not. I— I did it because—because—"

"Because he knew you'd be the ideal person to rescue us," Sandy said. "So we needed you to be outside the lair."

Bob cast her a profoundly grateful look that silently promised to name his firstborn after her. Mavis remained rigid, with her fists on her hips, and a suspicious look on her face.

"Well, we're all safe," Ruth said. "That's the important point. You do have the scale?"

Sandy's gaze snapped up. She slapped a hand to her grazed forehead. "Oh, shit! The scale. I don't believe it. We were inside a dragon's lair, and I completely forgot the stupid—"

"Here," Drusilla and Bob said simultaneously.

Both deposited a shiny dragon scale in Sandy's lap. The outside showed the burning orange-red of the dragon's hide. The inside flashed with glassy smoothness that really did act as a perfect mirror.

"You were absolutely right, dear girl," Drusilla said to Ruth. "There were lots of them just lying on the ground for us to pick up."

Drusilla stood and kissed Ruth on the cheek. Ruth looked surprised.

"That's for saving our lives," Drusilla said.

"Me?" Ruth said. "But I did nothing."

"Yes, you did. Ask Sandy about it one day." Drusilla flashed a grin at Sandy over Ruth's shoulder before she walked away whistling to herself.

Sandy frowned down at the top dragon scale as she tried to work that out. The scale clearly showed the perplexity on Ruth's reflection. Sandy remembered remembering Ruth smiling. "Your dimples."

Ruth's image abruptly looked flustered. She muttered about making a cup of hot tea and strode away.

"Why do I get the feeling that I'm missing half of what goes on?" Tyrone said.

"That's because you do," Mavis said. "But this one isn't wholly your fault. A large part of it comes with the chromosomes."

I never realised, from reading books," Sandy said, "how much walking was involved in adventuring. Or the way time seems to do odd things."

Drusilla brushed a yellow-brown leaf from her shoulder. "You mean how it was spring when we met Bob and his gladioli bulbs, and summer in dragon land, and now we're strolling through a forest picturesquely cloaked in the reds and yellows of autumnal splendour?"

"Don't forget how we managed to buy asparagus, marrows, pumpkins, cherries, and apples ripe all at the same time," Bob said.

"I wasn't actually going to draw attention to that," Sandy said. "Because I don't want whatever is causing it to get embarrassed and stop."

"Oh, good point," he said.

# L-J Baker

"I suppose," Drusilla said, "that the same goes for keeping quiet about the fact that we haven't had to do a shred of waged work to be able to pay for all our food and supplies."

"Although I have a great deal of admiration for verisimilitude," Mavis said, "I'm hoping we can skim very lightly over winter. I hate cold. Numb toes and fingers. And chilblains. The way ice and snow crust up your clothes. And how the front of you thaws and warms from the campfire, but your back stays frozen."

"But isn't it fun how your tongue sticks to really cold rake heads?" Bob said.

Mavis levelled a look of pure disbelief up at him.

"You do that, too?" Drusilla said. "How about snapping icicles off and using them as daggers? I used one once to slay a hapless gryphon that was hiding in wait for me in Mrs Blunt's rose garden. I thrust, thus! It died. *Argle aaarrgh.* And an icicle has the advantage of melting afterwards so the city watch will never find the murder weapon. I learned that tip from an assassin from the Brotherhood of the Stabbing Blade just before I killed him. Not with an icicle, though. I used my paring knife on him."

"You can't beat a really good snowball fight," Sandy said. "Remember last winter, Dru, when we made those ice forts in the back yard and pelted each other for hours? I secretly poured water all over mine to harden it and you accused me of using magic."

"Oh, that's sounds like so much fun," Bob said. "I never got to do anything like that as a boy, because my mother didn't like me playing in the snow in case I lost my mittens. She knit them specially. It's not easy holding knitting needles with ogre claws."

"Overgrown children." Mavis gave them all a disgusted look and fell back to walk beside Ruth.

"What about you, Tyrone?" Sandy said. "I bet, with your military training, you're a dab hand at snowball wars and assaulting ice castles."

150

"I am too mature for silly games," he said. "Besides, freezing weather makes armour unwearable. And I loathe the way ice melts on your clothes and makes wet stains."

Without waiting for a comment, he strode back to join Mavis and Ruth.

Sandy, Drusilla, and Bob shrugged.

"She might have a point, though," Bob eventually said. "Between the fun bits, hour after hour, day after day, week after week, of trudging through snow, slush, icy water and what-have-you would get old pretty quickly. Wet, cold claws. Damp sleeping blankets that never dried. Waking up to find your cloak stiff with frost. Breaking a layer of ice on the water before having a morning wash. Wet firewood that doesn't burn well. Constantly shivering."

Sandy frowned. "There is that."

"Another up-side," Drusilla said, "which my Gift for seeing the sunny side even of impossibly unpleasant and near-death situations prompts me to point out, oh gloomy ones, is that cold weather makes for a lot more snuggling together."

Sandy and Bob frowned at her.

"Not with me!" Drusilla said. "With others who might appreciate sharing a bit of body heat. Women you find rather attractive, for example."

Bob's onion-face split in a broad grin. He slapped Drusilla on the back and sent her sprawling in a pile of fallen leaves.

"That imagination of yours is wild enough to bring on the world's worst heartburn," Bob said. "But every now and then, you throw up a little gem."

"The trouble," Sandy said as she helped Drusilla back to her feet, "is that sometimes it's impossible to tell the insane from the brilliant."

"Is that not the very nature of genius?" Drusilla said.

Bob stroked his chin. "So, what is your feeling about the usurped throne and her being a princess in disguise?"

"Utterly whacked," Sandy said.

"Her marrying the Princess Maybelle?" Bob said.

"Dreaming," Sandy said.

"Her idea to hire a ship and sail around aimlessly until we get abducted off-board by a group of marauding merfolk who will conveniently take us, as captives, to the undersea coral palace of the Queen Under the Waves?" Bob said.

"Brilliant," Sandy said.

Sandy spat a last sour gobbet of bile into the waves, and sank down onto the deck with a groan. "Why does sea have to move so much?"

"Hydraulics," Bob said.

"The wind and moon," Mavis said.

"The way the planet spins," Drusilla said.

"No, no, no," Tyrone said. "Merfolk push and shove the sea from underneath to create waves. It's their first line of defence against unwanted intrusion from land-dwellers."

"Did you pick that colourful little snippet up in military training?" Drusilla said.

"Actually," Tyrone said, "I deduced it on the spur of the moment when I saw that gilled gentleman wearing a seaweed loincloth clamber over the side and shake his trident threateningly at us."

Sandy only managed to scramble upright on her seasick-weakened legs after the flurry of invasion activity ended. A dozen or so merfolk rounded up the passengers and crew, disarmed them, and herded them together near the mainmast using judicious prods with their harpoons and tridents.

"I'm not fond of that fish-woman's blue-green hair," Drusilla said. "But those scallop shells covering her nipples are kind of cute. Don't you think?"

"Dykes!" Mavis said. "Sometimes, you're just as bad as men."

"Blurble glurgle blub!" The merman shook his flipper-fist at them.

"Bob?" Sandy said.

Bob shrugged. "Beats me. They probably don't do a lot of gardening on the bottom of the sea. Fish-farming, perhaps, but it's not the same, is it? Different lexicon. Sorry."

"Shit," Sandy said. "What are we going to do now?"

"Glurgle blurb gargle blurble!" the merman said.

All of the crew, including the captain, pointed at Sandy and her friends and edged away from them. The merpeople began prodding them away from the crew.

"Hey!" Sandy called. "Careful where you're shoving that hook, cod boy. Captain Ahab! What's happening? What are they saying?"

The captain shrugged and spread his hands. "They need payment for our ship trespassing on the waves belonging to her Aquatic Majesty, the Queen Under the Waves. You're it."

"Us? That's not fair!" Sandy said. "We're paying you for this."

"How do you understand them?" Bob asked.

The captain reached in his ear and pulled out a small gold fish. "Organic Translator Module. A bit ticklish when you first put it in, but it works a treat. And keeps your ear-wax down. We got ours off this hitchhiker."

"Got any spares?" Drusilla asked.

"Sorry," he said. "Not that you'll be needing one for long. Unless you're a really, really good swimmer."

The merfolk had prodded them to the railing and tried to shove Mavis overboard. Bob grabbed a mer neck in each claw and lifted their flippers clear of the deck.

"Bob!" Sandy called. "Wait. Don't hurt them."

"They jabbed Mavis," Bob said.

"I can understand your chivalrous impulses," Sandy said, "but let's think this through. We're on this ship because we want to find the Queen Under the Waves. They want to take us to her."

"Oh. Right." Bob set the two mermen down. "Sorry, fish people. Slight misunderstanding. Which would not have happened, though, if you'd treated the lady with a little common courtesy."

"Lady is a loaded term, which I object to on several counts," Mavis said. "But thanks."

Bob grinned.

"I trust there is going to be some magical effect whereby we can miraculously breathe underwater," Ruth said.

"Probably," Drusilla said. "The infallible Oracle of Ring says nothing about me ending up in a watery grave miles and miles from any promontory suitable for a memorial obelisk of the sort normally erected for missing sailors, drowned fisherpeople, shipwrecked royalty, or misguided pioneer submariners. So, take comfort, dear girl."

"Of course." Ruth flashed her dimples, hitched her skirts, clambered onto the rail, and dropped.

"Ruth!" Sandy leaned over the railing. She saw the splash and Ruth sink. "No!"

"You're supposed to go after her," Drusilla said.

"I can't swim!" Sandy said.

"This isn't about swimming," Drusilla said. "You get to the bottom of the sea by sinking."

"Ruth!" Sandy still couldn't see her. "But— Aaarrgh!"

Drusilla pushed her. Sandy screamed as she fell. Cold salt water slammed into her and rammed itself down her throat and up her nose. Sandy flailed. Water tugged at her. She saw flashes of brightness from the sun above, and the darkness of the ship's keel. Something plunged down beside her. Sandy's legs and arms thrashed futilely. The surface was getting further away, not closer. She was going to drown. A hand grabbed her ankle. Sandy kicked at it and panicked. Her fists and feet connected with something firm. Her body contorted and convulsed with the effort to get to the surface. An angry merwoman darted up in front of her.

A hand grabbed the scruff of Sandy's neck. Sandy tried to jerk free. Her lungs burned. She was going to have to suck in something. A firm, warm hand on Sandy's cheek forced her head to the side. Ruth kissed her. Astonishment instantly negated Sandy's panic. Ruth blew water past Sandy's slack lips. Saltiness filled her mouth. Ruth broke off.

"What—?" Sandy said.

Ruth blushed furiously. "It— It was the only thing I could think of to get you to breathe the water and calm down. I— I'm sorry."

Sandy stared without a coherent thought in her head. Ruth turned away and let one of the merwomen begin pulling her further down into the ocean. Mavis, towed head-first by a merman gripping her well-muscled arm, glided down past Sandy wearing a broad, smug smile.

A flippered hand gripped Sandy's wrist. An unhappy merwoman glared at her. "Blurble glug blurble."

"Sorry," Sandy said.

The merwoman jerked Sandy's arm and began towing her down into the green-tinged depths.

"Aaarrgh!"

Sandy looked around. She saw a flash of silver, as if from the scales of an enormous fish. Tyrone plummeted down past her with a surprised merman swimming in hot pursuit. Drusilla, whose merman towed her close to Sandy, bubbled laughter.

"That might teach Captain Shiny to keep his armour on," Drusilla said. "You're looking dozier than normal, oh fearless and wet leader. You didn't seriously doubt that we'd be fine underwater?"

Rationally, that momentous impossibility should have been bothering Sandy and taxing her witch's knowledge of magic. Instead, though, she put her free hand to her lips. Maybe it was time to take that question mark off Ruth's sexual orientation. Or, perhaps, Ruth—practical and sensible—would have done the same for any of them.

Just when they were getting so far down that they could see nothing, the lights came on. Small ones. Drifting and darting this way and that. Sandy watched, amazed, as they descended through a moving constellation of luminescent fish and jellyfish. One big, ugly fish even had what looked like a lantern hanging in front of it. From the depths, a broader, stationary tapestry of lights resolved into a whole city of coral with gardens of swaying seaweed. The squeaks, clicks, and moans of whale song serenaded the watery home of the Queen Under the Waves.

The merpeople drew the humans and ogre down towards a magnificent sprawling confection of multi-coloured coral. The mer-denizens of the city and palace paused their swimming to stare at the newcomers. Mer-guards flanked the front opening to the palace. Their mer-captors slowed to a fast drift to navigate the highly decorative coral chambers, which looked like they had some rough edges. They passed merpeople wearing more elaborate seaweed garments, and adorned with pearls and decorative barnacles.

Their mer-captors towed them into a massive hall. Despite the myriad patches of luminescent slimy stuff and self-lighting starfish on the coral walls, the hall was so large that the corners remained gloomy.

In the centre of the hall, a group of very well-dressed merpeople, with their blue and green hair artistically styled around lobster claws, gathered near a massive bivalve shell. In the bottom of this, reclining on some sort of bedding like a living pearl, was the mer-queen herself. Sandy blinked when she saw Tyrone perched on the front edge of the bottom shell.

"Blurble glug," Sandy's captor said. She shook her trident.

This precipitated some bubbly, glurbling conversation, which the queen appeared oblivious to as she stared at Tyrone. Sandy thought the mer-queen's complexion a bit too pale, her eyes a little too bulgy, her gills slightly too prominent, and her hair a shade too blue for her reputation as the most beautiful female creature alive. But she did have extremely inviting breasts and graceful flippers.

"I wonder if the matriarchal aspects of this undersea society are deeply rooted and all-pervasive," Mavis said. "Or if she is merely a figurehead who must deny her femininity to play the part of a female-king."

"She appears to have plenty of femininity to me," Bob said.

Mavis gave him a sharp, unhappy look.

"In a fishy kind of way," he said. "Although, I'm sure, by the standards of her own species, she...she— Sandy?"

Sandy couldn't help a glance at Ruth, who seemed intent on studying their surroundings. "I— I think judging people by their outward appearances can be a deceptive and unproductive process."

"Exactly!" Mavis said.

Bob gave Sandy a "thanks for nothing" look.

"What I'm wondering," Drusilla said, "is where they get those weapons from. How would you build a fire to forge weapons under the sea?"

"Underwater magma vents or fumaroles," Sandy said. "I assume that's what they use to warm the water down here."

"Or magic," Ruth said. "Isn't that the legendary talking pearl earring she's wearing?"

"Blurble! Glug!" The merman signalled for them to swim closer to the queen.

Up close, the queen still looked fairly good, in a piscine fashion. Then she turned a smile on them. Sandy blinked. Dazzled. By the queen's pearly radiance and beauty.

"Blurble," the queen said.

She looked like she expected an answer. She turned her smile on Tyrone. "Blurble glug?"

"Glurgle," Tyrone said.

"Hey!" Sandy said. "How can you speak fish language?"

"I have one of those translator fish in my ear," he said. "It feels very strange. And I'll have you know, for the record, that I object most strenuously to being forced to wear any magical device."

"I don't think it is magical," Sandy said.

"It all sounds very fishy to me," Drusilla said.

Sandy stared at her in disgust.

Drusilla shrugged. "Someone had to get the bad pun out of the way. Now, I wonder if my royal briny cousin would care to bargain with us for her magnificent piece of jewellery. Ask her."

"Tyrone?" Sandy said.

"He's the one with the fish in his ear." Drusilla spread her hands. "There's not a lot we can do about that, is there? Besides, she seems quite taken with him. You know, even my imagination failed to cover the possibility of some sane woman running her fins through Tyrone's hair."

Sandy watched, stupefied, as the Queen Under the Waves petted Tyrone.

"She says," Tyrone said, "that she finds my exotic ruggedness and shiny exoskeleton fascinating."

"That's because she doesn't know you," Sandy said. "Ask about the earring."

One of the mermen swam up to Sandy and shoved something in her ear. It wriggled. It slithered. She shivered and cringed.

"…they, too, are humans?" the queen said.

"Of a sort," Tyrone said. "Very low class. Sandy is a witch. Drusilla is a shop-assistant."

"They, too, are handsome specimens," the queen said. "But the way their strange clothes are drifting around them in the currents, they do not appear the same as you. Perhaps I could have sex with them after I have worn you out."

"They're lesbians," Tyrone said.

The queen looked blankly at him.

"They're girls who like girls and not boys," Tyrone said. "You want a real man, not—"

"Oh!" The queen's large eyes widened. "How fascinating. Bring them closer! I must see these lesbians for myself."

Mer-guards prodded Sandy and Drusilla up to the edge of the bottom shell. The queen looked them both up and down.

"Look, she's mine," Tyrone said. "I got here first. And besides…I haven't done it before. So, it's my turn."

"You want to boink the fish queen?" Drusilla said. "I'm beginning to get some insight into some deeply-rooted sexual anxieties."

"Come and sit here," the queen said.

Sandy and Drusilla pulled themselves up onto the side of the shell. Tyrone reluctantly drifted to the side to make room. The queen reached out a cool fin to touch Sandy's cheek. Instead of slimy slipperiness or scales, the queen's skin felt rough.

"How interesting you are, little land creature," the queen said. "I think you and I will have sex first."

"Sex?" Sandy said. "Me and you?"

"You don't want me?" The queen seemed to suddenly radiate charm and overwhelming beauty. Desirability shone from her skin and limned her whole body.

Sandy swallowed. "Wow."

The queen smiled.

"You didn't used to have to do that," a thin, high voice said. "When you were younger."

The queen frowned and jerked upright. "Will you be silent!"

"I'm only saying," the voice said. "Speak up, speak out, speak the truth. That's my purpose."

"Perhaps you should have learned tact," the queen said.

"Time was when you used to be happy to hear me tell you how you looked," the voice said. "I'm not sure why you get so snitty about fine lines and grey hairs."

"Be quiet!" the queen said.

Sandy and Drusilla shared a look.

"Oh, mighty watery royal cousin," Drusilla said, "that wouldn't be the legendary talking pearl earring, would it?"

The queen flashed her an annoyed glance before quickly rearranging her radiant smile. "You have heard of it, have you?"

"Its fame has spread throughout the whole world, wet and dry," Sandy said. "Though secondary to your own legendary beauty."

The queen beamed at her and stroked Sandy's cheek. "I believe that I really rather like these lesbian creatures. Let's make passionate love and forget all life's little irritations."

"Erm..." Sandy stared at the finny hand that had strayed down to the front of her chest.

L-J Baker

"Oh, salty majesty," Drusilla said, "what would it be worth to you to permanently remove that little pearly, and inconveniently truthful, irritation from your realm?"

"You want my pearl?" the queen straightened and touched the large black pearl hanging from her gill. "It is priceless. Unique. Crafted by a young goddess when she had taken her temporary mortal form—as they often inexplicably do. What could you possibly give me of equal worth?"

"How about a hand-mirror made from the scale of an enormous fire-breathing dragon?" Drusilla said. "This will reflect your amazing beauty but not draw verbal attention to those few negligible imperfections, unlike—"

"Dru!" Sandy said. "We need the mirror to—"

"Relax," Drusilla whispered behind her hand. "We have two scales, remember?"

Bob pulled one of the dragon scales out of the front of his jerkin and passed it to Drusilla. The queen accepted it and admired herself.

"That's nice," the queen said. "A dragon? You don't get many down here. This would be quite something to have lying casually around for people to marvel at."

"If you look closely enough," the pearl earring said, "the mirror shows the wrinkles. It's not just me who notices these things, you know. Time has etched its inexorable passing even on you. And it's just going to get worse as— Aaarrgh!"

The queen tugged the pearl from her gill. She weighed it in her palm. "Okay. I'll be glad to be rid of the damned thing. I'll take the mirror. And sex with—"

"Me!" Tyrone flung himself to his knees. "Oh, please. I'll make this sacrifice for the good of our adventuring party."

Sandy and Drusilla shared a look which contained both amusement and relief.

"Sounds fair enough." Sandy held out her hand for the pearl. "You've got a deal, your royal depthness."

"No!" Ruth said. "The unicorn."

"Oh, crap," Sandy said. "I'd forgotten that. Ruth's right. What a good thing the merpeople gave her a translator fish in time for her to hear that exchange and point out our problem. If Tyrone pops his cherry, we can kiss the unicorn goodbye. It'll have to be you or me."

Drusilla flashed a smile at the queen before turning a faintly desperate look on Sandy. "Rock, paper, scissors?"

"This isn't fair!" Tyrone wailed.

"One, two, three." Sandy held out paper. So did Drusilla.

"How about both of you?" the queen said. "That could be extra fun."

Sandy did rock. Drusilla had stuck with paper. Drusilla smiled. Sandy tried to.

An ogre claw tapped Drusilla on the shoulder. Bob whispered something in her non-fish ear. Drusilla frowned and quickly looked around at Ruth.

"How could I have forgotten that?" Drusilla muttered. "It is a far, far better thing I do, than I have ever done. With no expectation of rest, and to save us getting our heads cut off. Sandy, I'll do it."

"Are you sure?" Sandy said.

"Oh, please!" Tyrone said. "Pick me! I have the shiny armour, though salt water is going to play merry hell with it. I am your little crab-man, remember?"

"Please don't tell Maybelle about this." Drusilla inhaled a large lungful of salty water and slid across to sit beside the Queen Under the Waves.

Sandy grabbed Tyrone and pulled him out of the shell. He was still kicking his arms and legs trying to swim back when the giant shell closed with Drusilla and the queen locked privately inside.

Bob frowned at the coral walls of the room they'd been prodded into. "I wonder where the privy is. I'm bursting."

"I expect you can just pee and it drifts away," Sandy said. "Only go over there to do it, will you."

Bob blushed. "I'd be too embarrassed."

"It's not as though you need to expose yourself," Mavis said. "I'm just relieved that I'm not menstruating. Imagine having that drifting around you wherever you swam."

"Wouldn't it attract sharks?" Sandy said.

"I hope so," Tyrone said. "Then you could all get eaten."

"Are you still sulking?" Mavis said. "You're going to be a lot of fun if you keep this up until spring."

"She was mine," Tyrone said. "So beautiful. I was there first."

"You ought to engage in physical intimacy with someone you know, like, and respect," Mavis said. "Not shag within half an hour of seeing someone. Although, I grant you, the rush of lust and that frisson of the unknown can be very exciting."

Bob stared at her.

Mavis looked oddly defensive. "Just now and again. I haven't done it for ages, myself. I don't recommend one-night stands as a way of life. It's far more satisfying to make love with your best friend. Which means you have to take the time to get to know someone first. Make sure he's Mr Right."

"Or Ms Right," Sandy said.

Sandy glanced across at Ruth. Ruth flinched from the eye contact, blushed, and looked away.

"She's rather plain," the pearl earring said from Sandy's palm. "Nose a bit too small. Eyes not— Oy!"

Sandy clenched her fist around the talking pearl. "Beauty is more than skin deep."

"Not to me," the pearl's muffled voice said. "I was made to judge people by their looks. Who's the fairest of them all? You just ask me. I'll tell you. And it ain't you. Your eyes are too—"

"Have you ever wondered what life would be like inside the stomach of a lesbian?" Sandy said.

"You wouldn't dare swallow me!" the pearl said. "I'm too valuable."

"And then you'd have to go through all my innards," Sandy said. "With the poohy stuff."

"I'm going to shut up now," the pearl said. "Not say another word. Not a peep. Nothing. Zilch. Nada. Zip."

The merpeople brought them some food. Most of it was fish or seaweed. Sandy noticed that Ruth only picked at hers and excused herself to drift up around the room to examine the coral and starfish. Sandy swam up to her.

"Are you all right? Sandy said. "You look…glum."

"I'm worried about Drusilla."

"Oh. Well, I'm sure she'll be fine. Who knows, the fins might be fun. And those gills could be like extra— Well, I'm sure Dru is coping."

"And Bill," Ruth said. "I wonder where he, Nameless, and the unicorn are."

"Ssh!" Sandy said. "I don't think any of us was supposed to draw attention to them. I bet we'll get safely back to dry land and they'll get mentioned as being with us. As if they'd never been missing. No questions asked."

Ruth flashed a dimple in profile.

"Erm," Sandy said. "Look. About earlier."

Ruth blushed and suddenly became absorbed in watching a small striped fish darting amongst the coral wall where someone had scratched the graffito: GRENDEL'S MUM WOZ HERE.

"Thank you," Sandy said. "You saved my life."

"Not really. You would've run out of air soon enough and learned that you could breathe the water."

Sandy frowned as she watched Ruth swim back down. Why did she have the feeling that everything she said to Ruth was wrong? Talking to women hadn't used to be Sandy's problem. On the contrary, doing it too well had brought them to the bottom of the ocean. Maybe Drusilla was right. Maybe this adventuring, with a death penalty over her head and that of all the people she loved, was changing her. The rest of her life wasn't looking too rosy if she developed out of the one real skill she had ever had. They'd better hurry up, collect the elven princess and the Green Hermit, and get back home before Sandy Blunt lost everything.

# Chapter Ten

Sandy screamed as the surging tidal wave threw her towards land and let go of her. She splatted onto hard, wet sand. The wave crashed over her, rolled her up the beach, and sucked away from her. Sandy coughed and spluttered salt water out of her nose and mouth. Air tasted light and thin after breathing the sea.

Bob's big claw gripped the back of Sandy's tunic and hauled her to her feet. Mavis picked seaweed out of her hair as water streamed off her tunic and breeches. Ruth stood tugging her bodice and sodden skirt into order. Something wriggled in her cleavage. She looked surprised, stuck a hand in, and pulled out a little silvery fish. She showed her dimples as she tossed the fish back into the water.

"Those merfolk really need to work on their public transport," Drusilla said. "I had hoped for something in the way of seahorses. I feel like I'm battered all over from that wave thing."

"If you do get some bruises," Sandy said, "maybe they'll make your fish-hickeys less noticeable."

Drusilla tugged her wet collar up around her neck and shuddered. "Fish? It was more like wrestling an octopus all night. You owe me big time. Big, big time."

"Oh, look," Bob said. "Do you think they'll have a funfair on that pier? With a Ferris wheel? And a haunted house? And candyfloss?"

"Is this another dream from your deprived childhood?" Mavis said.

Bob shrugged. "The closest I ever got was when a travelling circus strayed into the Wildlands. Unfortunately, Uncle Ted and Aunty Doris ate all the clowns and acrobats before I got there."

"That's actually quite sad," Mavis said.

"The really sad part," Sandy said, "is that we're in the wrong season. Sorry, Bob. It's all closed. We're going to be lucky to find a B & B open at this time of year."

Bob's massive shoulders sagged. Mavis clasped one of his claws and patted it.

"We can come back in summer," she said. "We can ride the merry-go-round together. And we can try to win each other a stuffed toy at the sideshows."

Bob instantly cheered and not even the spume-laden wind that knifed off the sea and blew gritty sand in their faces wiped away his smile.

Sandy squelched and slogged through the sand, past fishing boats beached for winter and piles of smelly seaweed, and towards the first row of houses. Drusilla, grinning, nudged her and pointed. Bob and Mavis had forgotten to let go of each other's hand and claw.

The stone, weatherbeaten houses crouched against the cold grey storms that blew in across the sea. Here and there wooden signs above doors creaked as they swayed in the wind. The "Home Away from Home" private hotel was closed. The "Just Like Grandma's Place" boardinghouse had a big CLOSED UNTIL SUMMER sign in the front window. Even the souvenir shops, with faded postcards and hand-made pottery sea-monsters crammed in the windows, were shut.

Sandy stopped to shiver at a street corner and wring some more water out of her tunic. Everywhere looked deserted.

"We could ask them if they know of a place." Drusilla pointed. "A walrus and a carpenter must be locals, don't you think?"

"It would be rude to interrupt them while they're eating," Sandy said.

"I wonder where they got the oysters," Tyrone said.

"Not that you need them for their aphrodisiacal properties," Drusilla said.

Tyrone glowered and stomped off down the street.

"He doesn't know how lucky he is," Drusilla said. "Having an insatiable merwoman with highly flexible fins as your first sexual experience could set some seriously unworkable precedents."

"Probably not nice to tease him about it, though," Sandy said. "I'll go and warn him that he's developing rust spots. That'll take his mind off sex and everything."

"Perhaps we could rent rooms in that place." Ruth pointed.

The Wishing Well Inn and Ye Olde Gifte Shoppe, plus Tea Rooms, was a large free-standing house a few hundred yards down the road. A white picket fence guarded fussily laid-out gardens. A sign on the gate warned: No BEGGARS, PIRATES, SMUGGLERS, SLAVE-GANGS, OR CREDIT. What Sandy had mistaken for an emaciated dog lying on the porch near the front door turned out to be a thick bristly doormat. A sign stuck on the door, handwritten in firm dark lettering, ordered: *Wipe your feet before entering.*

Sandy obediently wiped her boots and pushed the door open. A bell tinkled. The hall had a counter and portable screen blocking off the interior of the house to casual intruders. A crocheted tablecloth draped the counter. An over-decorated porcelain bowl containing a pot-pourri gave off a faint flowery scent which stood no chance against the aggressively uncompromising reek of beeswax furniture polish and mothballs. So many framed samplers and home-made sea-shell pictures covered the walls that it was impossible to tell what colour the wallpaper was.

A veritable snowstorm of handwritten signs covered the screen behind the counter. *Guests must not eat or smoke in their rooms. No alcohol on the premises except that purchased from the bar. No singing after dark. Dirty towels left in the bathroom will incur an additional 10% sur-*

charge. *Toenail clippings are not to be left on the floors. Guests who pinch soap, sheets, towels, or rolls of toilet paper will be cursed.* An official, yellowed piece of paper announced: These premises are licensed as a hostelry class 3A, in accordance with the Skull Coast Borough Council regulations section Q(cxxliv)2, to the Misses Priscilla and Charybdis Varnish operating as the Wishing Well Inn and Ye Olde Gifte Shoppe Co. Ltd Inc. By peering hard, Sandy could just make out that the health and safety inspection certificate pinned beneath it had expired eleven years ago.

"Oh, goody, breath mints," Tyrone said. "You could all do with some."

He strode to the counter and put his hand in the dish of peppermints.

"And what do you think you're doing?" a rotund, wrinkled old woman asked.

Sandy jumped as much as Tyrone. The woman, with purple-rinsed hair and wearing the faded black of old widow's weeds, seemed to have materialised from nowhere.

"Those complimentary mints," the woman said, "are for guests only. On the occasion of them settling their bills."

"Oh." Tyrone, red-faced, snatched his empty hand away. "Erm. I was—was—"

"We would like some rooms for the night," Sandy said. "If you have any vacant."

The old woman cast a sharp, penetrating stare over them all, lingering briefly on Bob. She sniffed discouragingly. "You look like a party of adventurers who've been washed up after a period of captivity on the bottom of the ocean."

"That's very perceptive of you, madam," Tyrone said. "For a woman of your advanced years, you— Ow!"

Drusilla kicked his ankle. The woman behind the counter glared at him with the look of someone contemplating a really nasty hex.

"Three double rooms, if you have them," Sandy said. "Please, ma'am."

The woman lifted a large ledger from under the counter. "Three rooms? For six of you? I'll have you know that this is a respectable establishment. We don't hold with none of that hanky-panky that young people get up to."

"Oh," Sandy said. "Of course not. W-We wouldn't dream of anything like that."

"Of course not," Drusilla said. "There are two sets of couples—sort of. But neither will sleep together if the boys share one room and the women take the other two. Three of us are gay, but the straight woman doesn't mind sharing with one of us. One of the two lesbians who would share a room is tentatively part of a couple, though she may not realise it yet, but not with the other lesbian. And the guys are straight, except for Tyrone who isn't anything yet because he's still a virgin. So, you see, ma'am, it's all quite simple and innocent."

The old woman muttered to herself as she filled in the ledger and demanded half the tariff as a deposit. Her corsets creaked almost as loudly as the stairs as she led them up to their rooms. She put Bob and Tyrone on the first floor; Mavis and Ruth at the opposite end of the house on the second floor; and Sandy and Drusilla in the attic room. As far as Sandy could tell, there was not another occupant.

"Bathroom on the ground floor," the woman said. "One at time using it. Hot water is extra and will be added to your bill. You're all bound to leave sand and bits of grit in the tub afterwards, seeing where you've come from. So make sure you rinse the bath after you empty it out. And no singing in the bathroom."

"I'll do my very best to repress the excess feelings of jollity," Drusilla said, "that this cheery and welcoming establishment fills me with and which would prompt me to burst into inappropriate song."

Their hostess's eyes narrowed dangerously.

"Am I correct in understanding that you serve meals?" Sandy said. "A bowl of soup or bag of chips would be great."

The woman sniffed. "You're too late for lunch. Dinner starts at six. We don't do room service. No eating in your rooms. I ask all guests to read the regulations and information sheets. Here's your key. If you lose it, it will cost you seventeen silver pieces for a replacement. Enjoy your stay."

She stomped away. Sandy and Drusilla shared a look that threatened to become a giggle. Drusilla dove to shut the door before they burst into laughter.

"I bet she'd make even Grob the Brave Barbarian Hero wipe his boots and clean out the bath," Sandy said.

Drusilla flopped on the bed. "It's as hard as a plank of wood. You'd probably end up with splinters in your knees and chronic backache if you did try anything."

Sandy turned her smile on the framed list of regulations and information. It was written in the same decisive hand as the ones below.

"*No spitting on the dining room floor,*" Sandy read. "*Guests will not leave pieces of armour outside their rooms in the expectation of an overnight cleaning service. Any lawsuits resulting from bodily injuries sustained by other guests tripping over said armour will be the sole responsibility of the guest.*"

"Better make sure Captain Shiny has read that one. Do you think that woman is a witch?"

"If you were asking my opinion of her," the pearl earring said, "I'd say—"

"We weren't," Sandy said. "Be quiet. I'm beginning to see why the fish queen was keen to get rid of you. And, yes, Dru, that woman is a witch or I've never had lessons in cackling over a cauldron. I'm thinking that Tyrone's sword had better still be working, or he's in grave danger of spending the rest of his life on a lily pad. How that man can be such a complete clot around women of all ages, species, and sexual orientations is a mystery."

Someone tapped on the door. Ruth and Mavis stood outside.

"We're going down to fetch our luggage," Mavis said.

"Luggage?" Drusilla said.

"It's in the stables with Bill, Nameless, and the unicorn," Mavis said. "I'm dying for a change of clean, dry clothes. Coming?"

Drusilla strode out.

"You were right," Ruth said to Sandy. "They have appeared. Safe and none the worse for wear. As if they had been with us all along."

Sandy put a finger to her lips. "Ssh."

Ruth smiled and turned away to head for the stairs.

"Okay, I'll grant you those dimples are cute," the pearl earring said. "Aren't they."

"But her hair could really do with— Hey!"

Sandy jammed the pearl into her pocket, grabbed the room key, and darted out to take the stairs two at a time to catch up to Ruth.

During the evening meal, they discovered that the stout, elderly witch was Miss Priscilla Varnish and her sister, and co-owner, was the stick-thin Mrs Charybdis Newt, née Varnish. The latter did the cooking.

"I'll have the catch of the day," Sandy said. "What are your seasonable vegetables?"

Miss Varnish glared at her. "No fish until spring."

"Oh, then I'll have the… Hubble Bubble Toil and Trouble Supper Special," Sandy said. "Since it's the only other item on the menu."

"Will that be with or without eye of newt and wing of bat gravy?" Miss Varnish said.

"Can I have tomato ketchup instead?" Sandy asked.

When faced with a large helping of gristly black pudding, burned mashed potatoes, and watery cabbage mush, Sandy discovered that, contrary to all her expectations, she did look back fondly on fish food. Bob, to Mavis's open dismay, confessed that half a year of camp food had given him a deep love of burned mashed potatoes and ended up eating everyone's helpings.

"Guests are allowed to stroll in the gardens free of charge," Miss Varnish said. "But not invite any non-guests after dark. Stay on the paths and no picking the flowers or dead twigs. We encourage all our guests to avail themselves of the wishing well. Remember that checkout time is two hours after dawn. And that the Gifte Shoppe will be open before then for you to make your purchases."

Bob cleared his throat. "Did— Did you want a stroll in the garden, Mavis?"

"For the purpose of teaching me more about genus and species of flowering plants, of course," Mavis said.

"Of course." Bob stood aside to let her lead the way. "There could be no other reason, could there?"

Sandy, Ruth, and Drusilla shared smiles.

Tyrone shook his head. "That ogre hasn't a clue, has he? Why would you take a chick out into a garden at night to teach her some dry, boring stuff about botanical taxonomy? Anyone for a stirring game of bridge?"

"It's easy to see why you opted for a military career," Drusilla said, "rather than clinical psychology or marriage guidance counselling. But you might let me have some of your metal polish. I've got a crown that needs a good shine put on it before spring."

Tyrone's eyes lit up. "Now you're talking. An evening spent polishing. Could there be anything more rewarding?"

Drusilla and Tyrone left the dining room together.

"Are you two going to sit there all night?" Miss Varnish asked. "I'd like to clear away this table before we serve breakfast."

"Oh," Sandy said. "Sorry."

Sandy and Ruth smothered their smiles until safely out of the room.

"She's a forceful personality, isn't she?" Ruth said.

"An old battle-axe, you mean. Look, did you want to check out that wishing well?"

"Sure. You don't happen to know its Latin name, do you?"

Sandy laughed.

The winter night air breathed crisp and chilly when they stepped outside. Ruth shivered.

"Here." Sandy took her jacket off. "Put this on."

"If I do, you'll be cold and take a chill."

"We Blunts can be very slow on the uptake, sometimes." Sandy draped her tunic around Ruth's shoulders. "I'll be snug in bed before I realise how cold it was outside."

Ruth flashed her dimples.

They had gone only a few yards across the lawn before Sandy thought her lips must be blue and her ears iced over. Chivalry had a lot of pitfalls that they must keep well hidden in the fine print.

Happily, the wishing well stood fairly close on one side of the lawn near some skeletal bushes that probably looked magnificent at any other time of the year. The moonlight was insufficient for Sandy to see more than a few inches into the well.

"I should have guessed," Ruth said. "It's coin-operated. Just like the privy."

"Here." Sandy passed her a copper coin.

Ruth dropped it in with barely a pause for thought.

"What did you wish for?" Sandy asked.

"A good night's sleep."

Sandy felt sharply disappointed, although she wasn't sure why. She frowned to herself as she trotted to join Ruth striding back across the lawn. Sandy escorted Ruth upstairs to her room and accepted her tunic back at the door.

"You— Erm." Sandy made an abortive gesture.

Ruth watched her with that unflappable expression which, Sandy now realised, radiated an admirable and endearing mixture of boundless patience and good sense tinged with a deliciously dry sense of humour.

"Is that all you wish for?" Sandy said. "Not that a good night's sleep isn't important. A lack of rest can make you irritable and tired the whole day. But— But I would've thought that… You know, most people might've gone for a big-ticket item. Wealth. Long life. True Love. That kind of stuff."

"There is something that I've wanted very much since I was twelve years old," Ruth admitted. "If I get it, though, I hope my success

L-J Baker

will be because I have worked to earn it, not because of a fake well. Goodnight, Sandy. Sleep well."

In the morning, the counter was unattended. Sandy might have called for assistance, but Drusilla pointed to the sign: *In the Gifte Shoppe. First Door on Right.*

"You didn't seriously think," Drusilla said, "that they'd let us check out without first coercing us into buying some expensive tourist tat?"

The Gifte Shoppe was an overstocked shrine to bad taste. Sandy's dubious gaze drifted over the range of Wishing Well Inn-branded sun-hats, t-shirts, shopping bags, waterskins, underwear, helmet covers, presentation packs of fudge, scabbards, and shade umbrellas. The shelves also groaned under an armada of ships in bottles, hundreds of collectible sea creatures made from shells, and oddly-shaped crocheted items that bore the unmistakable stamp of amateur manufacture.

Sandy picked up a ceramic dragon portrayed as sunbathing with a straw hat on. The humorous observation she was poised to make about it to Drusilla died in her throat when she saw Miss Varnish watching her. Sandy carefully replaced it beneath the sign: BREAK IT AND YOU'VE BOUGHT IT.

"Guests are entitled to a two-percent discount," Miss Varnish said. "Excepting items already reduced in price and those of a magical nature."

"Magic?" Tyrone recoiled.

The way Miss Varnish asked "You have a problem with magic?" came out sounding dangerously close to "I haven't cursed anyone for weeks, so say something stupid, sonny, and make my day."

"Perhaps you'd like to help Bob with the horses," Ruth said. "Only you can get the unicorn to move."

"Right," he said. "But I'd like to buy this letter-opener first. It's not magical, is it?"

A scowling Miss Varnish accepted the miniature sword stuck in a stone. "No. Not magical. That'll be ten silvers and eighty-three coppers. Unless you'd like it in a presentation gift pack. Which will be a silver extra."

"Wrapped in paper is fine," Tyrone said.

Drusilla tugged Sandy's sleeve and drew her towards the back corner. The magical section boasted such marvels as the Neva-Snap Do-It-Yourself at home hair extension kit—as used by Rapunzel, and shiny red apples with Super-Sorb™ skin guaranteed to take a thick, but invisible, coating of any poison.

"Ideal for getting rid of unwanted stepdaughters," Miss Varnish said. "Or making toffee-apples."

The selection of ladies' footwear included diamond shoes that meant you were never more than a heel-click from home, and glass slippers—sold singly or in pairs, one size fits all.

Drusilla picked up a wooden box. "The Astoundingly Awesome Zapadox's Miraculous Finger. What does it do?"

"One of our best sellers," Miss Varnish said. "Helps find those little misplaced objects that you know you put somewhere safe, can be used as a compass, and repels caterpillars with an effective radius of seven yards."

"Really?" Mavis said. "I'll take one. Gift wrapped, please."

"I count eleven boxes," Drusilla said. "Just how many fingers did this Zapadox have?"

Miss Varnish levelled a toxic stare at her. "His parents were cousins. Okay? Now, what were you going to buy?"

"I'll take this, please." Ruth set a tiny box on the counter. It contained a thick sewing needle with a faintly golden tinge. The "Prick-a-Prince" also turned out to be one of the cheapest items in the shop.

"We've always sold a lot more of these than the Princess Mattress Peas," Miss Varnish said. "Even when we had the discount for buying them by the pod load."

"That'll be because girls have been brainwashed into believing their lives can be fulfilled by marrying well," Mavis said, "so it's more important for females to identify princes. Whereas boys are encouraged to achieve their own successes. Marriage to a high-status woman is an auxiliary validation of their lives rather than the primary objective."

Fortunately, Miss Varnish didn't look like she understood much of that. She sniffed suspiciously and pointedly turned her attention back on Ruth.

"Time was we used to sell a lot more of these needles," Miss Varnish said. "When I was a girl, every woman wanted to find a prince and get married. I've lost count of the number of men I've jabbed with one of these things. They all bled, of course. Never did find one whose royal blood was immune. Young women these days have some strange ideas."

Mavis bristled.

"Actually," Ruth said, "I just wanted to do some darning."

"Oh." Miss Varnish grimaced, which Sandy belatedly realised was as close as the old witch got to a smile. "Darning is a respectable domestic skill. A girl after my own heart."

Drusilla elbowed Sandy and pointed to a display rack of knives, swords, and hand axes. "Does that look familiar to you?"

Sandy stared at the middle sword. It had *WWI* etched on the top of the blade. "Shit. It's exactly the same as Tyrone's."

Drusilla smirked. "Wizards and Witches Immune is actually Wishing Well Inn. Guess whose granddaddy spent a couple of weeks at the seaside getting a tan and ogling the girls in bikinis when he said he was off questing for dragons and slicing up evil wizards."

Sandy frowned and turned back to the counter.

"Your sister has arthritis trouble?" Ruth was saying. "Has Mrs Newt tried the Mildly Surprising Blunt's Embrocation Oil? Mavis, could you please fetch me the bottle from my pack?"

"Erm. Excuse me, ma'am," Sandy said. "These swords. Are they anti-magical?"

Miss Varnish blinked. "Of course not! They all have guaranteed enchantments on them. That model is the Romeo. Also known as the Babe-Magnet. It magically enhances the wearer's charisma by between two and five times."

# Promises, Promises

Drusilla laughed. "You mean that Tyrone is really half as appealing to women as we thought? Wow. Does he have problems."

"But if his sword isn't anti-magical," Sandy said, "how come I can't do any spells near him?"

"Oh, that'll be because he's an untrained wizard," Miss Varnish said. "They can be absolute nuisances. And there's always one in every questing party. The chosen one with magical abilities that he doesn't know about. The special destiny before him."

"Tyrone!" Drusilla and Sandy said. "The chosen one?"

"If you're really unlucky," Miss Varnish said. "He'll turn out to be a god. But that's not usually until book two or three."

Sandy and Drusilla stared at each other.

Mavis returned with the bottle and Sandy eventually emerged from her shock to hear Ruth discussing product lines with Miss Varnish and her sister.

"Water-purifying tablets?" Miss Varnish said. "Now that would be handy. You wouldn't need much marketing with those. Not with the amount of dysentery most adventuring heroes suffer by not boiling their water before they drink it."

"This embrocation oil is already doing my joints a power of good," Mrs Newt said. "I can feel it, Priscilla. Why haven't we heard of this Mildly Surprising Blunt before? Skin cream. Insect repellent. Furniture polish. Stain remover. Air Freshener. Privy Sanitiser. These products are amazing."

"WWI would like to be the Skull Coast stockist for the Mildly Surprising Blunt range," Miss Varnish said. "Exclusive, of course. If we can reach agreeable terms on the contract."

"Perhaps we might discuss it over a cup of tea," Ruth said.

Miss Varnish and Mrs Newt beamed.

"What a sensible young woman," Mrs Newt said. "A girl after my own heart. Come on through."

Miss Varnish herded Drusilla, Sandy, and Mavis out of the Gifte Shoppe, locked the door, and waddled off to hammer out a negotiation with Ruth in the sisters' private parlour.

169

"It's not even eight o'clock in the morning," Sandy said, "and I already feel as though the day has slipped from me completely."

Drusilla put a hand on Sandy's shoulder. "Very little normally surprises me. On this occasion, though, my secret royal self is inclined to join your dazed state. Who would've thought Ruth so enterprising a commercial saleswoman? And Tyrone an unrevealed wizard with half as much charm as we've been thinking? Let's hope there aren't too many surprises like that left for us before this is finished."

170

# Chapter Eleven

It must be about time I made some reference to the passage of time," Sandy said. "Green buds of spring and all that. Someone must've been listening when Mavis said she didn't like winter."

"Actually," Drusilla said, "I think it has more to do with building tension. Time pressure is one of the oldest tricks in the book."

"What do you mean?" Mavis said.

"When we set out, dear lady," Drusilla said, "we had a year to collect all these unlikely things that Sandy's libidinous imagination dreamed up, and return to the palace. Or we get our heads cut off. It's going to be a lot more exciting if we arrive in the nick of time rather than if we saunter back with several months to spare. My money is on us not getting there until the very last day. Just when they're sharpening the axe for Mrs Blunt."

"How do you know all this stuff?" Bob asked.

Drusilla shrugged. "Royalty in disguise are born knowing a terrific amount. Especially stuff like the intricacies of economy, political science, taxation, law, and international diplomacy. It must be hard-wired into our blue-blooded corpuscles. How else do you account for boys reared in protective obscurity on farms immediately becoming successful kings as soon as they get their bums on their thrones without the benefit of a shred of education and experience beyond knowing how to grow a good crop of potatoes?"

"You know, that is something I've wondered about," Mavis said. "I'm so glad that it has nothing to do with them being male. But you don't read about many girls plucked from secret hiding places to become queen, do you?"

"I was born to be a trendsetter," Drusilla said.

"It might have something to do with the majority of books and stories being made up for men," Bob said. "Female education has historically been far behind that of males. Literacy, which conveys the power to shape story-telling and history, was traditionally the preserve of men. So, stories were often for men and about men. At best, women got fed instructional and moral tales that told them how inferior they were and how they should be quiet, submissive, and obedient to men. Also, those often superficial action-based, plot-driven stories about the boy who becomes king tend to appeal more to men than women. Which is why you will find them considered of more intrinsic worth than, say, romances. Because men like to think what they read is naturally superior to anything that appeals to women—irrespective of the literary merits of any particular examples. Which is a load of bollocks."

Mavis stared at him with fierce pride. Her eyes glistened as if she were close to tears.

"I wonder where murder mysteries fit in that," Drusilla said. "Or travel guides. Which reminds me, I shall have to commission someone to write one of those when I regain my kingdom. Preferably a humorous one that includes mention of quirky local delicacies and amusing problems arising from misunderstandings about cultural differences in personal hygiene. That always makes for vastly entertaining reading and good publicity."

"You keep talking about this kingdom of yours," Tyrone said. "But how do we know it even exists? Where is it?"

"Funny you should ask that," Drusilla said. "It's just over there."

# Promises, Promises

Sandy didn't notice anything unusual about the peasants, farmers, merchants, artisans, or shop-keepers in the villages, manors, and small towns they passed. Drusilla, though, frowned a lot, scratched her pimples more, and muttered about oppression.

On the afternoon of their second day in the supposed kingdom, they arrived at a large town just at the right time to look for lodgings for the night.

"How about that place?" Sandy pointed to the Leaping Cow and Fiddle Inn.

"Not if you value my life!" Drusilla said. "It is infested with informers in the pay of the usurpers who would have us all arrested were they to guess my secret identity. Besides, they only have two stars in the Adventurer's Accommodation and Eating Out Guide."

Drusilla led them to the Dog and Tapeworm Tavern. She insisted on them sitting in the darkest, gloomiest corner.

"Isn't this going a little far?" Sandy asked. "I can't see what I'm eating."

"It's probably better that way," Mavis said. "I think something just moved on my fork."

"Even if you were the rightful uncrowned princess of this place," Sandy said, "you don't seriously think anyone is going to recognise you? Weren't you born in exile?"

"Ahem." A large warrior stood near their booth. "Keep your voices down. There are ears everywhere."

"He's not kidding." Tyrone scowled as he peered at his plate. "I think I just ate one. It was very gristly with a bit of wax."

"Ssh!" A slender assassin-thief type slid into the booth next to Sandy.

Sandy wriggled away from him and his strong odour of onions. "Who are you people?"

"We are the Blokeship of the Ring," a grey-bearded wizard said. Uninvited, he perched on the bench beside Bob.

Drusilla's eyes widened as Sandy's narrowed suspiciously. In addition to the warrior, the thief, and the wizard, a hooded ranger, a dwarf, and two rather childlike creatures crowded the booth. The thief helped himself to a drink from Sandy's tankard.

"As ill-assorted an adventuring party as ever I've seen," Drusilla said.

"When you say Blokeship of the Ring," Ruth said, "do you mean—"

"We mean blokes only," the warrior said. "No chicks. Not even ones who disguise themselves as men and are dab hands at killing really, really bad guys."

"Especially not those." The ranger shuddered. "They all want to marry me. It's the stubble, you know."

"Then why don't you shave?" Mavis said icily.

"I was actually wondering," Ruth said, "if you mean Ring as in a talisman of incalculable power that needs to be melted down for everyone's peace of mind, or if you mean the infallible Oracle of Ring?"

The men all stared at her and put their fingers to their lips.

"How did you know?" the wizard whispered. "Only those of wisdom drawn from a younger age of the earth, and with a reading knowledge of the Elder Edda, are familiar with the workings of the infallible Oracle of Ring."

"Actually," Sandy said, "Drusilla spouts on about it all the time. Look, I'm sure there are other tables free if you want to—"

"Drusilla?" The wizard's rheumy eyes glinted as he stared across the table at Drusilla. "Are you sure that you're not Marjory? Which is the name we have for the shape of the mouse on the small moon? It also works as a handy-dandy power word when you say it with a funny voice."

"My name is Drusilla," Drusilla said.

"But you are the dispossessed princess?" the thief said. "The one we've come to help regain her throne? The one prophesied by the infallible Oracle of Ring?"

"Look, her name was supposed to be Marjory," the wizard said. He rummaged in his robe to produce a scroll. "Crap. The light's really bad in here. I can't read. But it definitely says Marjory."

"Yeah," the dwarf said. "Staffelf is right. I remember Prolix saying Marjory, not Drusilla."

"Prolix?" Sandy said.

"A man of incomparable wisdom in the interpretation of arcane prophecies," Staffelf the wizard said. "And a terrific speaking voice. Great carry. Sounds unbelievably portentous even with the lousy acoustics you normally get in castle throne rooms. I don't know how he does it."

"This wouldn't be Prolix the Off-White, would it?" Sandy said.

"You know him?" Staffelf said. "I believe he also does part-time work as Master of Ceremonies for weddings and bar mitzvahs."

"I met him once in the Sword of Power, Helm of Invincibility, Ring of Greatness, and Staff of Ineffable Magic Tavern." Sandy grinned and glanced at Drusilla. "So, he's the guy who interpreted this prophecy? That really casts some light on things."

"I wish it shone on my plate," Tyrone said. "I've lost my spoon. I swear something tugged it out of my fingers."

"So, are we going to rouse the peasants," the warrior said, "gather the loyal lords and their retainers, and storm the castle of the usurper to put Drusilla or Marjory or whatever her name is back on her rightful throne? With a spot of burning, looting, and pillaging on the side?"

"Didn't the merchant's guild want us to secure her oath first?" the dwarf said. "To make her promise to reduce the wickedly high taxes and ease the other inflationary pressures caused by the record current account deficit and the crippling interest payments on the enormous loans from King Derek. Or else they won't arm their apprentices to help our cause?"

"But she's not Marjory!" Staffelf said.

"King Derek?" Drusilla said. "Does my future father-in-law bleed my poor kingdom white with his usury? Fear not. From what I saw, my darling Maybelle should be able to twist him around her little finger. Once we get those debts written off, we can reduce taxes and divert the treasury contents into rebuilding the country's infrastructure and encouraging investment in plant machinery and research and development."

"Wow," Mavis said. "You really do know all about economics and stuff."

"And get rid of the elves," the ranger said. "Everyone wants the elves gone, or it's no deal on the crowning."

"Elves?" Drusilla said.

"The king invited them in," the dwarf said. "He thought an elf settlement would be a nice little earner. You know, a bit of a tourist trap. Two hundred gold pieces for the complete elf experience. Spend a weekend with the immortal elves in fully serviced or self-catering cabins in the woods. And a way to stimulate the local film industry. With them already having the pointy ears and not needing special make-up."

"Elves!" Bob shook his head. "Misguided king."

"Is that species prejudice?" Mavis said.

"No, dear," Bob said. "It's experience. No one can trash a nice bit of forest faster than a bunch of elves. My claws curl at the thought one or two of them might have found my garden. More virulent than downy mildew and more destructive than an infestation of weevils."

"But I thought elves were tree-hugging good guys," Tyrone said.

"You haven't actually met any, have you?" Bob said. "When you're immortal, you have plenty of time to learn the finer points of public relations and spin doctoring. It's elves who run the liquor and tobacco industries. They never have to worry about dying of liver failure or lung cancer."

"Excuse me," the warrior said. "Was that a yes or no on starting the uprising?"

"Eager as I am to regain my rightful heritage," Drusilla said, "and thereby ease the terrible financial burdens on my poor subjects, now is not a great time."

"Oh." The warrior's armoured shoulders sagged. "I was looking forward to it."

"I have to help my friends here keep their heads," Drusilla said. "Sandy is the Great Obtuse Mage mentioned by the oracle. And while I'm gone, I'll marry Maybelle. Which, as I said, will give me great leverage when it comes to getting those loans cancelled. With a spot of luck, I should be able to return to general thanks and popular acclaim. And so effect the ousting of the usurper by a bloodless coup. Which will save a lot of money on the clean-up bill and make for a happier coronation."

"Bloodless?" The warrior's shoulders dropped even lower. "Oh."

"But you'll probably need some blokes handy with their fists," Bob said, "for evicting the elves."

The warrior straightened and smiled.

Don't forget that we need an elven princess," Sandy said. "Just to pop into the palace so that everyone can see that Princess Maybelle's hair is more lovely and golden than hers."

Bob shook his head. "Elves. They're bad news,"

"And the Green Hermit," Drusilla said. "Don't forget him."

"By an amazing stroke of good fortune," Tyrone said. "They're in the same woods. The elves moved into the Emerald Forest not far from the hermit's cave."

"How do you know?" Sandy said.

"Is this your wizardly nature asserting itself?" Drusilla said. "Can you feel the presence of elves just like you can sniff out dust? Those magical super-senses of yours—"

"I am not a wizard!" Tyrone stamped his foot hard enough to make his spur jingle. "I have my trusty WWI anti-magical sword. Nothing weird happens around me. I'll have you know that—"

"We read it in the Emerald Forest Tourist Board's Free Guidebook," Ruth said. "The map shows that we're nearly there. See."

Sandy smiled at her. "I don't know what we would've done without your good sense."

Ruth flushed. "You'd have managed quite well in the end, I expect."

"But it wouldn't have been nearly as interesting," Sandy said. "Or fun."

Ruth shyly flashed her dimples before turning to Bill and urging him to walk on.

Mavis smiled. "Wasn't that cute?"

"Nine out of ten," Bob said.

"I do believe," Drusilla said, "that our fearless leader is finally getting a few clues."

"About what?" Tyrone asked.

Mavis and Bob shook their heads at him and walked off after Ruth.

"Never, ever, ever lose that sword," Drusilla said to Tyrone.

W "hat is that horrible smell?" Sandy said.

"The kingdom's municipal services and grasp of community hygiene must be developing faster than I expected," Drusilla said, "for them to have instituted a rubbish collection and town tip several miles into the forest."

"Elves," Bob said.

Sandy looked in the direction the ogre pointed. She saw tree stumps, piles of half-burned rubbish, and dirt tracks worn towards drifting smoke. She frowned as she turned to pick her way along the muddy path. Bob looked disgusted as he bent beneath broken branches and tutted at the litter tossed carelessly into the undergrowth. The smoke came from the clearing ahead.

At first glance, Sandy thought that the half a dozen people lounging in exquisitely ornate carved outdoor chairs were thin, very pale humans. But the one standing in the middle broke into a strange capering dance which included movements that no human elbow or knee joints could make without the benefit of having been dislocated.

"Boo!" One of the audience hurled a goblet at the dancer.

The dancer dodged the missile and planted his hands on his hips. "I say. You might've waited until I'd finished. I had another year's worth to go."

"You're boring me," the goblet-thrower said.

"We've seen that dance before," one of the elven women said. "Etheleriellethel, pour me another drink."

"But this is new," the dancer said. "Well, as new as you can get when you've spent several thousand years exhausting your creativity and doing variations on the variations on the same theme."

"I'm so bored," the goblet-thrower said.

One elf pranced back to the female with a goblet. "I'm sorry, royal lady, the still is nearly empty."

"Whose turn was it to make the booze?" the elven princess asked.

The goblet-thrower yawned. "Mine, I think. Or was that three hundred years ago? It all blurs into one."

"Oh, how I wish another one of those time portals would suddenly open up near us," the elven princess said.

"Oh, yes!" the goblet-thrower said. "What I wouldn't give for another half a dozen humans to step through from another time and place."

"The ones who think they're from a more advanced society," the princess said. "Who think they're so smart because they've brought their guns with them. Their smug superiority when they think they can lick the poor backwards sods from yesteryear who can only fight back with bows and arrows. How big and brave that makes them feel when they can stand half a mile away and put a bullet through the brain of someone who hadn't a chance of hitting back."

"I just love the look on their faces," the goblet-thrower said, "when they realise that we're immortal. They fire and fire and fire at you as you calmly walk towards them. Then comes the point when their little guns go *click click* instead of *bang*. How desperate they look."

The other elves chuckled.

"Yeah!" the princess said. "You can tell the moment they realise that they've lost their unfair technological advantage. Suddenly, whizzing back in time isn't so much fun any more. And fighting isn't nearly as great a pastime when they're actually in danger themselves."

"Personally," the dancer said, "I prefer it when human youngsters wander through the forest asking if you know the way back to their wardrobe. They can be terribly trusting."

"Especially if you give them sweeties," one of the other elves said.

"Right now," the goblet-thrower said, "I'm so bored that I wouldn't mind another group of trade union organisers asking odd questions about working conditions in Santa's toy factory."

"Did we ever find out who that Santa was?" the princess asked.

"Apparently he's an overweight, elderly man who wears red and has a reindeer fetish. He keeps some elves as slave labour in some remote wintry location."

"Maybe we could find him and liberate our brothers and sisters," the dancer said. "As something to do."

The goblet-thrower yawned. "Nice idea, but he's a commercially successful myth. I need another drink."

"We're out," the princess said. "And it's your turn to make more."

"I'm so bored," one of the elves said, "that I think I could turn to stone."

"You could try what I did," the dancer said. "Hold your breath for as long as you can. My record is fifteen-hundred and thirty-eight years."

"You could use some of your time tidying up the place a bit," Bob said. "And yourselves, while you're at it."

The elves turned to stare at Bob.

"An ogre?" the princess said. "And humans. And a unicorn. We haven't seen anything like that for several hundred years at least."

"I suppose you've just been hacking the trees down whenever you felt like it," Bob said. "Without ever a thought to long-term forest management or undergrowth renewal."

"What is he talking about?" the princess said.

"He's not one of those tiresome health campaigners again, is he?" the goblet-thrower asked. "Look, onion-head, we didn't ask you to start smoking, did we?"

Mavis stalked past Sandy, brushed the slender dancer aside, and grabbed the goblet-thrower by the front of his grimy tunic. "You'd have thought that anyone several thousand years old would've had time to squeeze in a few lessons on rudimentary good manners."

"This might be entertaining," the princess said.

"And a bath," Mavis said. "Phew. You stink."

"Bathing?" the goblet-thrower said. "How very tedious. I need a drink."

Mavis let him go and wiped her hand on the back of her breeches. He eased out of his chair and minced away into the trees. His slender form disappeared with unnatural swiftness in the direction of the drifting smoke.

"At least you won't have to worry about the princess's hair being more beautiful than Princess Maybelle's," Ruth whispered.

Sandy glanced at the elven woman's lank, greasy hair and silently agreed.

"What about a game of torment the humans?" the dancer said. "That's always good for an amusing week or two."

The princess yawned. "Ennui. Whoever said that you could die of boredom wasn't immortal."

"Look," Bob said. "If you're so bored, why don't you go and find somewhere else to—"

An almighty bang smashed through the woods and reverberated around the campsite. Bits of shiny metal hurtled behind the sound. Sandy flung herself at Ruth. The pair of them tumbled to the ground together. The noise, smoke, and shrapnel flew over the top of them.

"What the—?" Sandy said.

"Shit!" The goblet-thrower stalked through the billowing smoke. He held a piece of twisted metal in one hand and was powdered from head to toe with soot. His clothes and hair smouldered. "Which one of you worm-meat mortals is responsible for this?"

"What happened?" The princess lazily picked a sizzling fragment of coppery metal off the front of her tunic and dropped it on the ground.

The elves still slouched in their chairs. None had so much as flinched at the explosion.

"The bloody thing has blown up," the goblet-thrower said. "And we're left with two hundred gallons of vinegar."

"Vinegar?" the dancer said.

"The explosion was entertaining," the princess said. "But I can't imagine swigging vinegar is going to be much fun."

The goblet-thrower scowled. "I didn't do it deliberately to relieve the grinding monotony. One of these walking corpses interfered with my magic."

"Oops." Sandy turned to glance at Tyrone crouching behind a tree.

Tyrone's face lit up. He leaped out and put a hand on his sword. He opened his mouth. Sandy knew she'd be too late to prevent whatever stupid thing he was about to say, but began to scramble to her feet anyway. Drusilla stepped behind Tyrone and clamped her hand over his mouth.

"Perhaps you'd like to take a trip," Drusilla said. "To break the boredom?"

"A trip?" The princess sighed. "I think we've walked all around the known world several times. What is there left to do?"

"We even did it once walking on our hands," the dancer said.

"Oh, yeah," the princess said. "Let's not do that again. Some things sound much more fun that they turn out to be."

"How about a cruise?" Drusilla said.

"A cruise?" the princess said.

"On a ship," Drusilla said. "With other swinging singles. Romantic nights. Shuffleboard. Fishing. Stopping every now and then at exotic locations so that you can buy souvenirs and risk getting food poisoning. Soft tropical nights at sea rocked gently by the waves. As well as hair-raising storms that toss you about and make you violently sick at unpredictable intervals."

The princess sat up. "Yeah? That doesn't sound so bad. Where can we find this cruise?"

"Captain Ahab," Drusilla said. "His ship, the *Grey Heavens*, can take you all over the ocean. Reasonably cheap, too."

Sandy frowned and turned to whisper to Ruth. "Isn't that the ship that took us out to be captured by the merpeople?"

Ruth flashed her dimples.

"All right," the princess said. "I'm game for a bit of novelty. How can we get to this ship?"

"Well," Drusilla said, "if you come with us, we can take you most of the way. And we could supply you with a complimentary pre-boarding cup of tea at a royal palace, too."

The princess stood. Scraps of food fell from her front and she dropped her goblet. "I had nothing else planned for the next few thousand years. Let's go."

"I still want to know who screwed up my magic," the goblet-thrower said. "If—"

"I've finished!" A translucently pale elf dragged a strange white carriage into the clearing. "Look, guys! Three hundred and forty years and eighty-six pots of glue. Now I can start on that life-sized model of an elephant made out of matchsticks."

The dancer tapped the side of the carriage and frowned. "Is this why you needed all our toenail clippings?"

"Forget the elephant," the princess said. "We're going on a cruise. Does this thing work? We can get the unicorn to pull it, then we don't have to bother walking."

After some discussion, including a whispered threat to Tyrone that they would tell the elf mage that Tyrone was an untrained wizard, they lent the elves Tyrone's nameless horse to pull the carriage. The elves piled into the back and flopped.

Bob grimly surveyed the littered clearing. Mavis put a hand on his arm.

"Drusilla has neatly got them all to leave," Mavis said. "When she regains her throne, she can hire some park rangers to put it all straight."

"As you know, Bob," Sandy said, "there are no gardens at the bottom of the sea for them to trash. So, let's hope the merfolk capture them and keep them. Here, look at this. It's the pot of gladioli that you gave me back in your garden. It's beginning to shoot."

Bob cradled the pot in his claws and smiled.

"How nice and considerate of you to cheer him up with that," Mavis said. "I wish I'd thought to do it. I'd completely forgotten we'd got that bulb."

"It hasn't been mentioned for so long," Sandy said, "that I think most people will have forgotten it. Seeing how we're going to need it soon, now was a good point to draw your attention to it."

"Also," Drusilla said, "if the bulb is growing again, that means we're heading for the same time of year as when we first met Bob. Which means we're running out of time."

# Chapter Twelve

Sandy frowned along the river, around the rocky clearing, and over the forested hills. "Are you sure this is where the Green Hermit's Hidden Secret Cave is?"

Ruth studied the map in her guidebook. "Yes. It should be that cave over there."

"Perhaps," Drusilla said, "it's the one with the sign saying: BUGGER OFF—THIS MEANS YOU. Do you think we should point out the spelling mistake?"

"It doesn't bode well for our encounter with the wise old man of the woods," Mavis said. "Although, I don't suppose a hard-won knowledge of the mystic and eternal ebbs and flows of life is necessarily incompatible with a weak grasp of language."

"He could be a phonetic speller," Drusilla said.

"From what I've heard about him," Sandy said, "we're going to have so many problems with him that a spelling mistake or two makes no difference."

"A man who has spent the last half a century meditating on grass can't be all bad," Bob said. "Unlike certain beings I could mention."

"Are we at the ship yet?" the elven princess asked. "Is that why we've stopped? We're all very bored in here. Some of us would like to try duty-free shopping."

Mavis shot the elven carriage a glare. "What sort of problems do you anticipate with this hermit? His personal hygiene can't be any worse than theirs. It'd be physically impossible for him not to have bathed for two hundred years."

"Erm." Sandy shared a nervous glance with Drusilla. "I'm thinking that, perhaps, Mavis, you might be the ideal person to escort our elven friends further along the river. Out of the way."

Mavis frowned. "Why me?"

"Because…" Sandy cast a desperate glance at Drusilla. "Because?"

"Because he has the reputation for being the world's worst misogynist," Ruth said.

Mavis bristled.

"Ruth!" Sandy said. "Why did you tell her? Can you imagine the bloodbath if Mavis and the Green Hermit start a tactile conversation about women's rights? We need to be nice to the old geezer to get him to agree to leave his cave for the first time in fifty years to come with us."

"Perhaps you ought to give Mavis a little more credit," Ruth said. "She knows how important this is to all of us. She'll continue to help us as much as she has, and won't endanger it for the sake of her principles."

Sandy thought Mavis looked as dubious about that as Sandy felt.

"Besides," Ruth said, "I'm sure Mavis will welcome the opportunity of discussing her theories with him all the way back here from the palace."

Mavis smiled ferally. "Oh, yes! I like the way you think. Elves, let's get out of the way."

Drusilla and Bob laughed. Tyrone, as usual, looked mystified.

Sandy beamed at Ruth. "I could kiss you."

"Perhaps later." Ruth flashed her dimples and turned away to lead Bill down to the water.

# Promises, Promises

Sandy stopped at the wooden sign and peered into the cave. She smelled something rancid and saw a pair of ragged underwear hanging from a vine to dry.

"Yep," Bob said, "this is a bachelor's pad. And that's a nice little veggie patch he's cultivating over there."

"Let's hope," Drusilla said, "that this isn't the one week in half a century that he's away from home."

"Hello!" Sandy called. "Mr Hermit? Mr Green? Are you in there? We—"

"Bugger off!"

"Nice to meet you, too," Sandy said. "We were wondering—"

"Can't you read?" the Green Hermit shouted. "Bugger off. This means you!"

"Shall I mention the spelling mistake?" Drusilla whispered.

"Look, sir," Sandy called, "there's something—"

"Go away! Don't you know what hermit means? It does not mean someone who would like every body within a three-hundred-mile radius dropping in for tea and a chat about the bloody weather! Hermit means I want some bloody privacy. Bugger off!"

"Maybe we should change our minds about letting Mavis at him," Drusilla said.

"Look, sir," Sandy said, "I need your help or my mother, me, my friend, and my girlfriend are going to get our heads cut off. If—"

"Good! Go away and die, all of you. Horribly. And don't bother me again."

Sandy scowled at the darkness inside the cave.

"Let me try," Bob said. "Oh, no! Look at all those slugs and snails on those cucumber seedlings! Eating them to nothing."

"Aaarrgh!" A wizened, bent old man with a flowing white beard and tatty robe scampered out of the cave and across to his veggie patch. He waved stick-thin arms. "Shoo! Get away, you nasty slimy things!"

Sandy and Drusilla shared a look of admiration for Bob. Bob shrugged modestly.

"Erm," Sandy said. "Excuse me, Mr Hermit."

The hermit spun around. He glared at her. "You're just as big a pest as them! Why can't you people leave me alone? Why is it that, as soon as you announce that you want to retreat from normal life, every man and his bloody dog takes that to mean that you want them traipsing around and bothering you with stupid questions? Look, sonny, I don't know the secret of eternal life. Or how many fairies can dance on the head of a pin. Or what you can do if one of your friends turns out to be an untrained wizard with an antipathy to magic. And if I did, I wouldn't tell you. So, there!"

The Green Hermit stomped past Sandy on emaciated legs and paused to stab a bony finger at Bob. "And another thing. I hate ogres. There's only one thing I hate worse than ogres, and that's women. If ever—oh."

The hermit put a hand to his chest. "I should never have eaten that nut cutlet for breakfast. If there's one thing that is worse than women for giving you heartburn, it's a leftover nut cutlet heated the next morning. Not that I know why I'm telling you. Pah! Now, bugger off."

"I've known women who gave me heart ache," Drusilla asked. "And who made my heart leap about in my chest in peculiar ways. And one who has stolen my heart with her first lovely glance. But never heartburn."

"You're young yet, sonny," the Green Hermit said. "You'll learn."

Drusilla smiled. "Learn what? Why do you hate women so much?"

The hermit's shaggy brows drew close together. "All right, I'll tell you. Anything to get rid of you. Women are evil. Stands to reason. They do wicked things to a man. Weaken him. Make bits of him behave in ways that he might not want those bits to behave. Everyone knows they'll suck you dry and spit you out afterwards."

"You dislike that?" Bob said.

"They chatter all the time. And aren't meek or quiet or submissive or anything. Not like they should be. Not like the gods made them to be. Inferior to man. But do they know their place? There's nothing worse than a woman." He passed a shaking hand over his face. "See. Just thinking about them has made me break into a cold sweat."

"Thanks for sharing that with us," Sandy said. "Now, is there any way we could get you to travel with us for a little while? To the palace. Not for long. And we'd bring you back straightaway."

"Have you known many women?" Bob said.

"That's all they want!" the Green Hermit said. "To get to know you. That means sex. They're insatiable. Voracious. Sex, sex, sex. They can't look at a man without thinking licentious thoughts."

"Really?" Drusilla said. "Your talents don't stretch to mind-reading, do they?"

"I should imagine you'll be safe from ravishment at your age," Sandy said. "Now, what—"

"You're never safe!" he said. "Not from women!"

"Actually," Bob said, "speaking male to male, I can guarantee that you're safe with this pair."

"Pair?" The hermit flicked his stare between Sandy and Drusilla. "Are they—?"

"Dykes," Drusilla said.

"Oh!" The Green Hermit clutched his chest.

"Women who love women," Drusilla said.

"Dru!" Sandy said. "This isn't very helpful. We—"

"You're perfectly safe from our hot, wet, slippery, girl-on-girl desires," Drusilla said.

"Oh!" The hermit's eyes widened and his face turned blue. "Girl on girl…"

"I only think about sex, sex, pulsating throbbing sex," Drusilla said, "when I see a really attractive woman. With large, soft, yielding—"

"Aaarrgh!" The hermit's eyes rolled back in his head and he toppled like a felled tree.

"Shit." Sandy crouched down beside the old man. "Mr Hermit?"

Bob pressed an ear to the hermit's chest. "He's dead."

Sandy stared across the skinny body. "You're joking?"

"No," Bob said. "He's dead. Gone. Curled his toes. Pushing up daisies. Deep sixed. Snuffed it. Heart attack, I'd say."

"Shit." Sandy frowned up at Drusilla. "You killed him. By making him think about steamy lesbian sex."

"Ironic, when you think about it," Drusilla said, "that he'll be getting stiff for the final time because of a dyke."

Bob grinned. Sandy looked at the corpse in despair.

"We're dead," Sandy said. "We can kiss our heads goodbye. Dru, I can understand the temptation to taunt the old bastard, but how could you— The elf mage! Go and fetch him. See if he can undead the old bugger."

Drusilla turned to jog away but stopped after a couple of paces. "Not with Tyrone around."

"Crap!" Sandy slapped a hand to her forehead. "I'd forgotten that. Let's kill Tyrone and then get the elf to whip up some resurrection magic."

The elf mage yawned as he sauntered to the cave mouth. He toed the corpse. "Looks dead. You see a lot of it when you're immortal."

"Can you bring him back to life?" Sandy said.

"Why would you want to?" the elf asked. "He was a miserable sod."

"It's not a question of wanting to enjoy the pleasure of his company," Sandy said. "We need him to be alive to visit a princess or we get our heads cut off."

"That's bad luck," the elf said.

"I absolutely refuse to ride away!" Tyrone stomped towards the cave. "In case you had forgotten, me and my anti-magical sword have a special commission from his Majesty to remain near you, witch, at all times specifically to make sure you don't to any tricksy, nasty, slippery magical stuff!"

The elf mage stared at him. "Anti-magical sword? Was it you who made my magic explode?"

"Crap," Sandy said. "This is all we need."

"Yes!" Tyrone said. "I am proud to counter all sorceries with my heirloom sword."

The elf's eyes narrowed. "Oh, really? I might have to modify the ideas I had for a spot of entertainment with you, handsome."

"Handsome?" Tyrone said.

"Handsome?" Sandy said.

The elf shrugged. "In a rugged and not terribly intelligent kind of way. The pillow talk won't be up to much, but I'm a sucker for shiny armour. Besides, I'm really, really bored."

"Wow," Drusilla said, "now I truly begin to understand the pitfalls of living forever."

"Stay away from me!" Tyrone patted his sword. "I can use it as a weapon. It's not just anti-magical."

"Is it really?" the elf mage said. "I've never heard of such a thing before. Magical swords that kill by themselves, or prevent their owners from bleeding to death. That sort of thing. Magical rings, goblets, talismans, helms, staves, gloves, key chains, you name it, which are imbued with all sorts of enchantments of varying utility and power. But an anti-magical anything is new to me. Which is, in itself, amazing."

"No, it's not anti-magical," Drusilla said. "He's an untrained wizard. Though he'll deny it till he's blue in the face."

"An untrained wizard?" The elf's jaded expression took on an interested twinkle. "Really? As in, someone who will need years and years of personal one-on-one tuition from a fully qualified mage?"

"I am not a wizard!" Tyrone said.

"I'm a little rusty," the elf said. "I haven't trained anyone for thousands of years."

"Oh, Tyrone's your man for getting rid of rust," Drusilla said. "There's no one better, eh, Captain Shiny?"

"You know, this might be just the thing I need," the elf said. "It's been millennia since I last had a hobby. Now, beefcake, what was your name again?"

Tyrone pulled his sword out and waved it at the elf. "Get away from me!"

The elf smiled and pushed the blade aside. "I'm immortal, remember? I don't cut into pieces very well. Now, about— Hey! Come back! I want to be your friend and mentor!"

The elf took off at a steady lope in hot pursuit of Tyrone's lumbering run along the riverbank.

"Do you think we should have told Tyrone that he could throw his sword away," Drusilla said, "and suddenly become half as attractive?"

"He'd never have believed you," Bob said.

"Tyrone is not our biggest problem," Sandy said. "What are we going to do with a dead hermit?"

"How about your magic?" Bob said. "Tyrone will be a mile and more away soon."

Sandy spread her hands. "My magical pedigree is a father who concocted insect repellent and furniture polish, and a C average at magical school. I'm not in the right league for revivifying cardiac-arrest victims. Shit. We're dead. I wonder what the chances are of my mother having nagged the king into changing his mind about executing us all?"

"On the bright side," Drusilla said. "I still have my wickedly sharp paring knife, and we now have Bob and Mavis along to help. With Tyrone out of the way, perhaps we could storm the palace, rescue Mrs Blunt, and I could carry Maybelle off in a terribly romantic kidnap. An elopement would have the advantage of not having to invite people we don't like to the wedding."

"Yes, well," Sandy said, "setting that aside as our emergency plan if every rational idea we have fails, what can we do about rigor mortis boy, here?"

"Did you say that he hadn't left his cave in fifty years?" Bob said. "Then it's simple. We just have to persuade some other old man to impersonate him. No one will know the difference, because no one will have met the real one."

"Brilliant!" Sandy said. "Let's bury the old bugger."

Bob dragged the corpse out to the side of the veggie patch. Sandy rummaged around in the cave to find a spade. When she emerged, Ruth stood with Drusilla and Bob near the body.

"We hadn't thought of that," Bob said.

"Hadn't thought of what?" Sandy said.

"The dear girl's quite right," Drusilla said. "The court wizard will be able to magically detect an impostor."

"That drunken old sot?" Sandy said. "Not if Tyrone's with us."

"You mean the Tyrone who has just run away?" Drusilla said.

"Shit," Sandy said. "The one time we need him…"

"All we need to do is take the hermit along," Ruth said.

Sandy stared at her. "He's dead."

"In addition to his current lack of life hampering his ability to do and say anything, dear girl," Drusilla said, "he'll begin to smell bad."

"He doesn't need to do or say anything," Ruth said.

Sandy frowned at her. Drusilla dug a crumpled piece of paper out of her pocket.

"Most beautiful woman in the world blah blah blah," Drusilla read. "Oh, here it is. Item seven. Green Hermit. The dear girl is right. All he has to do is prostrate himself at dearest Maybelle's feet."

"You don't get more prostrate than dead," Bob said.

"Are you sure?" Sandy said. "Okay. Then… Then let's sling him on the back of the cart with the elves."

"Yes!" Drusilla said. "Even when he does start to pong, those elves will never notice it over their own body odour."

"Bob," Ruth said, "would you and Mavis mind returning to the elf encampment in their carriage and fetching us that vat of vinegar?"

Sandy laughed. "Of course. We can pickle the old bastard."

"You're a genius, dear girl." Drusilla kissed Ruth.

Ruth pinked and showed her dimples.

"Wasn't I supposed to do that?" Sandy said.

"Not yet," Drusilla said. "But soon. When you two finally kiss, it'll either be the last thing you do before they cut our heads off, or it'll be the start of the happily ever after."

P lease move," Sandy said. "It's been so long since I slept with anyone that my virginity must have grown back by now."

The unicorn dug its little silver hooves into the ground and
refused to budge.

"Now what do we do?" Sandy said. "We're running out of time. We
have to be back at the palace tomorrow."

"Though I never thought I'd hear myself say it," Drusilla said, "we
need Tyrone. Or another virgin."

"If Tyrone has managed to defend his virtue from that elf mage,"
Bob said.

"These elves are not at all what I expected," Mavis said. "Perhaps we
ought to have made some attempt to rescue Tyrone."

Sandy cast a dubious glance over the elves. They sprawled in the
clearing like living litter. "I'm guessing none of them will have the necessary qualification to lead the unicorn."

"After a few thousands years of trying everything to avert boredom?"
Drusilla said. "Not a chance. Which is a bit of a nuisance. Since this
is hardly the place you'd expect innocents to be thick on the ground.
Not like in a school playground, for example."

"How about her?" Ruth said.

Sandy turned to see a young woman stomping through the woods
towards them. A dappled grey horse followed her. The unhappy
equestrienne looked about fifteen or sixteen years old.

"If nothing else," Bob said, "she looks like she's had plenty of experience with horses."

"Stop it!" the young woman said. "Damn it!"

Sandy wondered who she was talking to. "Erm. Hello?"

The young woman stopped and stared at Sandy with a peculiar
look on her face.

"Is something wrong?" Sandy said. "We have the Mildly Surprising
Blunt's Gripe Water, which is great for gas."

"Oh." The young woman smiled. "You're not telepathic. Thank everything! Hello. I'm Fiona and this is Penelope."

"Penelope is your horse?" Sandy said.

"Yes, she—" Fiona scowled and balled her fists. "Damn it, your name is Penelope! I refuse to call you *whinny-neigh-whinny-whinny-snort*. I'm the human, remember? I'm in charge. So there."

Sandy shared a mystified look with Drusilla and Ruth.

The horse halted close to Fiona and gave a soft neigh.

"You look like you have a way with horses," Sandy said.

Drusilla leaned close to whisper in Sandy's ear: "Think very carefully how you will attempt to ascertain if she has the right qualifications for the unicorn."

"You don't want to buy a horse, do you?" Fiona asked. "I could let you have one cheap. One careful female owner. Not much—"

Penelope the horse tossed her head and neighed.

"I can so too!" Fiona said. "You know, I always wanted a horse. Ever since I was a little kid. Especially a talking horse. All of my own. My special friend. That will do what I want, go everywhere with me, and always love me."

"Sounds perfectly normal," Mavis said. "Talking ponies, flying dragons. Who didn't want one as a kid?"

"Me," Bob said. "I wasn't allowed a pet."

"Isn't it something to do with a prepubescent girl's sublimated desires?" Drusilla said. "Or am I confusing horses with karaoke microphones?"

"What they don't tell you," Fiona said bitterly, "is how flaming annoying it can get. Always having this horse's thoughts keep popping into your head. And you're not going to get any intelligent conversation. Not from a horse. It's all: 'I want water.' 'I want to canter.' 'I want my nosebag.' 'I want a stallion.' 'I want to graze.' 'I want to go to my stable.' 'I want to be rubbed down.' All the flaming time!"

"I don't suppose, then," Sandy said, "there's much chance you'd care to help us out with our unicorn?"

Fiona shot her a glare. "Are you crazy, lady?"

Fiona stomped away. The dappled horse frisked and followed her. "Stop it! Oh, shut up! Get out of my mind!"

"Now we're in the pooh," Sandy said. "Ogre, tick. Elven princess, tick. Talking pearl, tick. Hermit, pickled and ready to be spread out on the floor, tick. Unicorn, no tick."

"While he's stubbornly standing still," Ruth said, "I might as well comb some of the Mildly Surprising Blunt's Blonde Rinse into that inconveniently white mane of his."

"Oh, that reminds me," Sandy said. "Do you still have that darning needle? Can you pierce my ear for me?"

"Pierce your ear?" Ruth said.

Sandy pulled the black pearl earring from a pocket. "I had the idea that I ought to wear it for a day or so. That way, we're guaranteed that it'll have to say that Princess Maybelle is prettier than its previous owner. Because that will be me."

"Finding a woman with more beauty than you ain't going to be hard," the pearl said. "The way your eyes—"

Ruth put her hand over the pearl. "Ssh! Beauty is in the eye of the beholder."

Sandy grinned.

Ruth handed the blonde rinse to Drusilla and fetched her "Prick-a-Prince" needle. Sandy sat and braced herself. She jerked out of reach at the first prick. Her fingers came away from her earlobe stained with a drop of blood.

"I barely touched you," Ruth said.

"Here." Mavis held out her hand. "Give the pearl to me. If we want to make absolutely sure there's no hitch over the comparison with the feminine beauty of its previous owner, we ought to let Bob wear it. He's already pierced."

"Bob?" Sandy stared up at the ogre's big yellow-brown ear lobes. "But he doesn't have holes in his ears."

"I didn't mean his ears," Mavis said.

Bob blushed. Drusilla roared with laughter.

Bob took the pearl, turned around, and reached inside his clothes.

"No!" the pearl shouted. "Please don't— Nooooooo…"

Sandy smirked, until Drusilla drew her attention back to the problem of the unicorn. The blonde rinse had worked a treat. The blindingly bright white mane now looked a dull, streaky yellowish colour.

"Maybelle's skin is definitely purer and whiter than that," Drusilla said.

Sandy frowned. She could not actually remember, but it seemed likely. "Unless she's contracted a bad case of jaundice. Which just leaves us with the problem of how to get the wretched creature to the palace. Any chance we could drag it?"

"Psst!"

Sandy turned and saw a tell-tale flash of sunlight off Tyrone's armour from behind a tree trunk. "Tyrone!"

"Ssh!" He looked wild-eyed toward the elves. "Has he gone?"

"We haven't seen him since he ran off with you," Sandy said. "Didn't he catch you?"

Tyrone edged out from hiding and kept his eyes on the elves. "I used all my military training to evade pursuit. And when he did catch up to me, I told him to go away."

"And he did?" Drusilla said.

Tyrone drew himself up straight. "Of course! I used my Officer of the King's Own Bodyguard tone of command. I saw that it made him gasp and shudder all over with fear. Then he scampered away. Ha! He was lucky he went before I did any real harm to him, I can tell you."

Sandy and Drusilla shared a look.

"Let's see," Drusilla said. "Captain Shiny's little masterful display made elf-boy weak at the knees. How much would you like to bet that the elf won't be back plying Tyrone with immortal love tokens?"

"Not a single copper piece," Sandy said. "I take it, Tyrone, that you didn't get up to any hanky-panky while—"

"Of course not!" Tyrone said. "I'm saving myself for the right woman."

"Or fish," Drusilla said.

"Perhaps you'd be so kind, then." Ruth handed Tyrone the unicorn's lead.

Tyrone frowned at Ruth. "You're such a very nice person that I might seriously begin to consider marrying you. Are you sure you're a lesbian?"

Ruth flashed him her dimples. "Oh, yes."

"Perhaps you just need the right man to cure you," Tyrone said.

"Funny," Drusilla said, "that's exactly what I was thinking about you. Now, shall we get moving? We do have a looming deadline. Literally."

"Mmmm! Mmmm!"

Tyrone started and stared down at Bob's breeches. "Your— Your trousers are talking!"

"It's not my trousers," Bob said. "It's what's inside. Doesn't yours?"

Tyrone paled and stared down at the front of himself. "Shit. No. The little chap has never made a sound. You don't think he's broken?"

Sandy, Mavis, and Drusilla laughed so hard they cried.

# Chapter Thirteen

The city gate guards needed some persuading that Tyrone was a captain of the king's bodyguard and that one of them should run as fast as he could to the palace to warn the king that Tyrone was bringing back the condemned witch as required on the day one year after she left.

People stopped to stare and point at the little cavalcade, especially the elves lounging in their unique conveyance. At least the elves had stopped moaning about having to make room for the large vat of vinegar containing the body of the late Green Hermit. One had made the mistake of asking why Mavis had taken a piece of charcoal and written CONTENTS: THE ONLY GOOD MISOGYNIST on the outside of the vat.

"How do I look?" Drusilla asked. She had been examining herself in the dragon scale mirror.

"Great," Sandy said, "if you were aiming for the patched, dusty, travel-stained, and rumpled, with pimples look."

Drusilla put a hand to a zit on her cheek and frowned. "If only we had taken with us a bottle or two of the Mildly Surprising Blunt's Acne Lotion. Still, my natural Gift for looking on the bright side reminds me that a few blackheads and a pimple or two aren't going to matter soon. Either we get our heads cut off, or my beautiful Maybelle will be whispering sweet nothings into my recently revealed royal ear. She could barely keep her soft, pale little hands off me when I wore a fake beard. Zits aren't going to deter her. True Love is strong enough to conquer a bit of acne."

"Of course," Ruth said.

Sandy shook her head and made a futile attempt to tug the worst creases from her tunic. "I hope I remembered to put on clean underwear. I've been gone a whole year, and travelled most of the known world, and faced dangers unimaginable, all the while with the threat of execution over me and those I love, but I just know that the first thing my mother is going to say to me is to ask if I'm wearing clean underwear."

"Probably," Ruth said. "It's because she loves you."

"Really?" Sandy said. "I thought it was because she wanted to embarrass the socks off me."

The fanfare of trumpets made Sandy jump. But not nearly as much as the platoon of palace guards who swooped and clanked around them and placed them under arrest. One jabbed Mavis with his pike. He found his neck snugly gripped in an ogre claw and his boots dangling several inches off the ground.

"Bob!" Sandy said. "Don't hurt him."

"But he hurt Mavis," Bob said. "And— Oh. We've done this before, haven't we? I have to put him down because we want to get into the palace and that's where they want to take us?"

"Exactly," Sandy said.

"Can I scare him and give him the little lecture about good manners first?" Bob said.

"Sure," Sandy said. "Go ahead. We've got a few more minutes before the year runs out."

The guards herded them into the big throne hall. Unencouragingly, a burly executioner stood in the far corner sharpening his axe. He made long, slow grinding strokes with his rasp that were a constant and irritating reminder of what he'd like to do to at least four of them.

## Promises, Promises

A brassy blast of trumpets heralded the approach of royalty. King Derek looked peevish as he stomped to the throne. Princess Maybelle swept behind him. Sandy stared. She saw golden blonde hair, pale skin, creamy bosom, pouty red lips, and perfectly symmetrically arched eyebrows. The princess was, without a shadow of a doubt, the most physically beautiful woman that Sandy had ever seen. All her extravagant compliments, when her brain had been lubricated with the Prodigiously Incredible Empericus's Cough Balm, suddenly made a lot of sense. How had time faded such perfection to the merest haze of memory?

One of the guards shoved Sandy. She tripped and landed on her knees.

"Hey!" she said. "Not this bloody floor again. It's murder on my knees. Why did you do that?"

He shrugged. "It's in my job description. Push prisoner to knees in front of king. Comes in the handbook right after keep pike nice and shiny."

Sandy shook her head. "I shall never understand the military mind."

"Right, let's get on with it." The king checked his wrist sundial. "You're just in time. A few minutes later and I would've cut your mother's head off—irrespective of whether or not the woolly vest she knitted for my royal self has worked wonders in reducing the number of chest colds I got this winter."

Sandy blinked. Ruth showed her dimples.

"Your majesty," Tyrone said. "At your orders, I have—"

"Oh, no," the king said. "You? Didn't you get eaten by a dragon or sink to the bottom of the sea? I ought to cut your head off, witch, for not managing to lose him."

"If it's any consolation, sire," Drusilla said, "an elf mage is even now planning how to sweep the good captain off his polished feet."

"Really?" King Derek said. "All right, then, I might let you off that. But there is the matter of this other stuff. Herald?"

"Allow me, highness." Drusilla pulled her crumpled piece of paper out of her pocket. "Item two—"

"Who are you?" the king said. "Oh, I remember. Aren't you the lunatic with the false beard and acne who acted as her lawyer?"

"I am, of course, technically still in disguise," Drusilla said. "But as we'll soon be on a first name basis, Pop, you can call me Drusilla."

"Pop!" King Derek's face turned apoplectic red.

"Item two," Drusilla said. "Tyrone, if you'd be so kind as to lead our little hoofed friend to the throne."

The men and women of the court went "ooh" and "aah" at the sight of the blindingly white unicorn. King Derek scowled.

"You will observe, royal highness," Drusilla said, "that, as the Great Obtuse Mage, Sandy Blunt, *promised*, everyone can see that the unicorn's mane is less pale and less pure than the beautiful Maybelle's skin."

Maybelle's eyes widened with wonder. "Oh! It is so, Daddy. Everyone. Can you all see? Look. I'm paler and purer and whiter than its mane. I must have a special stable made for it. Oh, aren't you a cute little horsy with a hornsy?"

"Shouldn't it be bigger?" the king said. "A lot bigger."

"It was," Drusilla said. "Eighteen hands. But it's melted a bit, since this kingdom is much warmer than the land of ice and snow where the frost giants live."

Sandy stared at her. Drusilla mouthed: "Trust me."

"Which is why, sadly," Drusilla said, "the unicorn must be taken immediately back to its home."

Mavis put a hand on Drusilla's arm and squeezed a thanks. Maybelle looked deeply unhappy.

"Moving right on to something to cheer the beautiful royal lady up," Drusilla said. "Item six. If you would but say something in your charming, irresistible voice, dearest, loveliest lady, I'm sure this ogre from the Wildlands will be amazed at the beauty of your tone."

"What about items three, four, and five?" the king said.

"Doesn't six come after two?" Maybelle said.

Bob stifled a guffaw with his claw. Mavis elbowed him in the side. He carried his pot of gladioli to the throne. Princess Maybelle stared up at him. Most of the courtiers had drawn back in terror.

"You're an ogre?" Maybelle said. "You must be. Your head is just like an onion. A strangely handsome onion."

"Oh," Bob said. "You think so?"

Maybelle smiled coyly and batted her eyelashes.

"Ahem!" Mavis and Drusilla both coughed loudly.

"Oh, that's right," Bob said. "Princess, your voice is so dulcet that… that I have carried this gladiolus bulb from the Wildlands to lay at your feet."

"Oh, how splendid," Maybelle said. "Oh, you handsome ogre. You don't have to go just yet, do you?"

"It's a *Gladiolus recurvus 'Purpurea Auratum'*," Bob said. "Don't over-water it. It needs a sunny position. Perhaps a little fertiliser when it starts flowering. If you like, I'm sure I can arrange for Sandy to send you some of the Mildly Surprising Blunt's All-Purpose Fertiliser Concentrate. Oh, and if it gets aphids, I've found that—"

"Thanks." Maybelle took the pot from Bob's claw and passed it on to a servant. "Lovely. Yes. I'll be sure to remember all that. Now, perhaps we could discuss something else. Something—"

"Item three!" Drusilla said. "Someone will give to the Princess the legendary talking pearl earring which was hithertofore the property of Her Aquatic Majesty, the Queen Under the Waves. Bob?"

Bob blushed. "Now? Here? In front of everyone?"

"Perhaps you'd like me to help you with it," Mavis said stonily. "Or your little bubble-headed princess there?"

"My— Oh! No, dear," Bob said. "I was just doing what I— Erm. Sandy?"

"Just give her the pearl," Sandy said. "And get back to Mavis as quickly as you can."

"Remember, witch," King Derek said. "If this pearl says something to upset my little Pumpkin, by way of an unflattering comparison to

the famed beauty of the Queen Under the Waves, your head is mine
for a bowling ball."

"We're fairly confident of a good result on this one," Sandy said.

"Who, indeed, would not be?" Drusilla said. "With such radiant
loveliness as dear, dear Maybelle. The fish-queen has no attractions
to compare."

"You'd know," Sandy said.

Drusilla shot her a pained look.

Bob turned his back to the princess and shoved a claw down into
his breeches.

"I have the strangest feeling that I don't want to enquire too deeply
into this," King Derek said.

"Oh, no!" the pearl said. "Give me death! Throw me into the depths
of the Abyss. Anything! Please. Mercy. Not that again. Don't ever—"

Bob offered the pearl to the princess. "Sorry, it's warm."

"Wow," Maybelle said. "It's black. And it really does talk. Oh… Let
me put it on. Now, pearl. How does my beauty rate?"

"Oh, glorious, effulgent, radiant, marvellous, beauteous, incredible,
gorgeous creature," the pearl said. "You are light after a horrible nightmare. You are the sun after a day in hell."

Maybelle clapped her hands together. "Oh! Daddy! Did you hear?
Did everyone hear? If anyone missed it, come closer and I'll get it to
say it again! Herald, write it all down so that I can have someone to
read it over and over to me."

King Derek patted her hand and smiled fondly at her, before rearranging his scowl for Sandy. "All right. I'll let you have that one, witch.
But you've still got four to go."

"Item four," Drusilla said. "Someone will give—"

"Is this the booking office?" The elven princess stopped near Sandy
and looked around. "These can't be the other passengers? You said
they were swinging singles. Shipboard romances. And where is the
duty-free booze? We're really going to need it by the look of this."

"Item five," Drusilla said. "Your royal highnesses, this is her royal
highness, an elven princess with an impossibly long name full of fluid

syllables and no harsh consonants. Now, if you would all be so good as to observe the distinct lack of golden loveliness in our guest's hair compared to that of the ravishing Princess Maybelle's incomparable tresses."

"You have a real problem with grease, don't you?" Maybelle said. "It's so difficult finding hair care products that really work. And which don't leave your hair limp and lifeless afterwards, no matter how long you get servants to brush and comb it for you."

"Have you tried the Mildly Surprising Blunt range of health and beauty products, your royal highness?" Ruth said.

"Oh, yes," Mavis said. "That moisturiser is to die for."

"Really?" Maybelle said. "How about a shampoo and conditioner?"

"Yes, ma'am," Ruth said. "We can offer you the choice of our complete range from hair care, skin care, cosmetics, and a gentle unwanted hair remover."

Maybelle's eyes widened greedily. "Really? How come I've never heard of this Mildly Surprising Blunt?"

"We could supply your needs free of charge," Ruth said, "in exchange for your royal endorsement."

"Free?" Sandy whispered.

"If we can get a little crown emblem for the packaging," Ruth whispered, "saying that we are the suppliers to royalty, you won't believe the boost to sales we'll get. It'll be worth far more than she could ever use, even if she bathed in everything daily. Trust me."

"And now, item four." Drusilla handed Sandy the piece of paper and tugged the dragon scale from her tunic. She stood before Princess Maybelle. "Dearest, loveliest princess, for a year and a day I have adored perfect female beauty. The memory of this beauty has sustained me through the terrors of dragons, sinking beneath the waves, and two highly indigestible meals at an over-priced seaside guest house. Only she kept me going. I would have perished a hundred times over if not for thoughts of her."

Maybelle's expression softened wistfully. "That's the vastly flattering sort of hyperbole that one's True Love is supposed to say, and which men never do. Are you going to mention unquenchable, unrequited passion?"

"Oh, yes," Drusilla said. "Lots and lots of it. Heart palpitations. Sighing. Brooding darkly. And seeking heroic deeds to be worthy of my secret love. Including collecting this dragon scale."

"Terrific!" Maybelle clasped her little hands together. "This really is just like in books. Who is this woman for whom you pine, pimply one?"

"The most beautiful woman in the world," Drusilla said.

Maybelle's pretty eyes narrowed dangerously. "Oh, really? You did hear my new pearl earring? I am the most beautiful woman in the world. Your girlfriend has to be second."

"She is second to none, lady." Drusilla handed Maybelle the scale. "See for yourself."

Maybelle's eyes snapped wide. "Oh! That's me! Daddy, look."

"Scale from a mature dragon to be used as a mirror," Sandy said. "I think you'll find that is in order, sire."

"Harrumph," King Derek said. "I suppose so. But what does your lunatic friend think she's up to with my daughter?"

"Drusilla is mostly harmless," Sandy said.

"If this is me…" Maybelle moved the mirror aside to frown at Drusilla. "Does that mean…?"

Drusilla nodded.

"Oh." Maybelle clenched a fist to her bosom. "Pining? Heroic deeds? Would have perished but for thoughts of me?"

Drusilla nodded.

"Oh…" Maybelle said.

"Dru can't be serious?" Mavis whispered. "That's the princess she wants to marry?"

"Isn't she a little superficial and vain?" Bob whispered.

"Can any of us predict who we will fall in love with?" Ruth whispered. "Let alone understand how it works on others?"

Mavis and Bob looked at each other and smiled.

"And let's not lose sight of the fact that Drusilla is not exactly normal herself," Sandy said. "Not that she is going to marry the bloody princess. Dreaming, remember?"

"But what about the infallible Oracle of Ring?" Bob said. "It hasn't been wrong yet."

Sandy smiled. "You didn't meet Prolix the Off-White, did you? He's a professional liar."

"What do you mean?" Mavis said. "He writes novels?"

"He'll make a prophecy say exactly what the person paying him wants it to say," Sandy said. "In this case, that means Dru's deluded, rampant imagination."

"That would definitely account for the oracle being highly colourful and dramatic," Mavis said.

"Yes," Ruth said. "But it doesn't preclude it being correct."

Sandy shot her an exasperated stare. "It can't be. For one thing, Dru is no more a princess than I am!"

"What about the other two promises?" the king said. "You're not out of the woods yet, witch. You, there, executioner. Keep sharpening that axe."

"Oh. Right." Sandy frowned down at Drusilla's paper. "Oops. Maybe we should've saved one of the good ones for after this."

"What is it?" Bob said.

"Ahem," Sandy said. "Item seven. The Green Hermit himself would emerge from his remote hiding place to prostrate himself at the feet of the most gorgeous woman created."

"Oh, dear," Mavis said. "I'd forgotten him. Do you think the princess might be so busy making eyes at Drusilla that she'll overlook the fact that he's pickled in vinegar?"

"She might be," Sandy said, "but Daddy isn't."

"Your year is nearly up," the king said testily. "Which one of you wants to get her head cut off first?"

Bob shoved the vat of vinegar across the marble floor.

"What's this?" the king said.

"Erm," Sandy said. "Item seven. The Green Hermit."

"He travels in a copper barrel?" the king said. "I didn't realise he was that eccentric."

"I wouldn't say eccentric, exactly," Sandy said.

Bob rolled up his sleeve and plunged a claw into the vat. He pulled out the corpse of the hermit. The courtiers and guards drew back with cries of "ew!" Bob set the corpse down on the floor near Drusilla and Maybelle. Maybelle shrank back. Drusilla took the opportunity to put a protective arm around the princess.

The king shot to his feet. "What is this! Phew! Are you trying to stink us out? Is this some trick, witch? Or some insult? I'll have your head for this! All of you!"

"Now, now, Derek," Mrs Blunt said. "You know that shouting is bad for your digestion."

Sandy turned to watch her mother stride across the throne room and march straight up to the king. "Derek?"

"Did someone forget to put your haemorrhoid cushion on your throne again?" Mrs Blunt said. "Is that why you're standing up and looking peevish?"

The king scowled at her and jabbed his finger at the Green Hermit's corpse. "Look! This is your daughter's doing."

"A pickled corpse," Mrs Blunt said. "Yes. When other women's daughters were playing with their doll's houses, dressing up, and experimenting with make-up, Sandra was forever bringing odd things into the house. Dead cats, old phoenix nests, criminals' amputated hands. I expect it's because she was a young witch. Or baby dyke."

"But— But—" the king spluttered. "It's an insult! To me and Maybelle."

"I'm sure it's not, Derek," Mrs Blunt said. "Sandra can be a little thoughtless sometimes, I grant you, and is not terribly tidy—you ought to see her bedroom!—but she's never malicious. Now, here's your cushion. Why don't you sit down and take the weight off your bunions."

The king sat but retained his deep scowl. "I'm going to cut her head off for this, you know. All of them."

"If it makes you happier to say so," Mrs Blunt said, "you go ahead."

"Mum?" Sandy said.

"Hello, dear," Mrs Blunt said. "How nice of you not to be late this once. Are you wearing clean underwear?"

Sandy blushed. "Mum!"

"Hello, Ruth," Mrs Blunt said. "I've really missed you. Still, I expect Sandra needed you more. Drusilla, you ought to have worn a cleaner shirt, dear. But don't mind Derek, his bark is worse than his bite. And his lumbago is playing up this morning, which makes him a little testy."

Sandy directed her bewildered stare at Ruth. Ruth bit her bottom lip and showed her dimples.

"Perhaps you guards there had better remove that dead old man, though," Mrs Blunt said. "He's leaking vinegar everywhere. That won't be good for the marble floors. Now, if that's all, I'll be off. I've got a meeting of the Patch Street Ladies' Bridge Club in ten minutes. Ermengarde's membership is up for vote. You remember Ermengarde, Sandra, dear? She was a prisoner here for years. She's the first success of my rehabilitation and community care program."

Sandy put both hands over her face.

"Hey, Sandy," Mavis said. "I really like your mother. What a strong woman. You're very fortunate to have grown up with such a positive female role model."

"Wait!" The king banged his fist down on the arm of his throne. "Betty, stop! I'm king here. And you and your daughter and these— these other two are condemned to death."

"Hasn't Sandra made all her ridiculous promises come true?" Mrs Blunt said. "Really, Sandra, dear, you ought not to be quite so extravagant where pretty women are concerned. Still, your father was just the same."

"I don't want to go there," Sandy said. "Look, sire, with the Green Hermit lying prostrate at the princess's feet, the promises have been fulfilled. There was nothing in the promise about him having to be alive."

The king scowled. "Harrumph. That can't be right. You can't have done all those ludicrous things. It should have been impossible. I was so looking forward to cutting your heads off. It looked a dead cert."

"Majesty," Tyrone said. "They have only done six out of the seven."

Sandy turned to scowl at him. "Whose side are you on?"

"His," Tyrone said.

"Which one did we forget?" Bob said.

Sandy frowned down at the page. "Unicorn. Pearl. Dragon scale. Elven princess. Ogre. Hermit. But that's all of them!"

"That's six," Mavis said.

"No, look," Sandy said. "The last one is item seven. We've got—Oh, shit, no. You're right. It starts at number two. Dru, you missed one! I don't believe it. A whole bloody year, and I never noticed that she'd only written down six instead of seven. And now we've only got seconds to go before time's up! What was number one?"

The king smiled. The executioner gave the cutting edge of his axe a long, slow, rasping stroke.

Sandy swallowed with difficulty. "Oh, shit. Sorry, Mum. Sorry, Ruth."

"Bob and I are with you," Mavis said. "We won't let them take you without a fight."

"Not a chance." Bob flexed large yellow-brown ogre muscles.

"Panic not," Drusilla said.

"How can I not panic?" Sandy said. "You forgot one of the bloody promises!"

Drusilla smiled. "No, I didn't. I didn't bother writing it down because I knew that we had it in the bag before we started."

"Oh, no," Sandy said. "I always suspected that your imagination was going to be the death of me. What is it?"

"Oh!" Maybelle shrieked. "Daddy! I know! That's right. The witch promised me that I'd be married. And I'm not. Look at my hand: no wedding ring!"

King Derek smiled.

"Oh, shit." Sandy slapped a hand to her forehead. "Just where did you imagine we were going to find someone to marry her at this short notice? What sort of— Tyrone! You could— No. What am I thinking? Your sword would need to be a much more expensive model to pull that one off."

Drusilla went down on bended knee before Princess Maybelle and gathered one dainty royal hand. "Dearest, loveliest Maybelle, I have travelled the world for a year and a day without my heart, for it has been, all this time, in your keeping."

Mrs Blunt sniffed and dabbed the corners of her eyes with a hanky. "That's very beautiful, Drusilla."

"It is, rather," Maybelle said. "And your acne doesn't look nearly as bad from this angle."

"Will you make me the happiest of women," Drusilla said, "and agree to marry me?"

"You want to marry me?" Maybelle said. "Oh! You know, the more I look at you, the handsomer you get. I rather think I—"

"Wait!" King Derek shot to his feet. "What do you think you're doing? Maybelle, are you out of your mind? You can't seriously think I'd let a daughter of mine marry some—some vagrant!"

"Drusilla is not a vagrant," Mrs Blunt said. "She works as my Sandra's assistant in the spell emporium. When she's not travelling the world having fabulous adventures, of course."

"But, Daddy!" Maybelle stamped a foot. "I want to get married. Today! I refuse to wither away as an old maid for a single day longer."

"Then— Then pick someone else," the king said. "There are dukes and countesses and all sorts in this place. For goodness sake, I'd rather you married the bloody witch than that pimply lunatic!"

"Me?" Sandy said. "Oh, no! Not me."

"You don't want to marry me?" Maybelle said. "Not that I would dream of marrying you, but I simply can't believe you wouldn't want me. That's not possible. I'm the most beautiful woman in the world. The pearl says so. The mirror shows it."

"I'd marry her if the alternative were getting my head cut off," Tyrone said.

"But…" Sandy looked despairingly at the princess.

"You don't think my daughter is good enough for you?" the king said.

"I do," Drusilla said. "And I'd very much like to marry her."

"Don't be ridiculous," the king said. "This witch has just insulted my daughter. Promises or no promises, I'll cut her head off for that!"

"Hold everything!" Drusilla stood and waved her arms in a dramatic flourish, pulled a battered but shiny gold crown from inside her tunic, and set it on her head. "Ta da! The time has come for me to reveal my true identity. I am Drusilla, dispossessed princess, and rightful ruler of the small but desirable kingdom just over that way. As mentioned in the infallible Oracle of Ring."

"Princess?" Maybelle's eyes shone and she clasped her hands to her bosom. "Oh! Better and better!"

"Over that way?" The king scowled. "But that would mean…"

"Yes," Drusilla said. "We need to have a little chat about how you're bleeding the economy white with those high-interest loans. I'm sure you wouldn't want your precious daughter to live in a country that you yourself are impoverishing so that you can afford to buy yourself gold-fringed haemorrhoid cushions. And she's never going to get enough beauty sleep if the peasants are continually groaning under the yoke of oppression."

"That crown really suits you," Maybelle said. "It brings out the blue tinge in your royal corpuscles. And your pimples don't show as much."

"Darling," Drusilla said, "will you—"

"Yes, please!" Maybelle said. "Kiss me. Where everyone can see."

"Not so fast!" the king said. "I'm not letting just any madwoman with a crown marry my daughter. How do I know you're this Princess Drusilla? And there's the small point that there's someone else sitting on that throne, not you. So even if you were her, you're not exactly a great catch for my daughter, are you?"

"Well, I've organised a popular uprising and bloodless coup," Drusilla said. "And I thought you might lend me some troops, reward my loyal followers, and pay for the wedding and coronation."

"*Me?*" the king said.

"Considering the vast amount of cash you've already extorted," Drusilla said, "I think it's the least you can do."

"Daddy, can you please stop interrupting!" Maybelle clamped her small, pale hands on the sides of Drusilla's head and pulled her close for a long, smoochy kiss.

"Stop it!" The king stomped down from his throne. "I forbid this. Pumpkin, you could be kissing no one more important than a delusional shop assistant."

"That would be my take on it," Sandy muttered.

"Perhaps I can help," Ruth said.

Sandy turned to frown at her. Ruth stepped towards the king and dropped a curtsy. He scowled at her.

"You're the plain, easily overlooked neighbour of the witch," he said. "What can you do?"

"I take it that you wouldn't have any objections to your daughter marrying Drusilla," Ruth said, "if she is a princess?"

"Daddy!" Maybelle clung to Drusilla's arm. "Please!"

"I suppose not," the king said gruffly. "How could you tell? You have to be very, very careful with magic around us royal types you know."

"I understand that, sir." Ruth flashed her dimples and held up a gold-tinged darning needle.

"Yoicks!" The king shuddered. "A 'Prick-a-Prince'! I haven't seen one of those fiendish things in years. Not since my bachelor days were terrorised by every woman wanting to stab me with one."

"You know how they work, then." Ruth pricked herself. "Blood. I'm not royal. Would you care to try it, sir?"

The king frowned, but he did take it from her. He jabbed the needle into his thumb. "Not a smear of royal blood."

"Dear girl," Drusilla said, "you are, as always, the solution to our crisis."

Ruth smiled. The king jabbed the needle in Drusilla's hand.

"Ow!" Drusilla shouted.

"Not a drop of blood," Ruth said.

"You're kidding?" Sandy said.

"She's not kidding!" Mavis laughed.

"Oh, darling!" Maybelle said.

"Oh, no," the king said.

Drusilla took Maybelle in her arms and kissed her. "I believe, royal father-in-law, that we can now tick off item one. Which means that Sandy and all of us are in the clear."

"Harrumph," the king said.

"Yoo-hoo!" The elf mage loped into the throne hall.

"Oh, no," Tyrone said.

"Am I too late?" the elf mage said. "Has my hunk-o-burning love already sailed on the cruise? I— No! There you are, you magical man, you."

"Get away from me!" Tyrone said.

"But I've brought my hard-to-get beefy a little gift." The elf mage quickly unwrapped the bundle he carried. Something flashed blindingly bright.

Sandy blinked away spots to see that the elf held up a shirt of mail that gave off a shine that must be more than just a reflection from polished metal. Each of the overlapping metal scales looked individually embossed.

"Wow," Tyrone said.

"It will never rust," the elf mage said. "It's made of elf metal, which, in the high elven tongue, we call elf metal. Extremely light and unbelievably flexible. You can sleep in it. And do other things. Lots of other things. It's for you, big boy."

"For me?" Tyrone licked his upper lip and glanced down at his scratched and battered breastplate. "Never rust?"

"You'll look great in it," Drusilla said.

"It's much shinier and more impressive than your old one," Bob said.

"Take it, man!" the king said. "You might as well go off with this elf man. You're not much use hanging around the palace."

"You're bound to make a better wizard than you are a soldier," Sandy said.

Tyrone pulled his sword out of its scabbard and tossed it away. He reached for the mail shirt.

"Oh," the elf mage said. "What happened to you, handsome?"

Mavis jogged across to pick up Tyrone's sword and gave it back to him. "Elf mail or no elf mail, you wouldn't be you without your phallic symbol."

"Good." The elven princess stifled a yawn. "Now that's all over, let's get on board this ship. I need a cocktail and a cabinboy. Or two."

Sandy smiled as she watched Tyrone walk out with the elves. The elf mage fussed as he helped Tyrone remove his old armour.

"Do you think we did the right thing encouraging that?" Mavis said.

"Well," Bob said, "if worse comes to worst, dear, he'll end up back at the bottom of the sea with the fish-queen."

"Isn't it about time," Drusilla said, "you called in the marriage celebrant, father-in-law? And ordered the palace kitchens to get busy on an impromptu but sumptuous wedding feast? And have the fairy godmothers roused from their afternoon naps?"

The king scowled and stroked his chin. "This hasn't gone at all as I expected. There must be something unpleasant I can save from this happy ending."

"You mean that we're all safe from getting our heads cut off?" Sandy said.

"Looks that way to me," Bob said. "Yippee! You did it!"

Bob clapped Sandy on the back and sent her staggering. She landed on her knees at the king's feet. The king jabbed a royal finger at her.

"That's right!" he said. "You insulted my daughter. You've still got to answer for that, witch."

"What?" Sandy said.

"Saying that my daughter isn't good enough for you," the king said. "That you wouldn't want to marry her. Not that I'd let her."

"No!" Sandy said. "I— I didn't say that, sir."

"Actually, you did," Maybelle said. "I remember it distinctly. Daddy, cut her head off."

"Dru," Sandy said. "Help me out, here."

"My father-in-law is quite right," Drusilla said. "You have insulted my bride-soon-to-be. We royal folk take things like that very seriously. Cut her head off!"

"Dru!" Sandy said. "What are you—"

"Executioner!" Drusilla called.

"No, wait!" Sandy said. "Drusilla! Are you out of your— I didn't mean— Shit. Look. Her Royal Highness is certainly very beautiful. That's true. Probably the most beautiful exterior of any woman in the world. But— But you see… Erm. No offence, you understand, princess, but…but I really wouldn't have wanted to marry you. Because— Because I prefer someone else."

"You prefer someone else?!" Maybelle's eyes flashed. "To me? Surely you mean that you'll settle for some lesser woman of your own class who is more suitable because you know that you could not hope to win my hand."

"Is that what you mean?" Drusilla said.

"Erm." Sandy licked her lips.

"That is what you mean, isn't it?" the king said.

"Well…" Sandy spread her hands. "Actually, no. I really do prefer another woman. She's very special. And amazing, really. In a quiet, thoroughly nice, sensible sort of way. But with a ruthless business streak that has only recently surfaced. And the cutest dimples. There's no one else quite like her. And I can't believe it took me so long to realise how wonderful she is. I'm— I'm deeply in love with her."

"Oh, finally!" Mrs Blunt said.

Drusilla beamed.

Maybelle pouted. "Who is she? I suppose it was some exotic demigoddess you met on your travels? Because no mortal could possibly compare with me."

"Erm." Sandy stood and turned around. "Actually, she was the woman right under my nose for years and I was too stupid to notice."

Ruth stood near the grinning pair of Bob and Mavis. She looked engrossed in examining the "Prick-a-Prince" in her fingers. Sandy strode back to her. She nervously wiped her hands on the seat of her breeches.

"Erm. Ruth? I—" Sandy remembered Drusilla's declaration and hurriedly knelt. "Ruth, I know that I should have a hundred compliments ready for you, because—because if any woman truly deserves them from me, it's you. But—"

Sandy heard a big, watery sniff. Bob wiped his eyes with a claw. Mavis passed him a hanky.

"I know I'm not pretty like the princess," Ruth said. "Or have perfect skin like Julie Smelt."

"Well, I think you are," Sandy said. "But in a completely different way to all that flowery stuff I used to spout. You're— You're lovely and kind and marvellous and great to be with and dependable and fun and a terrific friend and—and all the real stuff. Not just the outside. Oh, I'm making a mess of this."

"No," Ruth said. "I'm liking it."

Sandy smiled. Ruth's shy smile in return encouraged Sandy to hold one of Ruth's hands. "I love you. Really, I mean. Not just—"

Someone sobbed and sniffed.

Mrs Blunt had moved across to stand near Mavis and Bob. The three of them passed two damp hankies between them.

"Carry on, dear," Mrs Blunt said. "This is beautiful. Much better than your father managed when he popped the question to me."

Sandy shot her a despairing glance. Ruth smiled and squeezed Sandy's fingers.

"Look," Sandy said. "I know— I know I've been an idiot. Made a fool of myself with lots of other women. When— When I should've realised— But now I know— Oh. Ruth, I do love you. Would you even consider— If I tried really hard to— Perhaps, in time, you might learn to—"

"I have loved you for years," Ruth said.

"Oh. Really?" Sandy blinked. "You have? Wow. I had no idea. Does— Does that mean—"

"Gladly," Ruth said. "Happily. This is the wish that I didn't wish for at the Wishing Well."

Sandy took a moment to come to grips with that. "You mean—"

"Yes," Ruth said.

"Oh, I'm so happy I could burst into song!" Mrs Blunt said.

"Make that a double wedding celebration," Drusilla said.

Mavis put a hand under one of Sandy's armpits and Bob the other. Between them, they hoisted her to her feet.

"Oh, I'd forgotten them," Drusilla said. "Make that a triple!"

"Marriage?" Mavis said. "Sandy. Ruth. What can you be thinking?"

"What?" Sandy said. "Look, now is not a good time. She loves me. I love her. We want to kiss for the first time. We can discuss women's rights later."

"Marriage is a betrayal of women's rights," Bob said.

"While it may have originated in a contract designed to create a legal partnership to define and protect the property rights of the individuals and families involved," Mavis said, "it evolved into an institution controlled by men, for the advantage of men, and to the complete detriment and enslavement of women. Marriage stripped women of all rights to own property, to control any income they might make, to have any rights over their children, and even passed the right to control their bodies to their husbands."

"It's not that bad now, is it?" Sandy said.

"Surely you and Ruth want to enter a partnership of equals," Mavis said.

"Sharing everything between you," Bob said.

"Of course," Sandy said.

"We shall be," Ruth said. "Sandy is the witch, and she'll be in charge of the production of the Mildly Surprising Blunt range of products. And research and development. I'll look after sales, marketing, and distribution."

Sandy blinked at her. "Yeah. And— And I'll do the stuff around the house that I'm good at. Mending broken shelves. And fixing the water pump when it leaks. Shovelling snow. And Ruth will do what she's good at. Which is probably everything else. Oh, that won't work."

"I'm planning on hiring home-help," Ruth said. "Who will be paid a living wage and be able to negotiate flexible hours, will receive child-care supplements, sickness and maternity benefits, and be entitled to paid time off to attend career-development courses, personal-improvement seminars, and their children's school athletics days. That will free us both and your mother. Plus we'll be employing two or three people and empowering them to earn their own living."

"Wow," Sandy said. "You— You're amazing."

Ruth flushed and showed her dimples. "I'm afraid, though, we might not be able to fulfil your dream of being rich by your twenty-fifth birthday. Since it's only three months away. But my budget projections on our five-year plan are looking very promising. Plus there is the opportunity to expand into Drusilla's kingdom yet to consider. I hope you don't mind waiting a year or two longer than you wanted."

"That sounds like a fairly equitable partnership, dear," Bob said.

"Yes," Mavis said. "I think Ruth will manage it very well."

"She always does," Drusilla said.

"Oh, Ruth!" Mrs Blunt flung her arms around Ruth in a teary embrace and kissed her. "I have always hoped that you and Sandra would get together. I couldn't dream of a better daughter-in-law. Between us, I just know that you and I will keep Sandra comfortably in hand. And make sure she changes her underwear regularly."

"Thank you," Ruth said.

Mavis hugged Ruth and kissed her. "She got there in the end. I think you two will do very well together."

Bob wrapped Ruth in his arms, lifted her off her feet, and kissed her. "I hope you two will be as happy as me and Mave."

"I hope so, too," Ruth said. "Thank you."

"My turn!" Drusilla kissed Ruth. "Dear girl! I'm sorry about having to threaten to have your beloved's head cut off. I hope I didn't alarm you. But Sandy needs a kick in the pants sometimes."

"I know." Ruth flashed her dimples. "Thank you."

"Our fearless leader's lack of clues was—"

Sandy grabbed the back of Drusilla's tunic and tugged her aside. "Will you go back to your own fiancée?"

"I haven't kissed you, yet," Drusilla said.

"The only person I want to kiss is Ruth," Sandy said. "And it's about my bloody turn."

"Yes, please," Ruth said.

*And they lived happily ever—*

"No!" Sandy shouted. "That's not fair. Damn it, you can wait two more minutes. Or cut some of Drusilla's earlier dialogue if you need to make room. But you can let me kiss her!"

Ruth smiled and stepped forward to meet Sandy halfway. Up close, with their faces barely a breath apart, Sandy felt the strongest sense of wonder. She and Ruth closed the gap between their lips. By a magic older, stronger, and more enduring than any crafted by the hand of man, every woman in the world ceased to exist for Sandy Blunt, except Ruth.

And they might or might not live happily ever after. Realistically, they'll have their ups and downs, like any couple. But you get the idea that no matter how stupid and clueless Sandy will get, Ruth will sort it out in the end; and that Ruth will always feel she's getting a good deal, because she knows that Sandy really does love and value her for who she is.

# The End

# P.
# S.

In case you were wondering, Drusilla and Maybelle did return to the kingdom over that way on a wave of popular acclaim helped along by a large chest full of silver pennies from King Derek's coffers.

Bob accepted a job offer from Queen Drusilla to become her chief minister responsible for Forests, Fisheries, and Environmentally Sound and Sustainable Farming Practices. This meant that he could spend his lunch breaks with Mavis, since she worked in the same palace as Minister for Internal Affairs and the Sensible Use of People Resources Based on Merit and Need Rather Than Gender, Race, Heritage, Nepotism, Age, Alumnus Connections, Species, Size of Weapon, Sexual Orientation, or the Possession of a Powerful Magical Artefact.

And for those really nosy people: yes, when the time came, Bob and Mavis both reduced their working hours to make equal contributions to the raising of their children. (Two girls and two boys. One of the girls grew up to be a dyke who formed a life-partnership with one of Drusilla's and Maybelle's daughters after an unlikely series of amazing, death-defying, magical adventures. But that's another story entirely...)

The unicorn safely returned home. Nameless the horse, once liberated from pulling the elf wagon and with his master safely on board ship, cantered away to join the unicorn. The dragon did get to share a nest with his amour, but the relationship didn't last as long as one of his poems. One of Bob's nephews took over his garden and made a fortune growing dope, which thrived on Bob's composting technique and the Mildly Surprising Blunt's Special Formula Marijuana Fertiliser. Bill the pony lived to a plump, lazy, ripe old age without once suffering from the trauma of being near a mine entrance. He served as a first mount for all Ruth's and Sandy's children, and he never once bothered any of them with a single telepathic thought—no matter how sorely he was tempted.

And Tyrone? Well, six months after he left, Sandy received a postcard spotted with tanning oil and a strawberry margarita stain: *Having a magic time. Everyone loves my new armour. Must dash back to the conga line. Tyrone. BTW can't help you with unicorns any more.*

# P.
# P.
# S.

To finally put an end to the cruel, inhuman, nail-biting suspense you must still be suffering: yes, the ladies of the Patch Street Bridge Club did elect Ermengarde to full membership.

About the Author

L-J lives in New Zealand with her wonderful spouse, Fran. They have one dog, three cats, some cattle, and lots of chickens. Together they make cheese, brew beer, grow their own veggies, and laugh a lot. This is L-J's fourth published fantasy book, and her first attempt at a humorous one. L-J can be found online at the Lesbian Fiction Forum (http://www.lesbianfiction.org): new members most welcome.